[ANIMALS]
FIC
BREITROSE

MOUSENET

MOUSENET

by prudence breitrose

illustrated by stephanie yue

Disney • HYPERION BOOKS

NEW YORK

Copyright © 2011 by Prudence Breitrose
Illustrations copyright © 2011 by Stephanie Yue

All rights reserved. Published by Disney•Hyperion Books, an imprint of Disney Book Group. No part of this book may be reproduced or transmitted in any form or by any means, electronic or mechanical, including photocopying, recording, or by any information storage and retrieval system, without written permission from the publisher. For information address Disney•Hyperion Books, 114 Fifth Avenue, New York, New York 10011-5690.

Printed in the United States of America
First Edition

1 3 5 7 9 10 8 6 4 2

V567-9638-5-11152

Library of Congress Cataloging-in-Publication Data
Breitrose, Prudence E.
Mousenet / by Prudence Breitrose ;
illustrations by Stephanie Yue.—1st Disney Hyperion Books hardcover ed.
p. cm.
Summary: Sent to live with her chef father and his wife in Oregon after having stayed with her inventor uncle and scientist mother in Cincinnati, ten-year-old misfit Megan is lonely until she starts working with some computer-savvy mice to try to save Mouse Nation—and the planet.
ISBN 978-1-4231-2489-4 (alk. paper)
[1. Mice—Fiction. 2. Global warming—Fiction. 3. Computers—Fiction. 4. Inventions—Fiction. 5. Stepfamilies—Fiction. 6. Restaurants—Fiction. 7. Oregon—Fiction.] I. Yue, Stephanie, ill. II. Title.
PZ7.B84895Mo 2011
[Fic]—dc22   2011004801

Reinforced binding

Visit www.disneyhyperionbooks.com

THIS LABEL APPLIES TO TEXT STOCK

For Henry, Charlie, and Becky

MOUSENET

chapter one

There have been many milestones in the history of Planet Earth, like when the dinosaurs went extinct, and ice ages came and went, and the ancestors of humans first stood on two feet.

Then there was that afternoon in Cleveland, Ohio.

The crucial moment came in a cluttered garage, where a big man with a shaggy beard invented strange gadgets under the gaze of a row of watchers on a high windowsill.

And that afternoon, the watchers were in despair.

Their inventor had finally started to make something they could use—something that could elevate them from a hole-dwelling, crumb-hunting species to one that could rule the world.

Then he stopped.

"The computer!" they yelled at him. "Finish our computer!"

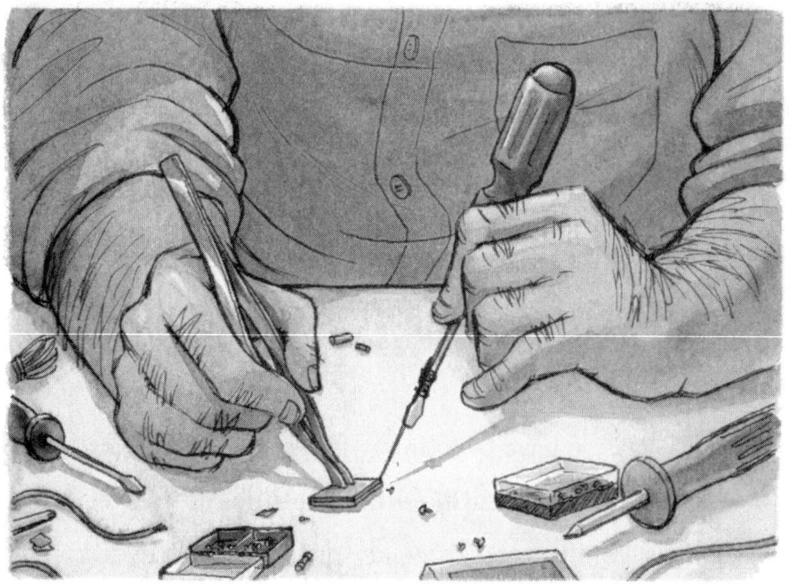

But they yelled in sign language, and the inventor didn't see them, and wouldn't have understood if he had seen them, so yelling didn't help.

They could only watch as the human turned the computer over in his massive hands.

"Way too small for my fat fingers," he mumbled. "Oh well, I can use the parts for other things."

The watchers held their breath as the inventor reached for the tiny screwdriver that would pick the world's smallest computer apart.

And they almost turned blue when he stopped with the screwdriver in midair.

"Wait a minute," he muttered. "I'll keep it for the wild child!" And he gave a rumbling laugh that made his beard shake. "I'll keep it for Megan. She can have some fun with it."

As the watchers breathed again, the inventor parked the unfinished computer at the back of his workbench, turned out the lights in the garage, and went off to bed.

When he was safely gone, the Captain of Clan 1578 led his group down from the windowsill to gather on the workbench. He was aware of a dozen pairs of eyes fixed on him, waiting for his wisdom.

"What did he mean?" asked one member of the clan. "What's a megging?"

"And are there really wild children out there?" asked another. "Young humans who have never been tamed?"

"A few," said the captain, not wanting to admit that he had no clue. "Mostly meggings. Take your positions, guys. We'd better e-mail the boss about this one."

Twenty-five years before this story starts, the watchers wouldn't have recognized a computer if it bit them in the foot. Back then, mice didn't know about anything much, except how to avoid cats, hide from humans, and hunt for Cheerios in the houses where they lived.

Then came the big breakthrough.

It happened in Silicon Valley, California, where hundreds of computer companies were just starting up. And these companies were different. The people who worked there were young guys who wore jeans instead of suits, and often ate food at their desks. Some of them didn't mind the fact that their leftover food attracted mice. Some of them even let the mice watch them work, day after day, week after week, month after month.

And that's all it took. After months of watching, the mouse minds sprang to life, recognizing first one word on a screen, then another, then more, until in time these first mice learned to read and write well enough to use computers themselves. They taught their friends, who taught *their* friends, and soon mice throughout the world had their own version of the Internet, carefully protected by passwords from prying human eyes. Now mice could e-mail each other, and write their opinions in mouse blogs, and post news about themselves on MouseBook, and check facts in Whiskerpedia, and take online courses on nutrition and safety and human behavior and world events.

But there was a problem.

Using human computers was a pain, and if there was a cat in the house, forget about it. There was no way mice could take their rightful place as the second most important species on the planet unless they had computers the right size—computers they could use in privacy behind the walls.

When Cleveland Clan 1578 first saw the world's smallest computer emerging on their inventor's workbench, they had e-mailed the news to the leader of the Mouse Nation, known behind his back as the Big Cheese. And the Big Cheese had been very excited indeed. But now they had to tell him that the little computer would be given to a wild megging who would probably hurl it across the room or stomp on it or flush it down the toilet.

The captain sighed, because who knew how the boss would react to such bad news?

"Ready?" he said. "Let's get this over with."

It wasn't easy to use a big desktop like the one on the inventor's workbench. The two strongest mice balanced on top of the monitor, holding strings that were tied around the bodies of the two smallest, who swung out over the keyboard so they could land on different keys in turn. Two other members of the team pushed the computer mouse, while another rode on top to click it. Still others were ready to jump on the space bar, or the keys for "Enter," "Shift," and "Delete."

The captain stood in front with a drinking straw, pointing to the key that someone should land on next.

Dangling, jumping, and clicking, they wrote out their message:

> From: Cleveclan1578@mousenet.org
> To: Topmouse@mousenet.org
> Subject: Our Computer
>
> Inventor has stopped working on computer and will give it to a megging, which we believe to be a wild female child.

When the message was finished, the captain gave the signal to send it, hoping he looked more confident than he felt. Would the Big Cheese blame *him* if the computer fell into the hands of a megging?

At Headquarters in Silicon Valley, a mouse from the Information Technology Team brought up the captain's message on the Big Cheese's computer and watched nervously, because you never knew. The boss had a quick temper, and if he got mad at you, it could shrivel your whiskers big-time. But he did not look too upset at the news.

"Bring in the Google team," he said.

When his best Googlers had arrived, the Big Cheese set them to the task of finding out more about this wild child. First they dealt with the problem of the name, and found that the closest human name to megging was Megan.

Next they Googled "Megan" and "wild" and "Cleveland" together, and got a big hit—a newspaper story that had run in the Cleveland *Plain Dealer* the previous week:

CHILD IN THE WILD

Megan Miller, 10, and her mother, Susie Miller, have spent two years on the island of St. Hilda in the Atlantic Ocean, where Susie Miller does research on wild sheep in a changing climate. She says: "Living in the wilderness wasn't easy for Megan at first, but now she's almost wild herself!"

The pair will be returning shortly to Cleveland, where they will reside with Ms. Miller's brother, the inventor Mr. Fred Barnes.

And there was a photograph showing a snowy landscape, with a girl-child all bundled up against the wind as she pulled sheep wool off some thorn bushes. The caption read:

Megan Miller, age 10, gathers wool that she and her mother will spin into yarn to make warm sweaters.

The Big Cheese did the slow pirouette that is the mouse equivalent of a huge smile.

"Bingo," he said, in the silent language mice use. "You are ours, Megan Miller, age ten. Together we will make history."

chapter two

It was mid-August when the mice on the windowsill got their first good sighting of the megging. She burst into their garage like a blaze of light, looking very wild indeed as the afternoon sun lit up her red hair, glinting off the front part that stuck straight up while two braids trapped the rest of it.

"Hey, Megan!" said the large inventor, holding out a bag of the chips he always kept around. "How was the doctor?"

"Great," she said, taking a handful of chips, "if you like needles." She showed him the Band-Aids on both arms. "He said I had to get two shots before they'd let me into fifth grade."

"Ah, fifth grade," the man said. "Bet you can't wait."

Megan sighed. "Know what, Uncle Fred? I *can* wait. I'm so out of it! There were some kids in the waiting room, and I had no clue what they were talking about. And they kept staring at my hair like I was from outer space."

She batted at the front part of her hair, which had stood straight up in front ever since her mom decided to cut it short all over, but stopped when she realized she was doing a really, really bad job.

"Not your fault that your mom gave you a bad haircut," said her uncle. "And don't worry about school. You have two weeks to get ready, right? Plenty of time for me to tell you what's hip, so you'll be up to speed. And another thing . . ."

He paused and reached for the tiny computer while the mice on the windowsill leaned forward so far that they were in danger of falling off.

"How would you like to be the coolest kid in the school," he asked, "with the smallest computer in the world?"

He held it out to show her.

"Wow!" she said, poking at it. "Does it work?"

"It will if you help me finish it," he said. "My fingers are kind of big for this sort of thing. Hey, wipe that chip grease off your hands, and let's get started."

Neither of them noticed a row of mice on the high windowsill, all doing slow, happy pirouettes.

. . . .

The Big Cheese had e-mailed:

> Learn everything you can. Observe humans at all times for clues as to their plans and their character.

So while some members of Clan 1578 were watching Megan and the inventor in the garage, the captain had ordered three others to keep an eye on the full-grown female who had brought the child to this house at midnight.

The female moved into the inventor's kitchen that first afternoon, shifting the piles of magazines and DVDs that had been comfortably roosting for years on the table, the chairs, and even the range top. Then she got out her laptop and began to write.

One brave mouse climbed onto the counter so he could read over her shoulder, hoping to glean some useful information about the wild child. And yes, the word "wild" did turn up, but it was only applied to sheep—special sheep who lived in changing climates. Not to meggings.

The mice felt more hopeful about picking up clues to the megging's wildness later that afternoon, after the big female had spent some time doing things to food that they'd never seen happen in this kitchen—slicing, steaming, chopping, mixing. When the girl and her uncle came in to eat, the mice looked anxiously at their inventor to see how he'd react, because the dishes that the big female had put on the table didn't look at all like his usual dinner, which tended to be either delivered or thawed.

But all the inventor said was, "Lucky us! Two vegetables—no, three—*and* salad!"

And the girl just said, "Wow, Mom."

The big female laughed. "Didn't know I had it in me, did you? I got a bit carried away, having a whole kitchen again—not just that wood stove. Get some water for us, will you, Meggy?"

Megan found some glasses and started filling them, though it took a while because she kept turning the faucet off and on, marveling at it.

"No water in the cabin, huh?" asked her uncle.

"Not in it," said Megan. "But just outside, in the creek."

"So no showers?" he asked.

"Sure we had showers," said his sister. "Right, Megan? In the waterfall."

"And the rain," said Megan. "Remember, Mom? That great storm when we washed our hair?"

The mice watching from the crack beside the range looked at each other. Was that what made humans wild? When you took away their plumbing?

Their inventor was talking as the humans sat down to eat. "Well, welcome to Cleveland, land of faucets. Bet you'll love this city, Megan, like your mom and me did when we were growing up."

"I dunno," said Megan. "I think it's trying to kill me."

"True," said her mother, with a smile. "We had an adventure on our way to the clinic. Megan had forgotten about traffic, hadn't you, my love? She started to cross the road right in front of a bus. Lucky I was there. You'll have to be a bit more careful, kiddo, when you walk to school."

At the mention of school, Megan drooped.

"Do I have to go to school?" she asked. "Couldn't you just keep on homeschooling me? It worked great, didn't it? I bet I've kept up in everything, except maybe fractions."

"Oh, those fractions." Her mother laughed. "All our stuff came up from the coast on a mule," she told her brother. "Including Megan's textbooks. One day he sort of lurched and the math book fell into the creek. Some of the fraction pages stuck together and we never did get them all apart."

"We had a deal," said Megan. "Me and that mule."

Which made the full-grown humans laugh loudly, but puzzled the mice because, as far as they knew, they were the only species (apart from humans) who could make deals.

"On homeschooling," Megan's mom was saying, when the laughter stopped, "the short answer is *no*. For one thing, I have to finish my paper on those sheep. Did I tell you, Fred? That Megan kept track of statistics for me, like rainfall? We have wonderful data, but it will take a while to write it all out. *And* I have to look for my next job. Another thing—you need to get socialized, young woman. A couple of months ago you said it would be great to go to a real school, remember? Make friends?"

"Seemed like a good idea at the time," mumbled Megan.

"And it's a great idea now," her mom said firmly. "You'll love fifth grade. I know it. Now, tell me what you two are working on, in that garage."

The listening mice leaned forward to catch every word as the inventor and the girl described the little computer, which they said should actually be finished sometime next week.

That gave the captain something to put in the daily report that the Big Cheese had demanded, even if he still had no clue what might happen to the computer if and when the wild child got control of it.

The humans soon fell into a routine. While Uncle Fred went to the computer shop, where he worked in the mornings, Megan and her mom sometimes shopped, sometimes did laundry, but mostly worked on the sheep paper. Megan would read out figures from the data she'd collected, while her mom wrote them into her laptop.

In the afternoons, Megan's mom usually went out looking for a job, while Megan and her uncle worked in his garage—which Megan thought might just be the coolest place on earth.

It wasn't like any garage she had ever seen. Uncle Fred had decorated one corner with big old pictures of himself playing football for Ohio State, and furnished it with comfortable chairs and a popcorn machine. He also had a stack of science fiction movies to watch when he took breaks. Actually, he claimed they weren't really breaks, because the movies gave him great ideas for things to invent—like the remote-control ant-zapper he'd made after watching *Planet of the Ants.*

The ant-zapper wasn't going to make his fortune, he said, because it could only zap one ant at a time, and it usually missed. He'd hung it from the ceiling on a piece of fishing line, with the corpses of other inventions that hadn't quite worked out, like the electric eyebrow tweezers that could give you a nasty shock, or the telephone in a barrette that sounded as if you were talking underwater.

One day Megan's mom came into the garage to see where

Megan spent so much of her time. It was late afternoon, and a ray of sunshine penetrated the dusty window, making the fishing line glow like spider silk as the inventions spun gently in the draft from the open door. Megan thought they looked magical, but her mom wasn't so sure.

"Those tiny things you invent," she said that evening, ladling a second helping of lentil soup into Uncle Fred's bowl, "they're cute, but everything is so small. I can't help wondering . . ."

"Let me guess," said her brother. "When am I going to hit it big?"

"Well, I've been waiting," she said, laughing. "Ever since that perpetual motion machine, remember, when you were six?"

"Yeah, well, not my fault the hamster got tired," he said. "I've learned a few things since then. And the computer *will* work, right, Megan?"

"Right," said Megan. "And I'll get half the profits for my college fund."

Her mom smiled. "Good luck with *that*," she said.

Day by day, the computer did indeed come closer to working. And night after night, the mice climbed down from their windowsill to report progress to the Big Cheese, who did pirouettes of mousely satisfaction, and thought about destiny.

If he'd had his way, of course, Megan and her uncle would have worked on the computer for sixteen hours a day—no, make that twenty hours—seven days a week. But that was more than you could expect from humans.

And some afternoons these humans simply vanished. Played hooky. Like the day Uncle Fred took Megan to the computer shop where he worked part-time. He introduced her to the guys he called his nerd posse, shaggy-looking men who teased her for being related to a genius—such a genius that not one thing he'd invented had ever earned a penny.

"Just wait!" he told them. "Now that Megan's helping me, we're going to hit it big."

Another day he took her to a science museum, where he spent so long working the hands-on exhibits that she had to pull him away because kids were waiting.

Then they stopped by the cafeteria. Big mistake. A group of girls was there, about Megan's age.

"No way I can go to school!" Megan told her mom at the dinner table that night. "It's homeschooling or nothing."

"What brought that on?"

Laughing, Megan told her about the girls, and how Uncle Fred had pushed her into starting a conversation.

"Sounds like a good idea," said her mom.

"He told me to use some of my trendy words," she said, looking sideways at her uncle. "The words he's been teaching me."

"So what did you say?"

"I said I thought that the solar system display was rad," said Megan. "And the thing about dissecting frogs was grody."

Her mom hooted with laughter. "Rad?" she exclaimed. "Grody? Freddy, my love, where have you been for the last thirty years? Even I know those words are prehistoric!"

"Anyway," said Megan, "the girls all said, 'Huh?' and stared at me. Specially my hair. And they laughed. I bet it would be even worse in school."

"Nice try, kid," said her mom. "But you'll do fine unless Freddy keeps filling up your brain with all that eighties stuff. Fred, did anyone ever tell you that you should get out more?"

But please, please, please, thought the listening mice, not yet! Not until you've finished our computer! Then you can get out all you like.

A few days later, Megan tightened up the last screw on the tiny computer.

"Yay!" she said. "Can we see if it works?"

" 'It'?" said her uncle, picking up the computer and balancing it on the back of his hand. "We can't just call it 'it.' We need a name. Any ideas?"

"Well, it's the same shape as a laptop," said Megan.

"Kind of small for any lap I know," he said with a beard-shaking laugh. "Closer to a palmtop."

"It's way smaller than my palm!" said Megan, taking the computer from him. "Look, I can balance it on my thumb. Let's call it the Thumbtop."

"Deal," said Uncle Fred, lifting a bottle of Coke in a sort of toast. "Would you do the honors, madam, and turn the Thumbtop on?"

Megan pushed a tiny button, and the watchers on the windowsill noticed that she crossed her fingers as the computer screen lit up. A couple of them crossed their front paws, just in case that might help.

"It's blank!" said Megan, feeling a thump of disappointment deep in her chest, and wondering if this invention, too, would end up hanging from the ceiling. "There's nothing there!"

"Of course not!" said her uncle cheerfully. "It doesn't have its software yet." He found a cord to connect the Thumbtop to the big computer on his workbench.

"It'll take a while to download stuff, so we have time to

eat," he said. "What do you think your mom has fixed today? Something organic? Another delicious salad, maybe?"

"Mom's out tonight, remember?" said Megan. "She's talking to someone about a job."

A grin spread slowly over her uncle's face, mostly hidden under his beard but showing up in the crinkles around his eyes.

"What a pity," he said. "That means we'll have to call on Mickey D."

"Who?" she asked.

"If you don't know my friend Mickey D, you've been away altogether too long," he said, and there was a bounce in his step as he led Megan to his battered car for the drive to McDonald's.

When they heard the car drive away, the mice in the garage came down from their windowsill. They gathered around the Thumbtop as it sucked up a browser for the Web, a word-processing program, a couple of games—everything you could want in a computer. Some of the younger mice reached out a paw to touch it, as if it was a living thing, but the captain shooed them away, afraid of anything that might interfere as their computer came to life.

. . . .

When Megan and her uncle came back from McDonald's, smelling of french fries, the Thumbtop was all loaded up.

"Can it send an e-mail?" asked Megan.

"Can't hurt to try," said her uncle. "Write me one. Here—you might need these."

He handed her a magnifying glass and a toothpick to write with, because the keys were definitely on the small side for human fingers. Megan was grinning as she picked out a message, letter by letter.

"Ready?" she asked when she had finished. "I'm hitting 'Send'!"

The large computer on the workbench jangled, as it always did when an e-mail arrived. Uncle Fred brought up her message on the big screen:

From: Meganbug2@gmail.com
To: Fbarnesinvent@gmail.com
Subject: Hi

Hi from the world's first Thumbtop.

The two humans met in the middle of the floor and gave each other high fives, while some of the younger watchers on the windowsill slapped each other's paws.

"We'd better record this moment," said Uncle Fred, fumbling in a drawer for his camera. "For history. Hold it out on your thumb."

If she had known how famous the photograph would become, Megan might have done something about her hair, which seemed to be sticking up taller than ever. But when Uncle Fred downloaded the photo to his big computer, it looked great, with the Thumbtop in the foreground and Megan's grinning face behind it, her freckles (and hair) in sharp focus. That's when the mice heard a car drive up.

"It's Mom!" said Megan. "Let's show her."

"Sure," said her uncle. "But you know what she'll say." He made his voice high and squeaky. "It's too small! Everything my little brother makes is wa-a-a-a-ay too small!"

He laughed as he turned out the lights and locked the door, leaving the garage to a bunch of mice who were almost too excited to breathe.

chapter three

When the humans were safely out of the way, the members of Clan 1578 came down from their windowsill to send the e-mail that would rock the mouse world:

From: Cleveclan1578@mousenet.org
To: Topmouse@mousenet.org
Subject: Our Computer

Humans have finished computer and it works.
They call it Thumbtop.

The captain paused while the dangling mice hung limp on their strings. The holders looked at their boss desperately, willing him to finish the e-mail before their muscles collapsed, but he couldn't decide whether or not to attach the picture. It made the child look so wild! For many mammals, having your hair stick up in front is a sign that you are about to attack, so the captain would like to have Photoshopped the picture, cutting out the human—or at least most of her hair. But he could see out of the corner of his eye that one of the holders was suffering from Trembling Whisker Syndrome, which was one step before collapse.

"I am sending a picture of the computer in the hands of the child, who is quite wild, as you can see," he dictated, and ordered his team to attach the photo, hoping for the best.

It didn't take long for a reply to come back from the Big Cheese:

> From: Topmouse@mousenet.org
> To: Cleveclan1578@mousenet.org
> Subject: Re: Our Computer
>
> Great news! Keep watching Thumbtop at all times.
> And see our Web site.

The members of Clan 1578 dangled, jumped, and clicked their way to the Web site of the Mouse Nation at www.mousenet.org. Their human female was already on the home page, her blue eyes gazing out beneath a spiky halo of red hair, and the Thumbtop held proudly toward the camera. Below it were the words:

The Thumbtop
Made by humans, meant for mice.
Coming soon to a mousehole near you.

The mice looked at each other in disbelief. Yes, yes, yes, it was made by humans. And yes, yes, yes, it was plainly meant for mice. But coming soon to a mousehole near everyone? How many mouseholes was that? Millions? Billions? When there was only one Thumbtop in the entire world?

It sounded crazy. But you didn't question the wisdom of your leader in Silicon Valley. You just went along and hoped he knew what he was doing.

When Megan brought the Thumbtop into the kitchen, her mom was standing with one foot up on the edge of the sink as she tried to sponge something off the leg of her only good pants.

"Mom, guess what!" said Megan. "We finished the computer and it really works!"

"Oh, honey," said her mom. She wobbled a bit as she brought her foot down from the sink, then gave Megan a hug. "I got a job! I was so excited that I spilled my soup."

"Great!" said Megan. "At Cleveland State?"

"That didn't work out," said her mom. "I'll be out in the field again, doing research on endangered animals. This time it's the hairy-nosed wombat. In Australia."

"Australia! When do we go?" asked Megan.

Her mom gave her a squeeze. "It's just me this time. I asked if you could come, but there's no way."

Something inside Megan went clunk. She'd never been away from her mom for more than a day or two in her *life*, and she had no idea what it would feel like.

Her mom was saying, "I'd much rather stay here with you, but there just aren't many jobs right now. And those wombats could really use some help. It's harder and harder for them, with that terrible drought. And it's only for six months."

"Six months?" said Uncle Fred, who had been listening from the doorway. "No problem! We'll manage fine, right, Megan?"

"Sorry, Fred," said his sister. "Not this time." She stroked Megan's hair. "It's your dad's turn. You get to live with him until I get back."

"With *Dad*?"

"You haven't seen him for two years, my love!"

"Not my fault," said Megan.

She'd been five when her parents split up. "We both followed our bliss," was the way her mom put it. Red Miller decided that he really, really needed to be a chef, and took off for France to learn how. Susie Miller really, really wanted to keep studying the effect of climate change on animals, so she finished graduate school at Ohio State. And Megan stayed with her because her dad was living in a sort of dorm in Paris that wouldn't work for kids. Yes, she'd heard he was back in America and was living in Oregon, but . . .

"You saw him in Paris, right?" asked Uncle Fred. "On your way to the island? Must have been fun, eh, Megan?"

"Not really," said Megan.

"Red couldn't get much time off," said her mom. "But you guys did go for a lovely walk by the river, remember, Megan? Then he smuggled you into the kitchen where he worked. That was great, wasn't it?"

"Bunch of people yelling in French," said Megan.

"Well, if anyone's yelling in his restaurant now, it's in English," said her mom. "I told you, didn't I, Fred? That Red married an American he met in Paris? Annie. She wanted to go back to her hometown—and that's where he's opened his restaurant."

"But Mom," said Megan. "You'll need me. You'll need me for your research. Like keeping track of rainfall."

"There isn't any!" said her mother. "That's the problem. That part's had a drought for years. Seriously, my love," she said, bending down to look Megan in the eyes—eyes that, to the watching mice, were starting to look a little runny at the edges. "I'll miss you like crazy, but it really is time you got to know your dad. I called him, and he's so excited. He says you'll love that part of the world. And I'll bet Annie has tons of relatives there, so you'll have step-cousins to hang out with. Instant family!"

At about this point, the watching mice noticed that Miss Megan's cheeks were starting to look quite wet, and the female parent also seemed a little damp around the eyes as she wrapped her arms around her daughter. And even the big inventor drooped in a way the mice had only seen when an invention turned out to be really, really bad.

For a while, the three humans stood like that, with Uncle Fred gently patting the shoulders of the two others. Then Megan's mom stood up straight.

"What's that about finishing the computer?" she asked.

"Oh, this?" said Megan, sniffing a bit and holding it out as if it wasn't important anymore. "We call it the Thumbtop. It works."

"It looks so *cute*," said her mom. "But isn't it too small? Bless you, Freddy, you've always so been obsessed with tiny things—maybe because *you're* so big. I remember when you were about eight . . ."

And she was off, remembering, which Megan normally liked. But there was so much going on in her head right now that she didn't really listen.

The next day, Megan's dad called and told her in his big boomy voice that it would be *great* having her in Oregon. She'd love it, guaranteed.

"It's beautiful out here," he said. "We're near the mountains. Do you like hiking?"

"I guess," said Megan, though she wasn't sure what it would feel like to hike for fun, because on the island it was just something you did to get around.

"Wonderful," he said. "We'll have some great hikes. And the beach isn't far. We can collect shells. Trouble is, it's not the greatest timing because I'm awful busy right now with the restaurant. But I'll try to make time for you. And there's always Annie. I know she can't wait to give you a great big hug."

Which made Megan think that Annie would be large and

soft compared to her own mom, who was sort of bony. And maybe she'd be great, if you wanted a stepmom.

But Megan didn't.

Up until the last minute she was hoping that her regular bony mom would change her mind and not go to Australia, or would decide to take her along.

But now here they both were in Megan's room, actually packing.

"Shall I take these?" asked Megan, pulling two sweaters out of a drawer as an alarming smell of large animal wafted under the dresser to the mice who were watching every move.

"Your sheep-sweaters? Absolutely," said her mother. "It gets cold there. But you won't need stuff for when it's really really hot."

"What about stuff that's really really short?" asked Megan, holding up a pair of pants. "With a hole?" She stuck her pinky through the hole in the knee.

"Oh dear," said her mom. "Those lovely pants we bought in Paris? You don't have much that fits, do you? My fault. I was going to look for some good sales this weekend. Too late now, but maybe Annie can take you shopping."

There was a *clump, clump* as Uncle Fred came up the stairs.

"Got room in your case for this?" he asked, handing Megan

a *Star Trek* T-shirt. "Kids will think it's really groovy. Oh, and I have something else for you."

He fished in his pocket and handed her the tiny computer. "You get to take the Thumbtop. And here's the power supply to keep it charged up."

He handed over the Thumbtop and its charger, plus a bunch of toothpicks to write with, and a small magnifying glass.

"Wow," said Megan. "You really want me to take it?"

"Why not?" he said. "Someone has to try it out in real life. That's called beta testing. It means you make a note if you have any problems, and we'll fix them when you get back."

Megan liked that bit about getting back. She wrapped the Thumbtop in a sock, put the power supply in another sock, and packed them in the middle of her suitcase. At least she'd have that one link with the only part of America where she felt at home.

There was panic behind the walls when the mice under Megan's dresser reported that their precious Thumbtop had vanished into a suitcase. It was bad enough to have it in the hands of a wild child, but with that child on the loose, it would be even worse. Who knew where the computer would end up?

And the Big Cheese had told them to keep watch over it at all times.

There was only one thing to be done: someone had to travel with the computer. The captain called a meeting in the warm space under the floorboards, just below the range.

"I want three volunteers," he said. "They must be brave. They must be smart. They must be prepared to travel with Miss Megan into the unknown."

He looked around. Nobody moved.

"Okay," said the captain. "I'll help you out. I want all the fours—the April guys."

The three mice whose April birthdays gave them a "4" in their name shuffled forward, first Mouse 48, then Mouse 42 and Mouse 47.

"Thank you," said the captain.

One by one, the other members of the clan came over and patted the three traveling mice as if they were saying good-bye forever, glad about their own birthdays, glad they would be staying in the warm, dry world they knew.

Next, a supply team gathered what was needed for the journey. They gave each of the mice two small plastic bags, one full of cheese crackers, and the other empty, for poop. As all mice know, few things in nature disturb humans as much as mouse poop, and a disturbed human can be the most dangerous mammal on the planet.

When the coast was clear, the three volunteers dragged their supplies to Megan's room. Her suitcase was lying open on the bed, and the mice clambered in and burrowed down through the pile of clothes, pulling their plastic bags behind them. One found an empty sneaker, two climbed into boots, and they settled down to wait for whatever was going to happen next.

Uncle Fred had sent out for some Chinese food as a good-bye treat for Megan.

"I don't think you'll get this at your dad's restaurant," he said. "You'll have yummy French food, like snails and frog legs and octopus."

"Barf!" said Megan.

"He's kidding," said her mom, pretending she was about to stab her brother with a chopstick. "Tell us you're kidding, Fred."

"I'm kidding," he said. "Your dad was a great cook even before he went to France. Right, Susie? Remember that time I came to dinner when Megan was about two? Ah, that soufflé. *Red Magic*, he called it."

Megan's mom smiled. "Red Magic," she repeated.

"So don't worry about a thing, Megan," Uncle Fred went on. "With the help of Red Magic, those frogs will taste just like chicken."

"You'll love his food, and it won't be frogs," said Megan's mom, as if it was an order. "You'll love everything about that part of the country. It's beautiful, and people there really care about the environment. While I'm off in the outback with dust up my nose, you'll be living a normal life with two nice, normal adults."

But as the watching mice knew, the girl's chance of a normal life was going to be zero to none. For an entire species, she was now the most important human on the planet, and the Mouse Nation had her squarely in its sights.

Later that night, the remaining members of Clan 1578 gathered around the big computer in the garage. It was time to confess to Headquarters that the Thumbtop was leaving. They knew it wasn't their fault, but would the Big Cheese understand?

Dangling, jumping, and clicking, they wrote:

From: Cleveclan1578@mousenet.org
To: Topmouse@mousenet.org
Subject: Bad News

> Wild child taking Thumbtop to destination unknown. Three volunteers are traveling with it. They will report if and when they arrive somewhere.

They clicked "send" and trekked back to their warm place beneath the range, wondering just how much trouble they were in. They would have been astonished to see what actually happened when the message arrived at Headquarters, and the Big Cheese showed it to the Mouse Council.

"Our computer is now completely under the control of the young female," he said. "That is excellent."

"But sir," objected the Director of Human Psychology, "this female is *immature.* At her age, the human young have very little power. And their brains aren't fully developed!"

"There's nothing wrong with young brains," said the Big Cheese. "Indeed, in the human species, young brains are often better than old ones. There's less clutter. Besides, young humans like to communicate with rodents, as we all learned from *Alice in Wonderland.*"

Some members of the council didn't look convinced.

"It is true that this young human lacks the means on her own to procure a computer for every mousehole," he continued. "But through her, we can approach the uncle. And it is he who can help us achieve our goals."

He looked around at his council, knowing that he had their full attention.

"In other words," he said gravely, "it is time. Once we know where the young female has settled, we will make contact."

Contact! The word hit the Mouse Council like an electric shock. It was indeed a solemn moment. After hundreds of thousands of years of hiding from the big mammal that ruled the earth, the idea of deliberate contact was alarming. No, make that terrifying. But as the members of the council knew, once the Big Cheese had set off in his chosen direction, there was no way any other mouse could apply the brakes.

They watched as their leader dictated the e-mail that would unleash a program still secret to all but a few mice:

> Tell TM3 to get ready. It is time.

TM3 got the message when he woke up a few hours later. "Yay!" he said, as loudly as he could.

chapter four

It took three planes to get Megan to Oregon. She wore a label around her neck so people with shiny smiles could march her off to the next plane, even though it wasn't rocket science and she could have done it by herself.

"You'll have a window all the way," her mom had said. "And you can do some research for me," she added, still trying to distract Megan from the fact that her whole life was about to change. "You'll have a great view from up there, and I want you to keep an eye out for damage from climate change, like dried-up rivers and dead forests."

Sometimes Megan hated to think about climate change because of what it did to animals—not just wild sheep and wombats and polar bears, but all the creatures that could lose their habitats and have to seek out cooler territory. But now, as she looked down, things didn't seem too bad. Although some rivers looked a bit skinny, others were full and shining in the sun. Some patches of forest were brown, but most were green and lustrous, and clean new snow had fallen on the Rocky Mountains. Maybe things weren't changing as fast as her mom thought? Maybe the planet could wait at least until she was old enough to do something about it?

Anyway, right now she had more urgent things to worry about, like how you survive when your whole life has been turned upside down.

In the baggage hold beneath Megan's feet, three much smaller mammals knew all about upside down, because that's the way Megan's suitcase had been loaded onto the plane. Squashed into a shoe and two boots, they couldn't even talk to each other in the sign language of the modern mouse. The only way to communicate was with the squeaks mice had used in the old days, before they got smart; and about all you can say with a squeak is "I'm hungry," "I'm scared," or "You're cute." None of that is very useful at thirty-five thousand feet.

. . . .

As the last plane crossed over the Snake River into Oregon, Megan thought about her dad. She still had memories from before he'd left for France, like the times when she'd run to him as he came home from work, and he'd pick her up and twirl her around, singing goofy songs. She remembered the prickly feel of his chin, and the smell of his shaving cream, and his soft voice as she sat on his knee listening to stories, and the scrunchiness of his curly red hair as she rode on his shoulders. Since then, of course, there'd been just that one short visit in Paris—not nearly enough time to feel she knew him, or what it would be like to live with him.

Her dad was waiting for her at the Eugene airport, and he hadn't changed much in the last two years, except for a few streaks of gray in his red hair. He picked her up and hugged her, and she noticed that he smelled of pastry dough and onions, with maybe a little garlic mixed in.

"Hey, hey, hey!" he said, putting her down. "You've grown!"

Megan thought, Well, duh! because of course she'd grown in two years, but she didn't say it because it suddenly felt so good to see him again, and she had a grin almost big enough to hurt.

She was still grinning as they drove a few miles south from Eugene on the interstate, then turned east toward the foothills of the Cascades. And she could see why her stepmother had wanted to come back to this long valley, the hills around it golden in the evening light.

"See why we love it here?" her dad was saying. "Great for hiking. What else do you like to do?"

"I dunno," she said. She knew that sounded feeble, but it was true because, compared to most kids, there was so much that she hadn't even tried.

"Trouble is, as I told you," her dad said, "I don't have a lot of spare time because of *that*."

They'd reached the edge of the town, and he slowed down as they passed a cartoony sign showing a chef with red hair, just outside a restaurant called Chez Red.

Megan thought the sign looked a bit cheesy, but her dad was beaming with pride. "That means *Red's Place* in French," he said, stopping the car so Megan could get a good look. "Not the classiest of signs, is it? But Annie's convinced that's what you need to bring in the locals."

He started the car again, with a sigh.

"One of these days, it's going to be the most famous French restaurant in the state," he said. "And then I'll put up a better sign.

Hire some real help. Now all I have is a couple of teenagers, so I have to be on duty almost twenty-four seven. But Annie will have more time for you. Bet you two will get along just great."

They drove a few more blocks through a neighborhood with tidy houses sitting in tidy yards. Then they stopped in the driveway of a house that had nothing tidy about it. There was new paint on some parts, but other parts were shabby, and the grass in the front yard grew wild. A boy with dusty-yellow hair that flopped into his eyes was shooting a basketball through a hoop that hung from the eaves of the garage.

Could this be the right place? No one had said anything about a boy. But here came a smiling woman wearing paint-spattered jeans and a big man's shirt, her dark hair pulled back tight under a scarf. It must be Annie, of course, except that she wasn't soft and bulgy, as Megan had imagined, but seemed quite thin under the baggy shirt. As Megan and her dad got out of the car, Annie looked as if she wasn't sure whether to kiss Megan or not, and waved her paintbrush as an excuse not to.

"*Wonderful* to see you," she said with a smile that showed perfect teeth. "I know we'll have a *great* time together." She bent down to gaze into Megan's face with deep blue eyes that went round and startled when they reached Megan's hair.

She stood up. "Joey!" she called to the boy. "Come and meet

Megan. She's been helping her mom do research on wild sheep!"

The boy came over, and like Annie's, his blue eyes went round, as if he'd never seen hair that stuck up quite like that. Now Megan could see he had freckles, though not as many as she had.

"Joey's in sixth grade," whispered Megan's dad. "He's a cousin of Annie's. His dad's away so he lives with his grandma, one street over, and grandma doesn't have a hoop." Louder, he said, "Hey, hey, Joey, pal. Won't it be great to have a step-cousin here in town?"

Megan wondered if there was anything she could say that would make Joey glad she was in town, but she couldn't think of anything, so she just smiled, and got a half smile back.

"Well, make yourself useful, Joe-Joe!" said Annie, putting an arm around his shoulders and giving him a squeeze. "You can take Megan's case upstairs."

Joey grabbed the handle of the suitcase and ran it into the house.

And the three mice inside felt every jolt as they were bumped up the three steps that led to the front door, then the eighteen steps of the staircase, until at last their world stopped moving, and the journey was over.

. . . .

Megan's room was at the back of the house. It was small and dark, with brown wallpaper that was peeling in places. A large pine tree blocked some of the light from the only window. There was a bed and a dresser, but no other furniture except for a cardboard box beside the bed, pretending to be a table.

"We haven't got around to fixing up this room," said Annie, from the doorway. "Maybe if your mom had given us a bit more notice . . ." She trilled a little laugh. "Anyway, when I have time, we can work on it together. Maybe some pretty pink curtains? I hope you brought some teddy bears or something to cheer things up!"

She peeled off the gloves she'd been painting in, and Megan could see that her nails were long and red and perfect—quite different from her mom's nails, which were short and sometimes chewed-looking.

Downstairs, the phone rang, and a minute later Megan's dad came halfway up the stairs to yell, "Gotta go! Scott burned the sauce again. Tonight of all nights. Oy, it's a hard life. Bye now!"

Megan heard the front door shut, then a car started up. "Will he be back soon?" she asked, missing him already.

Annie sighed. "We'll be lucky if he's home by midnight. So it's just little old us!"

She gave Megan a bright smile and went downstairs, leaving her alone in the dark room with her suitcase, which was upside down on the floor. She turned it over and opened it up. There were no teddy bears, but right on top was a map of St. Hilda Island, which had been on her bedroom wall in Cleveland. It still had tape on the corners—and still had a photo of her mom

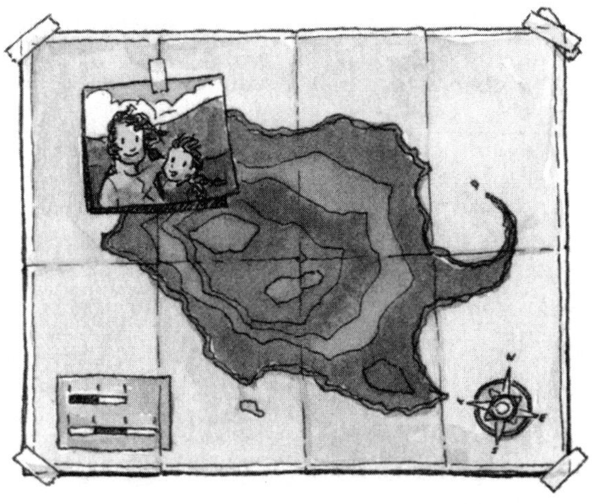

attached to it—so Megan stuck it where she could see it from her bed. Then she started putting away her clothes. There in the middle of the suitcase was the Thumbtop, her secret connection to her old life. Might there be an e-mail from her mom? There was no time to find out, because Annie was calling from downstairs. Megan hid the Thumbtop in a drawer under her sheep-sweaters. Then she quickly put away the rest of her stuff, threw her shoes and boots into the closet, and went downstairs as the smell of food seeped through the house.

When the room was quiet, the three mice untangled themselves from the boots and the shoe they had been riding in, and emerged from the closet. Where were they? They looked at the window, but all they saw was a tree. Were they in a forest? What forest? For all they knew, they could be on the moon, if the moon had trees.

They split up and checked the floor and walls of the room. Under the dresser, Mouse 48 found a gap in the floorboards that led to an easy climb to the ground floor. They clambered down as quietly as they could, pulling their plastic bags of poop to a corner where they would never be found unless the house was torn down. Then they made their way to a spot beside the refrigerator and settled down to watch their human in her new habitat.

The adult female was taking a couple of containers out of the microwave.

"It's leftovers from the restaurant," she said, tipping some food onto Megan's plate. "It's great that we get free food because things are a bit tight right now, and if I didn't have my job at the bank . . ."

Megan looked at her plate and wondered if it might be snails or octopus or frog legs, but she didn't want to ask. She took the smallest bite she could.

"Don't you like it?" asked Annie, sitting down opposite her at the long kitchen table. She made an exaggerated "sorry" face. "This is your father's best *coq au vin*."

"Like . . . like chicken?" Megan asked timidly.

"*Yes*, like chicken," said Annie. "It *is* chicken."

Megan noticed now that a whole chicken leg had been half buried under the sauce, so she fished it out to eat with her fingers, the way they had always eaten chicken on the island.

"Oh dear!" said Annie, putting up a hand as if to hide a smile. "I'm not sure *coq au vin* is meant to be eaten that way."

Megan felt herself going red and started using her knife and fork, but her fingers were slippery with sauce, and Annie was watching so intently that she got rattled, and a piece of chicken flew off the plate.

"Don't worry about it," said Annie, leaping for a paper towel. "We'll get you civilized by the time you leave!"

. . . .

To the watching mice, it was all very different from the humans-eat-dinner-together scene they were used to. In Cleveland, nobody worried if humans ate with their fingers, or if chicken flew off plates, or if food fell to the floor, where mice could retrieve it later. In this spotless kitchen, it was hard to imagine even a crumb being left for them. And the conversation was quite different, too. Back in Cleveland, everybody talked, including Miss Megan. Here she didn't say much at all at first, and then only when the larger female asked questions about living on St. Hilda—like, did they have a nice bathroom?

"It was okay," said Megan, "when it wasn't snowing."

"You mean it was an *outhouse*?" exclaimed the big female. "You had to use an *outhouse*? Oh, you poor thing." She went on to ask how you had showers on the island, and how you cooked, and where your water came from. Miss Megan sounded quite cheerful as she gave answers about creeks and wood stoves, but soon the big female had a look on her face that the mice recognized from the Chart of Human Expressions that all mice study. It matched Pity. Definitely Pity.

Apparently, Miss Megan saw the expression too, because she said, "You got used to it, and lots of things were really great, like when . . ."

At that point, the phone rang. Annie picked it up.

"It's my sister in Boston," she said, and took the phone into the hallway, so all Megan could hear from the kitchen was a laugh or two cutting loose above the mumble of words.

Mouse 47 heard a lot more, because when she saw the big female leave the kitchen, she scuttled around inside the wall and found a new listening post just as the female was saying, "She's a funny little thing. . . . Yes, she's cute, but really, she's, well . . . let's say some rough edges! Not surprising, given what she's been through. . . . Yes, quite the tomboy. What's that? A makeover? Well yes, yes, of course I'll make her over. That will be fun!"

And she laughed again, leaving Mouse 47 to wonder exactly what "making over" meant in this context, hoping for Megan's sake that it wouldn't hurt.

Back in the kitchen, the mice watched as the adult female gave Miss Megan a pat on the shoulder. Mouse 47 wondered if that was some sort of a signal for a "makeover" to begin—but all the big female said was, "So tell me what was *best* about the island."

Megan tried. She talked about climbing the mountain at dawn to check on the lambs, and leading the mule down to the port to pick up supplies, and sitting by the log fire while a storm raged outside.

But none of this wiped the expression of pity from her stepmother's face.

"Well, your life will be a whole lot easier here, you can be sure of that," she said. "We'll have a wonderful time, two girls together!"

Which seemed odd to the listening mice because, according to the class on human development that they'd all taken online, the big one should have progressed from "girl" to "woman" a long time ago.

After dinner, Megan wondered what came next. Back in Cleveland they'd watch one of Uncle Fred's science fiction movies, or maybe play a board game. But after brushing the last crumb from the long kitchen table, Annie sat down at the computer that squatted at one end of it.

"I do all your dad's accounts," she said. "And I've been getting behind. Do you want to watch TV? It's in the living room."

"I think I'll go to bed," said Megan.

Annie half got up from her chair. "Would you like me to

come up and, you know, tuck you in or something?"

"No thanks, I'm good," said Megan quickly, because the thought of being tucked in made her suddenly miss her mom more than ever.

As Megan headed upstairs, the three mice followed inside the wall, emerging under the dresser just as sneakers appeared in their view. They heard sounds of rummaging above their heads as Megan searched for something in a drawer. Then the rummaging stopped as she carried the Thumbtop to the bed, which was the only place to sit.

While Mice 42 and 48 watched from the shadows under the dresser, Mouse 47 worked her way around the edge of the room. By climbing up the curtains onto the windowsill, she found she could peer down and read the words on the screen as Megan picked them out with a toothpick. It was an e-mail:

From: Meganbug2@gmail.com
To: Smiller967@gmail.com
Subject: Hi

I'm here. Dad's going to be out a lot.

Megan paused as if she wasn't quite sure what to say next. Then she wrote:

> Annie's okay I guess.

"No!" Mouse 47 yelled, but silently. "You don't know that. She wants to *do* things to you!"

But Megan knew none of that, and finished the e-mail:

> Please please please can I come to Australia? You know I can help you with research.

Mouse 47 was so intent on the message that for a moment she forgot the windowsill rule, which says that you must never form a moving silhouette against the light, in case neighbors see a rodent shape and telephone the homeowner to come and kill you. When she remembered the rule, she froze—and although she didn't know it, she was just in time.

A pair of binoculars had just started pointing at Megan's window from the back of a house on the next street. At first the binoculars focused on what looked like a tiny stuffed animal on the windowsill. Then they moved over to Megan herself and the gadget in her hands. Could it be an iPod? But she wasn't wearing headphones—just jabbing at the thing with a little stick. Was she texting? The thing looked way smaller than a normal cell phone, but that seemed like the best explanation. The world's smallest phone. After a few minutes the binoculars saw Megan stand up and wrap the object carefully in a sock, as if it were very precious, and put it away in her dresser. Then she closed the curtains, shutting off the view.

chapter five

The sheets on Megan's bed were a bit damp, but nothing could have kept her awake—not the owl hooting in the dark trees, or her dad coming home at midnight, or the rumble of conversation in the kitchen while he and Annie drank hot chocolate, or the footsteps on the stairs as they finally came up to bed.

The mice under the dresser heard all those sounds, and when the house finally became quiet (except for the snores from the big front bedroom), they tiptoed down to the kitchen to start their night's work.

Their first job was to find out what part of the planet they were on, so they searched the kitchen until they came across an envelope addressed to the humans in the house. It said they were in a place called Greenfield, OR. *Or*? Or what? Headquarters would know.

They woke up the big computer on the kitchen table. It wasn't easy to write an e-mail with only three guys, but they found a shoelace in a closet under the stairs and tied it around Mouse 47, so Mouse 42, who was the strongest, could dangle her over the keyboard from the top of the monitor. Meanwhile, Mouse 48 ran around like crazy, operating the computer mouse and the space bar and the return key and the delete key and everything else. It was slow work, so they kept their message short:

From: Cleve3@mousenet.org
To: Topmouse@mousenet.org
Subject: Where

253 Cherry Street Greenfield Or.

They clicked "Send," put the computer back to sleep, and spent the rest of the night in the warm spot beside the refrigerator. They'd done their duty. If the Mouse Nation needed them, it knew where to find them.

At Headquarters in Silicon Valley, the Thumbtop Task Force had started to worry, to put it mildly. Most e-mail traffic in the mouse world happens after eleven o'clock at night, when humans are safely in bed, but the members of the task force had no clue which time zone the Thumbtop had landed in. They had been worrying ever since eight o'clock in Silicon Valley, which is eleven o'clock on the East Coast. By the time it was eleven on the West Coast, and there was still no news, some of them were basket cases.

So when the e-mail from Oregon finally arrived at 12:23 a.m., Silicon Valley time, it was good to have something to do after all that waiting.

One team Googled a map of Greenfield and zoomed in on 253 Cherry Street, while other members of the task force checked the Greyhound bus schedule. Then a messenger mouse was sent to wake up the Big Cheese, who hurried out to join the task force.

"TM3 could catch a bus from San Francisco this afternoon," they told him. "That would get him to Greenfield on Monday morning. Should we tell him it's a go?"

"Just give me a minute," said the Big Cheese. "This is a big step. We don't want to rush it."

Indeed, as everyone knew, this could be the most critical moment in the history of the Mouse Nation. If the Big Cheese said "Go!" it would mean that for the first time since the beginning of the world, a mouse would communicate with a human being. If that went well, the result might just be a computer in every mousehole, and a great leap forward for the entire species. But what if it went badly, and the young human betrayed them? What if she told Homeland Security that mice had evolved? That they were now right up there with humans, give or take a few things like thumbs and bank accounts?

There was no doubt that humans would feel shaken to the core, and would probably make every effort to wipe the mouse from the face of the earth.

The Big Cheese sent for the Director of Training. "Tell me about TM3," he said. "Do you think he's up to the challenge?"

"The head of the Talking Academy tells me he's the best of the bunch," said the director. "Excellent grades and good marks for initiative. And another thing—he trained on television programs that are popular with the human young, so he learned a dialect that they find familiar. Their slang," he added, seeing a puzzled look on his boss's face. "The way kids talk."

The Big Cheese took a deep breath.

"It's a risk," he said finally. "But without risk, there is no progress. We must take advantage of everything destiny puts in our path. Let's do it. We'll tell TM3 it's a go."

• • • • • • • • • • • • • • • • •

When the e-mail reached the Talking Academy in the basement of the Main Library in San Francisco, TM3 read it on one of the abandoned computers that provided the backbone of the academy.

> From: Topmouse@mousenet.org
> To: TM3@mousenet.org
> Subject: Contact
>
> You are hereby ordered to make contact with Miss Megan Miller at 253 Cherry Street, Greenfield, Oregon. Your first task is to win her confidence. Further instructions will follow. Travel arrangements are under the care of the Transportation Department.

TM3 looked around at the faces of his fellow students, who'd been reading over his shoulder. Those who had taken the Copying Human Expressions class were wearing expressions such as Envy or Fear or Wow. Mostly it was just Wow.

"Geenfield?" asked TM14, who hadn't got to the letter *R* yet. "Not Spingfield?"

Yeah, right, Springfield, that cartoon town in the Simpsons movie that TM3 had watched a couple of times because Simpson mouths move so much like mouse mouths. But no—Greenfield would be all too real, populated by real humans. And one of them would be the first human in the history of the world to communicate with a mouse.

The human in question woke up early the next morning to voices on the stairs.

Her dad's voice first, saying: "I just wanted to say hi."

Then Annie: "I think we should let her sleep, don't you?"

Steps, then the front door closed, and a car drove off. Was he gone *again*? It was very quiet. Megan imagined being stuck in this room for six months with nothing to do but look at the peeling wallpaper, with occasional breaks for leftover chicken with a stepmother who thought she was some sort of savage. She went back to sleep.

When she woke up again, the wallpaper was still peeling, and the house was still quiet, and her dad was still gone. But at least she had the Thumbtop, and for a moment she let herself hope. Maybe her mom had e-mailed to say the people funding her research had changed their minds and of course Megan could come to Australia.

Yes, there *was* a message from her mom, but it wasn't the one she wanted.

From: Smiller967@gmail.com
To: Meganbug2@gmail.com
Subject: Re: I'm Here

Sorry, my love, I miss you like crazy but no way you can come here. Trust me, you will have a great time in Oregon once you settle in. I know Red and Annie will **love** having you, because you are **great** to have around! Hang in there!

Got to run. I'm at Sydney airport, waiting for the plane to the outback. I'll e-mail when I get there this afternoon. Love ya!

Megan stared at the tiny screen for a moment, with a sharp longing to be with her mom on that plane to the outback. But she didn't have time to wallow in her feelings because Annie burst in with a big smile and a quick knock, giving Megan barely enough time to cover the Thumbtop with her hand.

Annie looked even more polished than she had the night before. She was wearing a clingy dress and bright makeup, with her hair scraped back tight enough to hurt.

"Good morning!" she said. "I forgot to tell you last night: we're going to Sunday brunch at the restaurant, so you should wear something nice."

Megan parked the Thumbtop under her bed and hunted around for something nice. There wasn't a lot to choose from. She settled on the *Star Trek* T-shirt Uncle Fred had given her, and her pants from Paris, even though they were a bit short and didn't zip up all the way, not to mention the little hole in one knee. She finished the outfit with one of the sheep-sweaters that her mom had knitted last spring from the wool that sheep had left on thornbushes as they thinned out their winter coats. Then she went downstairs.

The three mice under the dresser thought she'd looked fine, for a human, but apparently the full-grown female didn't agree, because phrases like, "Oh my dear girl, aren't those pants a little *tight*. . . ." and "Your sweater–what's that smell?" drifted up the stairs. Then the front door slammed, and a car drove away, and the mice had the house to themselves.

And the Thumbtop was still under the bed.

The three looked at each other. Nobody from Headquarters had given them permission to use the Thumbtop, but no one had said they couldn't. They sidled closer to check it out, but the lid was closed over the keys. They tugged at it, but it wouldn't open until Mouse 48, who was the most technically minded, found a button on the side and pushed it. The lid popped open while a soft hum emerged from the computer's insides, and the screen came to life.

Mouse 47 tapped the keys that brought up their e-mail program. This was amazing. No need for anyone to dangle. No need for anyone to strain himself (or herself) holding a dangler. No need for some old big-whiskers to tell you what key to land on next, and maybe swat your legs with a straw if you missed.

The Thumbtop might be on the small side for humans, but hey, it was perfect for mice. And there was even a message for them!

From: Topmouse@mousenet.org
To: Cleve3@mousenet.org
Subject: Re: Where

Have noted your address. Good work. Help is on the way. Prepare for TM3 on Monday. See Web site.

The mice looked at each other, puzzled. TM3? What was that? They clicked their way to the Mouse Nation's Web site and at first saw nothing that would explain TM3s. Then one of them noticed a button near the bottom of the screen that read "TM Program."

They clicked, and up came a picture of five ordinary-looking mice standing in a row. Below them was a caption:

> These mice are ready to graduate from our TM Program. You'll be HEARING from them soon.

That's a big help, thought the three mice. So *M* probably stood for *mouse*, as it usually did in their world. But what could *T* mean? They replied to the e-mail with "Message received," without admitting that it wasn't exactly "Message understood."

Then they took turns trying out the computer. And it was truly amazing. For the first time in the history of the world, a mouse could surf in private, without a whole team watching as you updated your page on MouseBook, or read a movie review, or checked college football scores.

They allowed themselves ten minutes each so they wouldn't drain the battery and set off alarm bells in their human's head.

Then they went back to their hiding place under the dresser to wait for the human to come home.

The mice were dozing when they were startled out of their dreams by a loud thump. Then came a bigger thump, causing a slight shake of the house itself.

Were they under attack? Did the Mouse Nation have enemies in this strange place? Mouse 42 ran to the big front bedroom, climbed onto the windowsill, and peered out. And he saw what was making thumps. Three half-grown human males were in the driveway, one with dusty-yellow hair that flopped into his eyes, one skinny and tall, and the third fairly round, with short hair that was sort of pink. And they were throwing a basketball at the hoop fastened to the garage.

The other mice joined 42 on the windowsill. At least the game gave them something to watch, as the young males threw the ball at the hoop, and missed, and taunted, and scored, and missed again, and yelled, and jumped in front of each other, and turned and headed for the house.

Headed for the house! An invasion! The mice ran back to Megan's room to protect the Thumbtop just as they heard a key turn in the lock of the front door, then feet on the stairs, coming closer.

The mice were not exactly surprised by the invasion, because they had learned in their classes on human behavior that humans were unpredictable. Any human could change in an instant from a harmless mammal minding its own business into a dangerous predator determined to kill you.

And of all the dangerous humans, young males were probably the worst.

Right now, the males were near the top of the stairs, and the mice could hear one of them saying, "I told you, the sheep girl's weird."

"Ba-a-aaa," said another male.

"And it looked like she was texting on something YAY small," said the first, and the mice could imagine his fingers an inch or two apart. "She hid it in her dresser."

"Like a Strawberry?" asked another male.

"It's BlackBerry, you moron," said the first. "No, it was way smaller. Anyway, those things are expensive, and when you live with sheep, you probably don't make a whole lot of money."

"Ba-a-aaa," said a third male.

Mice have always been at their best in times of danger. It helps them think with lightning speed, and now, at lightning speed, all three mice had the same thought.

After checking the dresser, the humans would look everywhere else, like under the bed.

Luckily, the bed wasn't new. Above the spot where the Thumbtop was resting, the mice saw a slit in the fabric that was just big enough for someone to crawl through. Quickly, 42 and 47 boosted 48 up through the slit. He dangled his tail down to wrap around the Thumbtop, and hauled it up out of sight. Then he lowered his tail again so the other two could climb up it to safety, just as they heard the sound of dresser drawers being opened.

"Hey, she brought along her own sheep!" a voice was saying, with a loud sniff. "That sweater still smells like one!"

"But that *thing's* not here anymore," said another male. "Maybe under the mattress."

The bed shook as the humans picked up the corners of the mattress, then one said, "How about under the bed?"

The mice held their breath as the boys jumped on the bed, and three faces appeared upside down at the edge of their space.

"Nah," said the face with the dusty-yellow hair. "She must have taken it with her, whatever it was."

In an instant, all three faces disappeared, and the bed shook wildly as the boys rolled off.

"Hey, you guys want cookies?" said one. "Annie says it's okay."

The humans clattered back down the stairs, and the three mice relaxed a bit because the immediate danger seemed past. But they decided to leave the Thumbtop where it was for the time being, just in case.

Only when they heard a car drive up late in the afternoon did they lower it gently to the ground so Megan would find it right where she'd left it.

chapter six

It felt like an earthquake when Megan hurled herself onto the bed that afternoon, almost dislodging the mice beneath her.

They guessed she was not in a great mood, and they were right.

First had come brunch at Chez Red, where Annie had sat her at a table near the kitchen so no one could smell her sweater or see the hole in her pants.

Annie brought her something that turned out to be mostly eggs, then went off to help show customers to their seats, and take their money when they had finished. Red Miller himself came out of the kitchen, looking good in his chef's outfit, and sat at Megan's table for a few minutes, asking how she liked her brunch. She said if he meant the egg thing, it was great, and he laughed and said, "I'll give you some lessons in French food, starting with the name for 'egg thing.' *Oeufs à la florentine.* It means . . ."

He broke off, looking toward the entrance to the restaurant. "Hey, look who's here! Didn't know you were in town, pardner."

Megan noticed a tall man with dusty-yellow hair coming toward her table. "That's because I'm not in town," he said. "Not really. Just on my way to the airport—back to Dallas. But Joey told me there's a new cousin in town and I guessed she'd be here."

He sat down opposite Megan, which revealed that Joey was right behind him.

"Welcome to Greenfield," said the man. "This place could use some more cousins. You're ten, right? And Joey's only just eleven. Great to have someone his age in the family."

"This is Jake Fisher," Megan's dad told her. "Annie's first cousin. Joey's dad. Be nice to him because he owns a share of the restaurant."

"Good to see our place so full," said Jake. "At least for brunch."

"Jake! Joey!" It was Annie, swooping over to give Jake a quick hug and pat Joey on the shoulder. "Brunch for both of you. On the house!"

"Have to take a rain check," said Jake, standing up. "And next time I'm home, I want to see *you*," he said, pointing a finger at

Megan, who grinned up at him. "Until then, you and Joey will be friends. That's an order. Right, Joe?"

Joey mumbled something; then, as they walked away, Megan heard him saying, "Dad!" in the tone of someone who doesn't want to be locked into friendship with fifth-grade girls who have strange haircuts.

When the last customers left, Megan hoped she could spend some time with her dad, but instead it was Annie who walked her briskly to the car.

"We're going shopping," she said. "Won't that be fun? We'll get you some really snazzy clothes for the first day of school—well, it'll be *your* first day."

"You mean school's *started*?"

"Last week. Didn't your dad tell you? Don't worry—we explained, so you won't be in trouble."

Depending on your definition of trouble, of course. As if being new wasn't bad enough . . . coming *late*?

The thought silenced Megan for most of the ride, but that was okay because Annie did all the talking as she drove. She started by telling Megan how important it was to look nice at school because the other kids at Fairlawn Elementary would know her dad had opened that new restaurant in town, and she should *look* as if the restaurant was a success, even if it wasn't yet. That wasn't really her dad's fault. He was a great chef, but so far the people of Greenfield didn't seem to appreciate good French food.

The restaurant might have done better ten miles northwest of the town, in Eugene, because the University of Oregon was there, and people at universities know about French food. At least they can read the *menu*, for crying out loud. But they'd settled in Greenfield because that's where she grew up, and she loved this valley. Not that she had much family here anymore—only Joey and Jake, and Aunt Em, who was Jake's mom. Joey's own mom had been killed in a car crash about five years ago. So sad. And now that side of the family had fallen on hard times. Until last year, Jake had run a great little business making parts for computers. Keyboards, mostly. And he was working on solar stuff, on the side.

"Like what?" asked Megan. "Solar panels?"

"Not exactly," said Annie. "See this earring?"

She reached up to touch her right earring, which actually looked kind of boring—just a lump of yellowish-greenish glass.

"And see this one?" said Annie.

To Megan's alarm, she swung her head all the way around,

while the car swerved, and Megan could see something astonishing. The left earring, the one that had been in the sun as they drove, was illuminated from inside by a brilliant fire, glowing in the densest shade of yellow-green.

"Wow!" said Megan.

"Neat, huh?" said Annie. "Jake made these. He was working on what he called his solar blobs. Not only jewelry but blobs to charge cell phones and things."

"Wow," said Megan again. "But if they only work when they're in the sun . . ."

"That's a problem," agreed Annie, with a smile. "He told us he was this close to solving it." She took both hands off the wheel to hold her index fingers an inch apart. "But he had to stop because his keyboard business collapsed, like a lot of businesses around here. Poor Jake. Now he's working for a company in Texas, and he has to travel all the time, which is why Joey's living with his grandma."

As they approached the mall, Annie started to get a gleam in her eyes that almost matched her left earring.

"I'm *so* looking forward to this," she said. "That's one reason I was glad your dad had a little girl—so we could go shopping together. Girls' clothes are so *cute* nowadays."

But their first stop at the mall wasn't for clothes.

Annie put her arm around Megan's shoulder to pull her gently toward the window of a hair salon, where there was a picture of a girl with short hair in little fronds coming down all around her face.

"Wouldn't that look good on you?" asked Annie. "I'll bet it's years since you had your hair cut properly, so let's get you a cute new style. I called from the restaurant and we're lucky—they can fit you in."

Before she could object, Megan found herself sitting in a chair with a wrap fastened around her neck, while the stylist reached for a braid and started to unwind it.

That's when Megan freaked. This was way too much, way too soon. A whole new state, a whole new family, a new school, *and* new hair?

She tugged at the Velcro at her neck and jumped down from the chair, looking up at two astonished women.

"It's just that . . ." she began, braiding up her hair again.

She didn't finish because she didn't really know what came next, but Annie got the point.

"Oh dear," she said. "You probably need to ask your mom?"

"I guess," said Megan, because that seemed as good a reason as any.

Annie's mouth had a definite droop to it as she led Megan out of the salon and into the first of many department stores. And (from a stepmother's point of view) things didn't get much better. At the very first store, Annie seemed to realize that if you wanted to buy cute clothes for someone, this was the wrong kid. She picked out one garment after another and exclaimed how precious they were, or sassy, or just *darling*, but when Megan tried them on, they didn't look that way anymore. For instance, there was a top with a big frill that made Megan feel like a clown, and another with skinny sleeves that turned her into a stick figure, and something with purple sparkles that was just plain wrong.

"You know what?" said Annie finally. "You should have had that haircut. The part in front . . . it's so distracting. Nothing's going to look really great. Who cut it like that?"

"My mom," said Megan. "It'll grow."

"Well, let's just save our money until it does," said Annie. "Or until you let me get you a cute new style. Then we'll buy you some clothes that are really *scrumptious*."

They settled on plain skirts and pants and T-shirts and sweaters with no frills or sparkles, but no holes either, which was fine with Megan, though she couldn't help feeling she'd let Annie down.

As they drove home through a light rain, Annie listened to music and didn't talk. And more than ever, Megan missed her own mom, who knew how to make her feel good no matter what.

The Thumbtop was under the bed, where Megan had left it, but there were no e-mails. Nothing from her mom.

Surely she should have arrived in the outback by now? So why hadn't she e-mailed? Megan had a quick vision of a broken plane lying on a sand dune with kangaroos sniffing at it. With the help of her magnifying glass and a toothpick, she sent off an e-mail saying, "Mom, where are you?"

So far, this was not turning out to be the best day of her life.

For a much smaller mammal, a few hundred miles to the south, this *was* turning out to be the best day of his life—the day he would embark upon the biggest adventure in the history of his species.

A transportation team led him to a Greyhound bus in San

Francisco, and as he climbed aboard, TM3 couldn't stop grinning (mice don't normally grin, but he'd taken a smiling class for extra credit). Following the instructions of the transportation guys, he headed for the third seat from the front, on the right. There, in every Greyhound bus, you find the mouse cabin—a hollowed-out nest in the bottom of the seat that's equipped with soft bedding, a container of water, some cheese crackers, and plastic bags for poop.

As TM3 settled down in comfort for the long ride northward through the night, he thought back to the last time he'd ridden in a mouse cabin, when he was a frightened young mouse being whisked away from his family into the unknown.

It happened when the captain of his clan in Elko, Nevada, noticed that he'd been born with "talk mouth," the slightly floppy mouth that occurs in about one mouse in a million. With a mouth like that, you can learn to make sounds way beyond the usual squeaks and grunts. With a mouth like that, you get trained to talk. An escort mouse had come all the way from Headquarters to hustle the young mouse onto a Greyhound bus, stuff him into the mouse cabin, and take him to the Talking Academy in San Francisco.

Of course TM3 missed his family and his clan, but there hadn't been much time for that, because the Talking Academy was very intense. In addition to the talking classes, you had to take all the regular online courses that are part of every mouse's education. And each evening, you practiced talking along with DVDs borrowed from the library collection.

Only once had TM3 ventured outside into the streets of San Francisco—and that had been a mistake. The Main Library is not in the best part of town, and he'd had a brief scuffle with a rat, who took a tiny piece out of his ear.

Now, as he settled into the mouse cabin for a long drive north, he thought about how much he had changed since that first ride. No longer a scared baby mouse, but a mouse with a mission. Perhaps the most important mission in the history of the world.

It was Annie who drove Megan to Fairlawn Elementary School that Monday morning, because her dad was off doing his marketing.

"You'll love Fairlawn," said Annie, who was dressed in a suit for her job at the bank. "Oh, I made so many friends at that school! I'm sure you'll meet some really nice girls to hang out with."

Megan didn't feel sure about anything except that there'd

be no other new kids to hide among. She was IT. As they approached the low buildings of the school, buzzing with the sound of kids, she felt her stomach tighten up. For a moment she thought of telling Annie that she had a stomachache, real bad. But that had never worked with her mom, and she had a hunch it was even less likely to work on someone who thought that Fairlawn was the greatest place on earth.

The school secretary marched Megan to Room 15 and handed her over to Mrs. Fitch, a teacher who smelled of lavender soap and peered down at Megan through thick glasses that made her eyes look enormous.

Megan got a full-strength whiff of lavender as Mrs. Fitch stood with her arm around her at the front of the classroom.

"This is Megan Miller," Mrs. Fitch said. "She will be a great addition to our class because she just had a wonderful adventure. So exciting. Two years on a lonely island in the Atlantic Ocean, wasn't it, dear? So what were the lessons of the wild? What did you learn that you can share?"

Megan thought of all the research she'd helped her mom with, like how hard it was now for the sheep to find enough food, and to protect their lambs from the fierce new storms. But as she looked out at the twenty-seven pairs of eyes fixed on her, all that came out was, "I learned a lot about sheep."

Giggles rippled around the class, and Megan felt herself turning a deep, deep shade of red.

At about this time, a garbage truck was lumbering slowly through the streets of Greenfield, with a mouse wedged behind the driver's seat.

It wasn't a great ride, but as the local mice who met TM3's bus explained, his only other option was a very long walk. So there was really no alternative to this slow, smelly journey to his destination.

The escort mice signaled for him to jump off at the end of Cherry Street, and a waiting team led him through a series of backyards, where the damp grass wiped some of the garbage smell from his coat.

When they reached 253, the Greenfield mice waved good-bye. TM3 took a deep breath, found a crack near the door, and squeezed his way in.

The three Cleveland mice had been dozing in the gap beside the refrigerator when a strange sound brought them wide awake. It was a voice, right there beside them, saying, "Yo, dudes!"

They'd been taught that only humans and the occasional parrot have the power of speech, but there was no bird in sight,

and nothing that looked human in their space. How could there be? There wasn't room.

"It's only *moi*," said the voice again. Although whispery and soft, the voice sounded definitely human, even if the dim shape they could now make out was definitely that of a mouse.

"I'm TM3," said the shape. "I believe you've heard of me. The Big Cheese asked me to come."

The Cleveland mice went into shock.

"If you are struck dumb, that's understandable," the stranger said. "After all, you are the first beings from any species to hear a mouse talk, apart from the dudes at the Talking Academy."

The three mice had never heard of the Talking Academy, because the Big Cheese had kept it secret until he was sure the graduates wouldn't emerge sounding like Donald Duck. So right now, although the mice heard human sounds, their brains told them there was no way those sounds could come from another mouse. This mouse-shaped object must be a robot, or a toy, or an illusion.

"Hard to believe, huh?" said TM3, guessing their thoughts. "Come into the light."

He led them out onto the kitchen floor.

"Now read my lips," he said, turning around to face them. "You guys got anything to eat that's not cheese crackers?"

When the three mice had recovered from their shock, and had shown TM3 where to find some Cheerios, it was time to send an e-mail to Headquarters. There was no way they could get at the Thumbtop, hidden away in Megan's dresser, so they made do with the big computer on the kitchen table. While the three Cleveland mice dangled and jumped and clicked, TM3 told them which letter the dangler should land on next as they wrote:

From: TM3@mousenet.org
To: Topmouse@mousenet.org
Subject: Arrival

I'm here and will observe human subject prior to making approach.

After they'd sent the message, the four mice gathered in front of the refrigerator, ready to dive into the gap beside it at the first sign of a human.

"Tell me everything you know about this female," said TM3. "Just how wild is she?"

"Looks pretty wild," said Mouse 42.

"She's different from other humans," said Mouse 48. "She doesn't know all the rules, like what to wear."

"And the full-grown humans don't treat her like you'd expect," added Mouse 47. "The female doesn't touch her as much as the parent in Cleveland did."

Then there was the young male. As they told TM3, in spite of kinship ties that involved something called a "step," he seemed hostile.

The Cleveland mice expected that TM3 would be discouraged by the news of this family's strangeness, but all he said was, "No problemo! It's all good. If she's not having a great time with her humans, all the more reason to make friends with *moi*."

And they saw something they'd never seen on the face of a mouse before. It was an extra-wide grin, the one that had earned TM3 an A in his smiling class.

chapter seven

Megan survived her first day at Fairlawn by pretending to be invisible at the back of the class, and at recess she kept walking around the edge of the school yard as if she was going somewhere. She sort of hoped kids from her class would come up and talk to her, and sort of hoped they wouldn't, but she didn't expect it, because she knew she'd sounded pretty weird, talking about sheep like that.

So she just watched, imagining that the *kids* were sheep and she was helping her mom do research on their social structure. It didn't take long to spot the alpha male. With sheep, it was always a big ram with huge horns, but at Fairlawn it was a large boy called Brandon, who the other kids seemed a bit afraid of—except for the posse of boys who hung around him, as if for protection.

After some more watching, Megan found she could identify several other social groups—like the tight little bunch of giggly girls who must be the popular group, and an athletic group playing hopscotch, and a nerdy group carrying books. That's probably where I belong, thought Megan. But even the nerdy group didn't look particularly welcoming, so she remained a social group of one. The invisible group.

When her class reassembled in Room 15, she went quickly to her desk at the back, hoping to stay invisible, but a soft "Ba-a-aaa" came from some boys in a corner. Then others picked it up, and soon the whole class was ba-a-aaaing, and Megan went red again, wanting only to survive to the end of the day and go home, even if it didn't yet feel like home.

She could hear the house on Cherry Street before she saw it. It was making a thumping noise, punctuated by occasional yells as Joey shot baskets with a couple of boys she guessed were from his middle school—one of them skinny and tall, and the other one rounder, with pinkish-blond hair.

"Hi," said Megan, and sat down on the front steps to watch. Maybe Joey would remember she was family and ask her to play, but it didn't look very likely. He sort of mumbled "Hi," and sort of smiled in her direction, but kept on playing.

"Is that your cousin?" asked the tall boy.

"Kind of," said Joey.

"I'm his step-cousin," said Megan. "My dad married his dad's . . ."

"Right," said Joey.

"Hey, you guys hungry?" asked Dustin, the tall one.

"There's some pizza at my place," said Spike, the round boy. "Let's go!"

He grabbed his bike and set off, and Dustin followed.

"Wait up, guys," yelled Joey as he parked the basketball beside the garage, and with a slightly apologetic look toward Megan, pedaled after them up the street, leaving it very quiet.

Megan stayed on the step, listening to the silence. Maybe she should have taken the initiative. Maybe she should have just grabbed a rebound and scored, because she'd actually gotten quite good at basketball, playing in Uncle Fred's driveway, and had often beaten him one-on-one, because he mostly stood in one place while Megan scooted around him and scored again and again.

But thinking "what if" didn't help. Right now she had to face the house, which seemed very empty because Annie wouldn't be home from her job at the bank until after five. Some days,

Annie said, Megan could go the restaurant after school. Her dad would love that. But not today because he was off in Salem talking to a guy about meat.

She had said, “You're old enough to look after yourself after school, aren't you?”

Megan said yes of course she was old enough, and now she let herself in with the key Annie had given her. The house felt a bit spooky, and Megan felt almost as if she were being watched. She took a handful of cookies and hurried upstairs to the safety of her room.

And TM3 followed her by way of the secret mouse route inside the walls.

When Megan and TM3 looked back at that Monday afternoon, they had very different memories.

Megan remembered sitting on her bed trying not to think about being alone in the house, trying to do homework, and trying not to worry about her mom.

TM3 remembered the extraordinary excitement that came with observing his human for the first time. He'd seen her picture on the Web site, of course, but the colors on the real Megan were much brighter, especially her hair, and he could see now that those little brown dots that humans call freckles were almost too many to count.

The high point of his afternoon came when she took the Thumbtop out of her dresser drawer and sat down with it on the bed. He scooted carefully around the edge of the room and up to the windowsill, where he could watch over her shoulder as she started up the tiny computer. When it came to life, he knew why the leaders of the Mouse Nation were so excited about it, because it was plainly intended for mice. His paws twitched with envy as he watched Megan jab at the keys with a toothpick and check her e-mail.

And yes, there was a message. TM3 leaned over as far as he dared, to read it over her shoulder.

> From: Fbarnesinvent@gmail.com
> To: Meganbug2@gmail.com
> Subject: T-Top
>
> What's shakin', kid? Everything hunky-dory? Hope the Thumbtop is working well. Next thing I'll invent could be a new green power supply for it. Your mom would like that. Any ideas?

As she read the message, the young human's expression went from Sad on the mouse Chart of Human Expressions to Interested. She quickly pushed "Reply" with her toothpick, then picked out a message about solar blobs and someone called Jake.

She ended:

> Things are okay but I miss you.

Then she hit "Send" and her expression drifted to Anxious. She stared at the Thumbtop for a couple of minutes before stabbing it to start another e-mail:

> From: Meganbug2@gmail.com
> To: Smiller967@gmail.com
> Subject: Are You Okay
>
> MOM. You said you'd write, I hope your plane didn't crash.

She hit "Send" again, and then as TM3 watched, she signed out of her e-mail program and Googled "plane crash Australia." Apparently the search didn't produce anything, because she started a new search for "Susan Miller." Pages and pages of Susan Millers came up, and TM3 could see words like "artist" and "novelist" and "winner of the 10K" and "Grandma Sue" before his human added "sheep" to the search box. And that must have given her what she wanted, because she clicked on several sites about sheep and the climate, reading bits of them through her magnifying glass. Then she sighed deeply and stood up so abruptly that TM3 had to sprint for cover behind the curtain, his heart racing.

He heard the opening and closing of a drawer, as she put the Thumbtop away. Then came the *phlump* of a body hitting the bed. Then stillness.

It was a few minutes before he dared creep out again, and peer down at the massive creature stretched out below him. She seemed to be deeply absorbed in a textbook called *Oregon: The Place and the People*, so he had time to study her.

"Make contact." Those were his orders. But he'd bet that whoever gave those orders had never been this close to a human, never seen the sheer size of the thing. He watched the huge chest going in and out with each breath, saw the size of the monster legs as she crossed and uncrossed them. And this specimen was only half grown!

What if he gave up? What if he told his bosses that he was sorry, but not this time. Not this mouse. Except that mice obey orders. Period. End of sentence. If they don't, they are severely punished. He didn't know what the punishment would be for chickening out on a mission like this, but it would probably be

exile, at least—getting sent as far as a Greyhound bus could take you, with orders to never come home.

Bottom line: there was no way out. He'd have to make contact. And that would mean using his brain as it had never been used before.

Think, he told himself. *Observe.*

He started his observations with her face. He could see that her mouth turned down at the corners, which meant she was not happy.

And no wonder.

As all mice know, young humans stay under the care of adults for a ridiculously long time. But here was his human all alone in the house, not getting the strokes and pats that the human young seem to need. Would that make her eager to talk to someone else, even if that someone was a mouse? There was only one way to find out: He had to introduce himself. But how? What if he tapped her on the shoulder and said, "My name is Talking Mouse Three, or TM3 for short, and I want to be your friend"?

Would she smile and say, "Oh, I am so glad to meet you!"

Sure, he told himself. *In your dreams*. She might *look* a bit different from most humans, but she was probably the same on the inside. That meant she'd probably scream and tell her adults about the weird mouse in her room, and they would attack with all the usual weapons, like traps and poison, and bring in cats to eat anyone left over.

Somehow, he had to plan an approach that would get past her scream reflex. But first, he had to know how strong that reflex was. And there was only one way to find out.

He would give her the EEEK test. And he'd set it up tonight—just as soon as he could get to a computer.

TM3 got his first glimpse of the adults in the household later that afternoon, when the front door opened to a male voice calling, "I'm home!" closely followed by a female one with a "Yoo-hoo!"

He took the route inside the walls to reach the viewing spot beside the refrigerator just as his human arrived to get a major hug from the male, followed by a minor one from the female.

"I only have a couple of minutes," said the male, "but I wanted to hear all about your first day. How did it go?"

"Okay, I guess," Megan said.

"Have you made any friends yet?" asked the woman.

"Not exactly," said Megan. "It's kind of hard to get started."

"Well," said the woman, "here's what always worked for me.

First, listen to what the others are saying. Then join in! Ask an intelligent question. You'll be part of the group before you know it!"

"Here's another idea," said the man. "And this one works for me every time. Just go up to someone and start a conversation. People really like that! Talk about things *you* know about. Like in my case, cooking. Or in your case, sheep. . . ."

"That might not work so good," said Megan, thinking of the *ba-aa-aa*-ing from this morning.

"Okay," her dad went on, "how about islands? Or your mom's research? Or the fact that your dad runs the best restaurant this side of Portland?"

And as he headed back to the restaurant, he called over his shoulder, "You're an interesting kid, my dear. Don't sell yourself short!"

If you think she's interesting now, thought TM3, just wait a couple of days. Then she could just become the most interesting human in the universe—if he did his job right. And if she passed the EEEK test.

That night, when everything was quiet except for gentle snores from the front bedroom, TM3 led the Cleveland mice down to the big computer. They brought up the Mouse Nation's Web site, clicked on "Tests," and scrolled down the list to "EEEK."

Yes, this was what he needed. First came some cartoons showing human females standing on chairs yelling "EEEK!" while harmless rodents gazed up at them. Then came the test itself:

Human Response to the Mouse

How Human Responds	Grade
Talks to or touches mouse: no EEEK	A+
Approaches mouse: no EEEK or soft EEEK	A
Watches mouse: medium EEEK	B
Jumps on chair: loud EEEK	C
Runs from room: multi-EEEK	D
Faints	F

Where should he give Megan the test? It couldn't be in this house, because if she flunked and told her adults the house had mice, they'd declare war. The test should be done at her school. But where was that? He organized the guys from Cleveland to find out. Two of them climbed into Megan's backpack as it lay in a patch of light from a streetlamp, and in a little while they emerged with a sheet of paper that was headed:

FAIRLAWN ELEMENTARY SCHOOL

How We Show Respect for Others in Room 15

So the EEEK test should be administered in Room 15 at Fairlawn Elementary School. But who should be the test mouse? Obviously, TM3 couldn't do it himself. He was far too valuable to his nation to take that kind of risk. And he couldn't spare any of these dudes from Cleveland.

He would have to trust the local talent, so he dictated an e-mail to the Commander of the Greenfield Region:

From: TM3@mousenet.org
To: Greenfieldboss@mousenet.org
Subject: Testing, Testing

We need EEEK test administered to human in Room 15 at Fairlawn Elementary School (see www.mousenet.org/tests/EEEK). Subject is female about 2/3 size, red hair in ropes at back, crested in front. Please report results as soon as possible.

The Commander of the Greenfield Region was delighted to help. He'd heard a rumor that the Thumbtop was in his town—that magical little computer he'd seen on the home page of the nation's Web site. And TM3, that mouse his guys had met at the bus and guided to Cherry Street? Clearly a secret agent from Headquarters. Put two and two together, and Greenfield might just be at the center of the mouse universe right about now. And if all went well, maybe a certain local commander could get his picture on the Web site.

He forwarded the e-mail to all clans in the Fairlawn neighborhood. By dawn he had a volunteer, and the EEEK test was ready to go.

chapter eight

Megan's second morning at school didn't start off any better than the first. In fact it was disastrous.

First, she'd decided to follow Annie's suggestion on how to make friends. You listen, then you ask an intelligent question or two. And she got her chance. A group of girls in her class were talking about this and that while Megan listened carefully, hoping to find a place where an intelligent question might work.

And here it came. One of girls mentioned the Melody sisters, giving Megan a natural opening to ask, "Are they at this school?"

There was a moment of silence, then the girls collapsed in laughter because, as one of them told her, the Melody Sisters was a really hot group that was about to perform in Eugene.

So much for Annie's advice.

At recess, Megan decided to try what her dad suggested—simply to start talking about something she knew a lot about. And hey, her dad was right when he said she'd had an interesting life, for a kid. She had a lot to talk about. But gazing around the school yard, she couldn't see anyone who looked as if they wanted to be talked to right now. So she decided to do the next best thing. She'd *do* something she knew about, and kids who shared that interest might join in.

Her mom had said people in this state were really interested in the environment, right? Recycling and all that good stuff? She noticed that some of the kids were just throwing their old water bottles in the trash, instead of the bins that were clearly labeled "Recycling," so she started fishing some of the bottles out of the trash bin and putting them where they belonged.

True, recycling three or four bottles wouldn't save the planet, but as her mom always said, you have to start somewhere. And it could maybe attract the attention of someone else who was interested in the environment. And maybe together they could start a campaign to make the whole school greener, then the school would make the city of Greenfield greener, then Greenfield would be an example for other cities in Oregon, and who knew how far it could go?

And it seemed to be working. Some kids were strolling toward her. When they came close, she saw that it was Brandon the alpha male, with his posse. But the conversation, when it started, was not what she'd hoped for.

"Did you just take stuff out of the trash?" asked Brandon, as his posse gathered around him. "That's pretty gross, sheep-girl."

Now was her chance. "It's not gross, and it helps in two ways," she began, remembering a short lecture her mom had given Uncle Fred. "It keeps plastic out of the landfill and it saves the resources for making new bottles."

"So?" asked Brandon, taking a step closer.

She shrugged because the answer was so obvious. "It all helps with climate change—global warming. And that's important because—"

"Global warming? You really believe that stuff? It's all a hoax, don't you know that?"

"Biggest hoax ever," said one of his followers. "It snowed in May. My dad says that proves it's a hoax."

Megan knew her mom could flatten them with a few facts, and she remembered one that might work. "Sometimes climate change just makes the weather weird, so that . . ."

But she was talking to backs, as the boys ran off, leaving

Megan to think that perhaps the idea of making friends through recycling might have to wait a while.

It was after lunch that her whole life changed.

While they were waiting for Mrs. Fitch, a tall blond girl called Caitlin was telling some friends about a new book she'd just read. Then she stopped talking, and her blue eyes grew huge as they focused on the floor.

A mouse was walking slowly up the middle of the classroom.

Caitlin yelled "EEEK!" and jumped up on her desk. Some of the other girls screamed and jumped up on desks too, while the boys pulled back. The mouse kept coming. It passed Caitlin's desk and walked all the way to the back of the classroom, stopping in front of Megan.

"Kill it!" shouted one of the boys. "Stomp on it!"

Megan wasn't crazy about mice. She had never wanted one as a pet, and for a moment she was tempted to jump up on a desk too. But this one reminded her of the little chipmunks she'd watched for hours on the island, and it was trembling with fright, and everyone was looking at her.

"It's not hurting anyone," she said. She knelt down and scooped up the mouse in her hands. Then she carried it to

the open door, put it down, and watched it scuttle away to the safety of the bike shed.

She turned back to the classroom and saw twenty-seven pairs of eyes turned her way. She'd hoped to see a little admiration in those eyes, but the kids were staring at her with amazement, as if she was even more weird than they'd thought.

TM3 had been nervous all day. No, make that terrified. Suppose Megan failed her EEEK test? What then? Would they have to switch to Plan B? What was Plan B? He made the Cleveland mice check his e-mail every ten minutes, which drove them nuts. Finally, at about 1:30, a message came through from the Commander of the Greenfield Region:

> From: Greenfieldboss@mousenet.org
> To: TM3@mousenet.org
> Subject: Re. Testing, Testing
>
> EEEK test of female human completed. Human passed with A+.

TM3 did a very slow, very happy pirouette. "Yay!" he said, while the Cleveland mice gave each other high fives. Now they could proceed with Plan A.

Together, they wrote the first-ever e-mail from a mouse to a human:

> From: TM3@mousenet.org
> To: Meganbug2@gmail.com
> Subject: The Mouse In School
>
> I'm glad you like mice. I'll see you at 3.

It looked a bit short. Was there something he could add that would make her want to meet him? He knew that when kids e-mail or text each other they sometimes write things like LOL or BFF or MOS or TTYL. But it wouldn't help to say he was laughing out loud, and he wasn't yet her best friend forever, and there was certainly no mom over his shoulder. But "Talk to you later," that would work. So he added:

TTYL. Your friend

Something was still missing. . . .

"Hold it," he said. "I need a good name."

TM3 didn't sound right. He needed a name that was a bit more human. One of his teachers had sometimes called him *Trey*, because it was an old word for *three*. That would do nicely. He signed himself "Trey."

When school was over for the day, it was just starting to rain. Megan sped up as she ran to Cherry Street, hoping the rain wouldn't keep Joey from shooting baskets today. She wanted to tell him about the mouse, because maybe he'd be impressed if he knew she wasn't the sort of girl who yelled "EEEK" and jumped on chairs. But the wind had started whipping at her in fierce gusts and throwing rain hard in her face, and the driveway was empty.

The house felt different from yesterday. It didn't have that quiet scary feeling. Instead it had a noisy scary feeling, as the wind tugged at it and made its loose parts clatter and creak. The trees that loomed behind the house were dancing and bending in the wind, while somewhere a tree limb thumped against the house hard enough to make it shake.

Megan thought about going upstairs to get the Thumbtop, but that would bring her closer to the wind and the trees. Besides, the big computer in the kitchen really was easier to use.

When she checked her e-mail, she found there was still no word from her mom, and she tried to ignore the knot of worry in her stomach. There was only one message, and it was from someone she didn't know. Her mom had always told her not to open e-mails from strangers, but the subject of this message was The Mouse In School, so it must be from a kid in her class. Who else would know?

She clicked on the message, which read:

From: TM3@mousenet.org
To: Meganbug2@gmail.com
Subject: The Mouse In School

I'm glad you like mice. I'll see you at 3. TTYL. Your friend, Trey

That was weird. What did that mean—TTYL? It looked like the sort of thing kids text, but she'd never texted. And who was Trey? She hadn't heard that name at Fairlawn. And how did he know her e-mail address? She hadn't given it to anyone yet. Three o'clock was about when she came out of school. Did that mean someone would be waiting for her tomorrow? Would it be someone she wanted to be friends with?

She pulled the class list out of her backpack. No one there called Trey. No name that even came close. She felt goose bumps starting to prickle at the back of her neck. She closed down her e-mail without answering the message, took out her homework, and tried to concentrate on math. And today she was really glad when Annie came home from the bank.

chapter Nine

The wind was still blowing when Megan went to bed, and she fell asleep to the sound of pine needles brushing against her window. When she woke up in the middle of the night, she'd been dreaming that the pine needles were brushing her face.

She opened her eyes, which usually made dreams stop, but the soft stroking went on until she sat up sharply. All she could see was the glowing face of her clock, which read 3:01. She listened to the silence for a minute, then lay down again. And that's when she heard an odd whispery sound.

"Miss Megan. Megan Miller. Meganbug."

It was so faint. Had she really heard? Was she going nuts? It was such a strange sound. It wasn't quite like a real voice, but more like the noise she'd hear when Uncle Fred was listening to the radio through headphones, and put them down for a minute.

There was silence for long enough to make her think she'd only imagined the voice. But then she heard it again, closer to her ear: "Miss Megan, I'm Trey. I sent you an e-mail, remember? I even watched you read it."

Now Megan felt awake enough to feel real fear. It started near her feet and raced up her body like an electric shock. The fear had reached her head, and she was just about to scream when she heard the voice say, "Please don't eeek. I'm your friend."

She forced herself to turn on the lamp on the cardboard box by her bed, even though she was afraid of what she might see. But when she saw it, she almost laughed. What had she been expecting? A ghost? Some guy standing there with an ax? Instead, right there on the edge of her pillow was an ordinary mouse sitting up on its haunches. It must have been squeaking in a way that sounded like human talk, if you were only half awake.

"Boo!" she said. The mouse didn't move, but kept on looking at her.

Oregon seemed full of weird mice—first the one at school, and now this guy in her bedroom. They seemed much braver than regular mice, or maybe much dumber, because they didn't run away. Unless maybe this wasn't a real mouse at all, but some sort of robot her dad had put on her pillow as a joke?

She peered down to get a better look, but that didn't help. In fact, what she saw started another wave of shock rippling through her body. The mouse's lips were moving as it said, "Don't worry! I won't hurt you."

She felt dizzy and lay down. But that put her eyes even closer to the mouse, which she now saw had a little piece missing from one ear. Its lips kept moving. Words kept coming.

"That's better," the mouse was saying. "Sorry I had to shout."

At last she managed to talk. "No," she said.

"No what?"

"You. You're not talking. You're not real."

"What makes you think I'm not real?"

"Well, mice don't talk," she said.

"So what am I, chopped liver? A human in a mouse suit?" he asked. "Lady, believe it. I am a mouse and I talk."

"That's not scientifically possible," she said. "I'll wake up and you'll be gone."

"I've got news," he said. "You're awake."

"Prove it," she said.

He scratched his head. "Why don't you get up and walk around. Do whatever it is that helps you wake up."

She went to the bathroom to splash water on her face, sort of hoping to find her dad in the corridor, laughing because she'd been fooled by his robot. But there was no one there. When she got back, the mouse was lying on her pillow looking very relaxed.

"So?" he said.

Megan couldn't think of anything to say.

"You probably want to know how I learned to talk, why I learned to talk, how many mice can talk, why you're the first human in the history of the world to hear a mouse talk, stuff like that?"

"I guess," said Megan, feeling that everything she had ever

learned about the natural world was turning upside down.

"There's a lot to tell you," said Trey, "but we can make a start tonight. Come with me."

"Where?" She imagined being led through a mousehole into a secret world, like Alice following the white rabbit to Wonderland.

"Just to your kitchen," he said.

She stood up and pulled a blanket off the bed, because the house was cold. Back on her pillow, she could see Trey was jumping up and down and saying something. She bent down to him.

"A ride would be nice," he said.

She sat on the bed so he could run up her arm to her shoulder, where he grabbed a braid.

"That's one reason we picked you," said Trey. "Great handles." And he gave a little whispery laugh, unlike any sound she had ever heard.

She could feel him holding on to the braid as she walked downstairs as quietly as she could. There was a faint glow coming from the kitchen. As they reached the doorway, Megan saw that the light was coming from the computer screen, illuminating three more mice standing near the keyboard.

On the screen were the words:

Welcome, Miss Megan!

She sat down heavily on the chair in front of the computer.

"Hey, careful!" came the voice from her shoulder. "Lucky I was holding on. Well, what do you think?"

"Who wrote that?" she asked.

"What's short and cute and has a long tail and a very good brain?"

"A mouse?"

"Mice," he said. "And lady, you ain't seen nothing yet. Hit it, gang!"

One of the three mice leaned over and clicked the "Return" key to start a presentation that began with a page headed:

Home of the Mouse Nation

For the next ten minutes, the presentation led Megan through the recent history of the mouse. It explained how mice have always been much smarter than they look, but they couldn't do much about it until the big breakthrough in Silicon Valley, when they had first learned to read and write and use computers.

"Do *all* mice know how to use computers?" she asked.

"Well, most of us," said Trey. "There are still a few wild tribes we haven't reached yet. But we'll get to them all eventually."

"I never knew," said Megan lamely.

"How could you?" said Trey. "No humans did."

The presentation was still going on, showing how mice all over the world could now e-mail each other, and visit mouse chat rooms, and communicate with their friends on MouseBook, and write mouse blogs, and take courses in politics and geography and history and English and math and mouse safety and understanding humans.

A picture of Planet Earth came up—one of those taken from space, making it look like a big blue marble. And with it came the words:

There is no limit to what we can do.
We are ready to help mankind.

Then that screen dissolved into another:

But there is a problem.
We don't have our own computers.
We have to borrow them from humans.
This is hazardous to our health!

Now the screen showed scenes of terrible things that can happen when a mouse borrows a human computer. In one, mice were so busy working at a big desktop that they didn't see the cat flying through the air toward them, its claws extended, its teeth bared. Another scene showed a woman standing on a chair screaming while a man chased mice away from her computer with a broom. Next came a picture of four mice working at a laptop so diligently that they didn't notice a human hand about to close the lid on them.

Then Megan gasped, as her own face filled the screen.

It was the photo from Uncle Fred's garage. Above her face were the words:

The Solution!

And below the picture:

The Thumbtop
Made by humans, meant for mice.
Coming soon to a mousehole near you.
Thank You, Miss Megan

Then the presentation ended, and Megan found she wasn't making sense. "No, but . . . we didn't . . . Who put that on the

Internet? I don't see how *my* Thumbtop, I mean, Uncle Fred . . ."

Trey patted her ear. "You must admit," he said, "that the Thumbtop is a whole lot better for mice than for humans. Paws yes, fingers no."

"But there's only one Thumbtop in the world! There's no way you can get one in every mousehole. That's impossible!"

"For mice," said Trey, running down her arm to stand in front of her, "there is no such word as impossible, as you will learn tomorrow."

"Tomorrow?"

"Tomorrow, the most important mouse in the world will answer your questions," said Trey. "Until then, not a word to anyone. Deal?"

"Deal," she said weakly, and shook the tiny paw that Trey held out to her.

It took her a long time to get back to sleep.

chapter ten

Megan was having a picnic with the dormouse from *Alice in Wonderland*. Then Stuart Little drove up in his car, with Johnny Town Mouse in the passenger seat. Stuart crashed his car into the dresser, which woke Megan up as the sound turned into a banging on her door.

"Wake up, sweetie!" said Annie, sticking her head into the room. "I called you three times! You're *late*."

So it was all a dream. No dormouse. No Stuart Little. No talking mouse leading her downstairs in the middle of the night.

Megan staggered out of bed and said, "EEEK!" A mouse with a piece missing from his ear was sitting on top of the dresser, looking straight at her.

"It *was* a dream, wasn't it?" she asked.

"Anything you say, lady," said the mouse, with a goofy grin.

"Not a dream," said Megan. She sat back on the bed, hard.

"It seems not," said Trey. "For one thing, dreams can't use computers, even little tiny ones. That's a hint."

"Oh, the Thumbtop." She took it out of the drawer and put it on the floor, beside the dresser, where no one could see it from the doorway. Trey stretched out a paw and pressed the ON button.

Megan saw that the Mouse Nation was right. The Thumbtop was a perfect size for mice. Trey's paws flew over the keys.

"Do you know just how great this thing is?" he asked her. "It's the greatest thing since sliced cheese, that's all."

"Glad you like it," she said.

Footsteps stopped outside the door, and Annie stuck her head in again.

"Who are you talking to?" she asked.

"No one," said Megan, thankful that Trey was out of sight.

She took her clothes to the bathroom, because somehow it didn't feel right getting dressed in front of a male who could talk, even if he was a mouse. When she was dressed, she ran down to the kitchen, where her dad was making breakfast.

"Are you lucky, or what?" he said, tossing some pancakes. "The greatest chef between Roseburg and Albany stayed home this morning to show you his Red Magic—breakfast edition."

"But there's not much *time* for breakfast," said Annie. "She's running late, aren't you, sweetie? Too busy talking to an imaginary friend!"

"You still have one of those?" asked her dad, dumping a stack of pancakes onto Megan's plate. "An imaginary friend?" He laughed. "I remember you had a little buddy when you were about three. Rosie, wasn't it? You were so cute, you and your Rosie."

"I don't have an imaginary friend," said Megan, but felt

herself going a bit red as she took a mouthful of pancake. Then she realized it was better to be heard talking to an imaginary friend than to a real mouse, so she changed it to, "Well, not exactly."

"What's that?" asked her dad. "Your mouth was sort of full."

"R*un*, girl!" said Annie. "Look at the *time*!"

Cramming in one last mouthful of pancake, Megan grabbed her backpack and took off up the street, followed by the rather plaintive voice of her dad calling out, "We'll talk tomorrow, okay? Tomorrow afternoon, you can help me at the restaurant. Learn some of that Red Magic. Is that a date?"

Megan turned to yell, "It's a date," then took deep breaths of the clean damp air as she ran up the street, glad to be away from human questions, glad to have time to think.

And upstairs at 253 Cherry Street, her unimaginary friend tapped out the message that his species was waiting for:

From: TM3@mousenet.org
To: Topmouse@mousenet.org
Subject: Yessssss!

I have made contact, and so far it's all good! Miss Megan has promised to help us, and she will keep our secret.

But what a secret it was! That morning, at the back of the classroom, Megan felt as if her head would burst with the size of it. It was way too big for any one kid. She found herself wondering, *Why me?* Why out of all the millions of kids in America did it have to be her? She longed to tell somebody, except of course she had promised not to, and besides, who would believe her? If she told any of the kids in this class, they'd think that her time on the island had addled her brain. And adults would march her straight off to have her head examined.

What had she gotten herself into, anyway? If she *did* help mice get computers, what then? How much would the world change? Might mice secretly want to hurt human civilization? Uncle Fred had told her about a nerd who'd hacked into one of the government's computer systems. If he hadn't been caught, he could have done a huge amount of damage.

And that was just one guy.

What if you had a million mice, all with computers, all hacking, all wanting to hurt your civilization? They'd be able to bring banks and businesses and hospitals and colleges and armies crashing to the ground—and if she was the one who let it happen, it would be all her fault.

How much *could* she trust mice? How much could she trust

Trey, even? Oh, if only she could tell Uncle Fred about him. Or her mom. They'd know what to do. Where *was* her mom?

THUMP!

A bony hand landed on her desk.

Mrs. Fitch had worked her way to the back of the room, and must have noticed that Megan was not exactly focused.

"Megan, dear, I'm sure you can give us the answer," she said. "What is the main product of Oregon?"

Megan looked up into the blue eyes behind the thick glasses and smelled the lavender soap and had no clue.

"Is it rain?" she asked. Everyone howled with laughter. That might have been fine if Megan had been trying to be funny, but she wasn't, and she went bright red one more time.

At last it was time to walk home, and that walk did a lot to calm Megan's fears.

The first mouse she saw was perched on a gatepost. It showed no sign of shyness as she approached, but made a deep bow in her direction. As she looked more closely she saw a second mouse bowing, half hidden in a clump of grass, then three more standing on a mailbox. Four or five were nestled among some leaves at the foot of a tree, while others peered out from bushes and flower beds, all bowing or waving their tails as she passed. Megan started off by waving back to each mouse and saying, "Hi there," but there were so many that she found it easier to waggle her fingers as if she were a queen waving to her subjects.

By the time she got home, she was sure of one thing: at least one species was on her side.

Four members of that species were waiting for her on the kitchen table.

"Greetings," said Trey. "We have work to do, but first I want you to meet my three friends from Cleveland. Last night you weren't properly introduced."

"Cleveland!" Megan exclaimed. "That's where I came from!"

"Well, duh!" said Trey.

"How did they get here?" she asked.

"In your suitcase," said Trey. "How else? But don't worry. Your modern mouse travels clean."

"Wow," said Megan, glad to meet anyone from Cleveland. "Can they talk?"

"Not with their mouths," said Trey. "Very few of us have been trained to make human sounds. Everyone else does MSL."

"Huh?"

"Mouse Sign Language. It started with some dudes who

hung out in a school for deaf kids. They copied the signs. Some of them weren't much use—all that stuff with fingers—but there's a lot you can do with ears and tails. Show her, guys!"

One of the Cleveland mice stepped forward and went into a graceful dance. He waved his front paws, formed changing patterns with his tail, and waggled his ears, sometimes together, sometimes separately.

"What did he say?" Megan asked.

"He said, 'My name is Mouse 48, Clan 1578, Cleveland Region, Mouse Nation,'" translated Trey. "'I enjoy action movies and am interested in world affairs.'"

Next came Mouse 42, same clan, same region, and interested in sports, especially college football.

And Mouse 47, who loved reading, especially stuff on Web sites that explained human behavior.

"Could we give them real names instead of numbers?" asked Megan.

"Okay with you guys?" asked Trey.

The three waggled and waved and swayed in a way that seemed to say, "Cool."

"So what shall it be?" asked Trey. "The Three Mouseketeers? No, that's been done to death." He thought for a minute, and remembered a video from the Talking Academy with so little dialogue that even beginner mice could talk along with it. "Let's go with the Three Stooges," he said, turning to the three mice and counting them off with his paw. "You can be Curly, you're Larry, and you're Mo. Any questions?"

Mouse 47, the one he'd called Mo, made some quick, agitated signs.

"Okay, okay," said Trey. "Mo is a female," he explained, "so she doesn't like that name. I've seen movies with girls called Mo," he said to the mouse. "You can pretend it's short for Molly or Maureen or something."

The mouse made some more signs.

"Okay, okay, fine." said Trey. "You can be Julia, if that's what you've always wanted. So we have Curly, Larry, and Julia. That's fine with me."

"There's still a problem," said Megan. "I can't tell you guys apart. Mind if I put little marks on you?"

She found a yellow marker, and each mouse in turn stood in front of her while she dotted their ears in alphabetical order—one for Curly, two for Julia, and three for Larry. As they got their dots, each mouse went into a slow pirouette of joy, because looking like every other mouse in the world can get a little old, and it was great to have a sign of personal identity.

And as Trey also pointed out, Megan could recognize *him* any time, thanks to the piece missing from his ear. He was about to describe the huge San Francisco rat that had chomped it, when the big computer on the table beeped. Curly, Larry, and Julia rushed to their positions, with Larry holding, Julia dangling, and Curly running around like crazy doing everything else.

"You're about to meet that important dude I was telling you about last night," said Trey, as the mice clicked their way to a screen that showed part of an office. "That's headquarters in Silicon Valley. A company went broke and the humans walked away. Left their gear behind, just like that. Is it impressive, or what?"

The webcam swiveled around to focus on a mouse sitting up on his hind legs with a chain of office around his neck.

"That's the Big Cheese," said Trey. "The guy with the bling. It's okay. He can't hear us."

"The Big *Cheese*?"

"That's what we call him behind his back," said Trey. "His real title is Chief Executive Mouse. He's the boss. Very important dude."

"He looks like he's waiting for someone," said Megan.

"He is. He's waiting for you. Tell him we're ready, guys!"

Curly clicked on a key that sent a signal to Silicon Valley.

The Big Cheese looked around as if to make sure he was meant to begin, then he started the graceful dance of Mouse Sign Language.

When the waggling and swaying stopped, Trey took over. "Okay, here's what he said: 'Welcome, Miss Megan, at one of the most important moments in the history of the world. A moment when two species that have always regarded each other with fear and loathing join forces for the good of all. There will be almost no limit to what we can do together for the benefit of the planet we share, once we have a computer in every mousehole, because although we are small, we are many, and we are very, very smart.' "

Megan remembered her fears from the morning.

"Is it okay if I ask him a question?"

"Sure," said Trey. "Shoot!"

"Ask him if he'll promise not to harm humans—like making our computers crash."

The three mice slowly tapped out the question.

"Madam," the Big Cheese began, stretching his back to make himself look as tall as possible. "We *need* your computer systems to work. We *need* your civilization to function smoothly. Indeed, it is in our interest to keep the human race as contented and peaceful as possible. You have my word that once we have suitable computers, the Mouse Nation will be a major force for good on this planet, because when humans prosper, we prosper."

Megan let that sink in, then remembered another of her thoughts from the morning.

"Can I tell my family about you?" she asked. "Like my uncle? He's the one who invented the Thumbtop."

"Tell no one—and *especially* not the uncle," replied the Big Cheese, with the little hop that puts emphasis on a word in MSL. "As the inventor of the computer, he will be vitally important to us, because we will need his help if we are to acquire sufficient computers for our needs. Any approach to him must be made with the greatest of care, and certainly not until we are ready to show him our plans."

"What plans?" asked Megan.

The Big Cheese looked a little impatient, as if the answer should be obvious to her.

"Why, plans for the production of the computer!" he said. "Our engineers are confident that we mice can learn to manufacture the computers ourselves—with some assistance from a human, such as the uncle. And we will then be in a position to usher in a new era that benefits the whole planet. And you must admit, humans could use our help. They are not doing a great job on their own."

Megan's mind was spinning. *Mice* making Thumbtops? *Mice* ushering in new eras? *Mice* helping humans to run the planet? It would take a while to sink in.

"Quick," Trey was saying. "He's waiting for you to say something."

"How about, 'Okay'?"

"He's expecting a bit more than that. Maybe something like, 'I am grateful for your confidence in me. I promise to tell no one, and will do my best to pave the way toward mass production of the computer for the benefit of both species.' Sound good?"

"I guess," she said.

Trey waved to the three Cleveland mice, and they laboriously wrote out the message. When it reached Silicon Valley, the Big Cheese gave a low bow, then made a few more signs.

"Now what's he saying?" asked Megan.

"He says that's excellent news," said Trey, "and he will reward you for your trouble. He has a gift for you right now, and he's telling me where to find it."

"A gift?" said Megan, and she looked around the kitchen, half expecting to see a package. But as the picture of the Big Cheese faded away, Curly, Larry, and Julia were opening Trey's e-mail program.

"Here it is!" said Trey. "Historic moment coming up right now. The first demonstration to a human of the power of the modern mouse. It's your gift," he explained, as Curly clicked to open a message:

From: Ozmice@mousenet.org.au
To: TM3@mousenet.org
Subject: Missing Parent

Tall female stiff yellow hair seen in outback, near habitat of hairy-nosed wombat. Can't e-mail because of sand in laptop.

"That's my mom!" yelled Megan. "You found her! It's like magic!"

"Magic?" said Trey. "You don't need magic when you have mice, and Australia has a *lot* of mice, so . . . Yikes!"

Annie's car was turning in to the driveway. There was a quick scuttle, a flash of fur and tails, and the four mice vanished into the space beside the refrigerator. Megan had plenty of time to shut down the computer, because Annie stopped to talk to a neighbor before she came into the kitchen.

"Are you okay, honey?" she asked as she came in. "Mrs. Coleman just told me you were talking to some bushes. Is that what you did in the wild? Or is something worrying you?"

"I'm fine!" said Megan, with a grin. "No problems! In fact, things are going just great."

She gave Annie a quick hug before running upstairs to her room, where her new friends were already waiting for her.

chapter eleven

"I have excellent news," the Big Cheese told the Mouse Council that night. "I have personally spoken to Miss Megan, and she has assured me that she will do her best to help our nation acquire computers."

This was indeed great news. Everyone started to talk at once in MSL, turning the tabletop into a graceful whirl of paws and tails and ears.

The Big Cheese raised a paw, and the random ballet simmered down. He turned to the Chief Engineer. "How long will it take to complete your plans for the computer's mass production?"

"I need to know much more about it," said the Chief Engineer. "Do I have your permission to talk to the mouse on the spot?"

"You do," said the Big Cheese.

The engineer waved to the team of mice standing around the computer in the corner of the conference room. They went into action to summon Trey.

He was asleep in one of Megan's shoes, exhausted from his night and day of educating her. Curly was on duty guarding the Thumbtop, and heard the little beep that meant a message was

coming through. He woke Trey to tell him that someone from Headquarters wanted him for instant messaging right now.

"They couldn't wait for a civilized hour?" Trey muttered. But he staggered over to the Thumbtop.

"Greetings, mouse!" dictated the Chief Engineer, as the rest of the Mouse Council watched the words of the conversation roll across the monitor screen.

"Yo," replied Trey, his paws not yet wide awake enough for long words.

"First," wrote the Chief Engineer, "tell us whether the small computer is good to use."

"It's way cool," wrote Trey.

"Do you mean it does not overheat during use?" asked the Chief Engineer.

"I spoke figuratively," wrote Trey, privately thinking that the dude should get out more. "It's a delight to use. Perfect for paws."

The engineer glared at the two youngest members of the council, who were making the MSL sign for "laughing out loud" (it's the right paw in front of the mouth).

"Describe the device," he continued. "Please do not speak figuratively."

"Think of a laptop that has shrunk to mouse size," wrote Trey.

"Is there a mouse-sized mouse?" asked the Chief Engineer.

"No," wrote Trey. "Just a paw pad. Touch pad, they call it."

"I will need information on the components," said the Chief Engineer. "Can you open it up and describe the parts?"

Trey turned the Thumbtop over. Without thumbs and a screwdriver, there was no way he could look inside. "Can't do it," he wrote. "Not enough thumbs."

"Then have your human make a list of the parts for me as soon as possible," replied the engineer.

When Megan woke up, she wasn't much help. She knew Uncle Fred had taken parts from lots of different places, like old cell phones and thumb drives and remote controls, but she didn't know their technical names.

"I'll ask Uncle Fred," she said, and just had time to send an e-mail before school:

From: Meganbug2@gmail.com
To: Fbarnesinvent@gmail.com
Subject: Thumbtop

Some people

Then she remembered that mice aren't technically people, so she deleted "people" and wrote:

Some friends want to know how we made the Thumbtop, like what parts we put in it, and I don't know their names. Could you please e-mail sometime today?

The trouble was that while "sometime today" was okay for Uncle Fred and Megan, who operated on human time, it wasn't nearly fast enough for the Chief Engineer, who was on mouse time. That morning he e-mailed Trey three times asking why the list had not yet reached him. And three times, Trey told him that there was no chance before evening, because his human was to spend the afternoon with her male parent, and would not even check her e-mail until late in the day.

Megan's dad was waiting for her in his car after school, and whisked her off to the restaurant to help him cook while they had a father-daughter chat.

The afternoon was so busy—cutting up vegetables and rolling out pastry and skimming fat off a stew—that Megan almost forgot about mice and Thumbtops and chief engineers. As she and her dad worked, they talked, and he kept making her laugh with some of the lamest food jokes she'd ever heard. Like, "Did you ever hear about the chef who made the soup so thick that when he stirred it the room went around?" Or, "What do you call a cat that ate a lemon? A sourpuss."

Megan groaned with such pain that he dropped the jokes and started asking her about the island and her mom. She was glad to find that he wanted to know more than just where they went to the bathroom, and he listened intently as she told him about hiking all over the island, and scrambling up damp mountains after the sheep, and helping her mom with research.

"It's great, how Susie wants to save the world," he said. "I really admire that. Someone has to do it. Have you heard from her?"

"Well yeah, but she can't . . ." Megan stopped herself because she'd been about to mention the sand in the laptop before she realized that there was no way she could know that officially—no way without the magic of mice.

So she backtracked. "She e-mailed from Sydney," she said.

That seemed to be enough for her dad. As they started to cut up vegetables for another dish, he began to talk about Paris, and how hard it was being an apprentice chef, but how great it was when he finally got a job at a world-class restaurant, where he specialized in fish.

And that's how he met Annie, who was a model at the time. She was at a table with a bunch of other Americans and had a question about the fish. He came out to explain, and she was so beautiful that, well . . . well, the rest was history.

Which left Megan wondering where she'd be right now if

Annie'd had a question about the dessert instead of the fish, and she'd married some other assistant chef. But for today, at least, Megan was glad about the way things had worked out.

Megan was still at the restaurant when the first customers came in, including Joey and his grandma—a white-haired woman who looked a bit wobbly and held on to Joey's shoulder as she walked.

"So you're Megan!" she said, coming up to peer into Megan's face through very thick glasses. "Annie's told me all about you."

Which made Megan a bit nervous until Annie herself arrived and gave her a huge hug and said, "Aunt Em, I see you've met my lovely stepdaughter."

And yes, Annie did look like a model, with her huge blue eyes carefully made up, and her lipstick perfect.

There weren't many customers, so Red Miller sat with them to eat the stew, pointing out it was special because Megan had helped.

"Are you going to be a chef like your dad?" Aunt Em asked her.

Megan almost said no way, she wanted to do something much more important, but she guessed that Annie and her dad thought cooking *was* important, so she said, “It looks like fun, but I think I’ll be a scientist.”

“Have you ever thought about being a spy?” Joey asked.

“A *spy*?” said Megan, astonished. “Why would I be a spy? Who would I spy for?”

And Joey gave her a half-smile and a shrug that she didn’t begin to understand.

“What about you, Joey?” asked Megan’s dad. “Going to be an inventor like Jake?”

Joey shrugged. “Seems like a hard way to make a living.”

“It’s not your dad’s fault he had to stop working on those solar blobs,” said Annie. “But he’ll get back to them, won’t he? In this new job? Jake’s working for a company that makes Tick-Tock-Clicks,” she explained to Megan. “Show her, Joey.”

Joey unwound a clunky-looking watch from his wrist and aimed it at his grandma. There was a click, and her picture appeared on the dial.

“Isn’t that neat?” said Aunt Em.

“The trouble is,” said Annie, “everyone in the company has to start out selling. And Jake isn’t crazy about that.”

“But if he does well,” said her dad, “his boss promised he could get back to his blobs. Which would make sense because they'd be a great power source for Tick-Tocks—maybe for things like cell phones too."

"And if that doesn't work out," said Aunt Em, "he can always rely on his investments. Like this restaurant. Right, Red?" She laughed.

"Yeah, yeah, yeah," he said, reaching out to pat Aunt Em on the arm. "One of these days I'll be able to pay him back. With interest. Just as soon as we start making a ton of money."

"We *will* make money," said Annie firmly. "We *will* come out of this bad patch. Then we'll be fine, and Jake will be fine. . . ."

"And I'll be fine," said Joey. "Get my college fund back."

Red Miller sighed. "It's hard. People around here aren't used to French food," he told Megan. "Then there's the cost of everything I have to get from France. Like truffles from Périgord, cheese from Normandy. . . ."

"Do you *have* to get food from France?" asked Megan, because that was one of the things her mom worried about—all the fuel it took to send food halfway around the world. "Doesn't it grow in Oregon?"

Everyone turned to stare at her.

Annie gave her trilling little laugh. "Truffles?" she asked. "Camembert?"

But Megan's dad took her seriously.

"Some restaurants do great business that way," he said. "Just buying local food and cooking it, you know, sort of fresh and natural. And yeah, that sort of restaurant could do well. But that's not *moi*. That's not the way I was trained. And there'd be so much to learn. I'd have to look into business models—cash flow—all that stuff. And it's not like I have an MBA."

"A what?" she asked.

"A business degree. Master of Business Administration, I think it's called."

Megan laughed. "Hey, I can help you. I have an MBA."

"You have *what*?" said Annie, with the little smile you use on someone who is probably nuts.

"An MBA, sort of," said Megan. And it was true, if you meant Mouse Business Assistance.

Annie and Joey and Aunt Em all laughed because it had to be a joke. Right? But Megan noticed that her dad was deep in thought, not laughing at all.

chapter twelve

"You've got mail!" said Trey, running to meet her as she came into her room.

His day had not gone well. The Chief Engineer had kept up his barrage of e-mails, barking things like, "I expect the courtesy of a reply" and "Where's that list?"

"You could have opened it yourself," said Megan. "You know my password, don't you?"

"Well, duh," said Trey. "Of course I do, because I know everything, but I thought you might have a cow. *Mice* have cows if you go near their e-mail."

Megan was in a great mood after the dinner at the restaurant, where her family had really started to *feel* like a family, and the vision of mice having cows gave her a fit of the giggles loud enough to bring Annie scurrying upstairs to see if she was okay.

When Annie was safely downstairs again, Megan clicked onto her mail. There was a message from her mom, finally, as well as one from Uncle Fred.

"Okay," said Trey. "Your mom first."

He could hardly sit still while she quickly read her mom's e-mail telling her that she was safe, and missed Megan, and had gotten the sand out of her laptop, and had been observing her first hairy-nosed wombats.

Megan quickly replied, saying that things were going much better here in Oregon.

"Now," said Trey, "the next one? Please please please?"

And there it was:

From: Fbarnesinvent@gmail.com
To: Meganbug2@gmail.com
Subject: Parts

Why do you want this stuff, kiddo? Have you come across some rich dudes who want to invest in Thumbtops? That'll be the day! Hey, thanks for telling me about your step-cousin Jake. I Googled around and found his e-mail and now we're in touch. Told me all about his blobs. Sounds like my sort of guy.

He added a smiley face and attached a list. Megan quickly replied to say thanks, and after Trey had forwarded the list to the Chief Engineer, they celebrated with a high five, or a low five, or a five-four, or whatever it is you do when you tap your hand to the paw of a mouse. Then Megan had to dive into her math homework, with a little help from Trey, who had done well on fractions.

As she lay down to sleep that night, with Trey in a slipper on the cardboard box by her bed, Megan felt exceptionally good about the state of her world. This family was turning out to be okay. Joey seemed to like her somewhat, even if that question about being a spy was a bit weird. And it was terrific to have a friend to whisper to after she'd put out the light, even if that friend was a mouse.

Perhaps it was just as well that she was fast asleep before that nice world started to fall apart.

Larry had been on guard duty, and woke Trey with the news that the Chief Engineer wanted him urgently for some instant messaging. Again.

"Now what's chewing your tail?" is what Trey wanted to write, but instead he tapped out: "How can I help you, sir?"

"The list you sent is useful, but I need more information," wrote the engineer. "I must see how the parts fit together. Have you learned yet how to take the back off the computer?"

"Still not enough thumbs," wrote Trey.

Which produced an order: "Your human has thumbs. Have her in front of a webcam at 3:15 tomorrow afternoon."

"There's no webcam in this house," wrote Trey.

"Find a house that has one," replied the engineer.

Then he signed off before Trey could point out that humans weren't mice. You couldn't just tell them what to do. But with a sigh, he went to work.

Locating a house with a webcam away from prying eyes wasn't hard. All it took was an e-mail to the commander, who e-mailed all the clans in the neighborhood. By dawn Trey had the address of a house on Spruce Street with a webcam and no cats, guaranteed, and no humans either, because they were away in Florida.

But as he looked at the Megan-shaped bump in the bed, he got a bad feeling inside. He'd been afraid it would come to this—that he'd have to ask Megan to do something that was fine for mice, but not so great for humans, not for her. Just how far could he push her to follow the rules of *his* world—especially the rule that says you have to obey an order from a member of the Mouse Council no matter what?

. . . .

When Megan woke up, Trey was standing on her pillow, giving her his best grin (actually, it was his second-best grin, but she didn't know him well enough to see that he was forcing it).

"Hey, human," he said.

"Hey, mouse," she said, tickling him behind an ear.

Good, thought Trey. She seems to be in a friendly mood. "You're in luck," he said, remembering his course on Human Persuasion, which said you should always try to put a positive spin on things, even if you don't feel very positive yourself. "You get to see the Chief Engineer today."

"Is he coming here?" she asked.

"Not exactly," he said.

"Then . . ." she began.

"You're wondering how mice learn to be engineers?" said Trey, remembering another part of the persuasion course. His teacher had told him about "Distraction Theory." If you want to get people on your side, try distracting them. Give them so many facts that they won't know which ones are really important.

"Mice learn by watching," he continued. "Eavesdropping. Our engineers mostly hung out in computer companies, like Hewlett-Packard and IBM, but some of them learned their stuff in universities. I think this guy went to Stanford."

The engineer wanted to look at the Thumbtop on a webcam, Trey told her. Yeah, he knew there wasn't a webcam here on Cherry Street, but some local guys had lined one up. Wasn't that great? All she had to do was to find a tiny screwdriver and put it in her backpack. Then take the Thumbtop to school with her. Oh yes, he'd have to ride in her backpack too. Could she please make a hole in it so he could look out? He'd always wanted to see a human classroom.

Later, Megan thought she should have asked more questions, like where was this webcam? And did she have human permission to use it, as well as mouse permission? But she trusted Trey, and did what he asked. She put the Thumbtop in her backpack and poked a little hole in the fabric with a sharp pencil so a mouse could see out.

Downstairs, she told Annie that she needed a tiny screwdriver for a special project, which was true. When Annie produced one, Megan slid it into her backpack, next to the mouse that was trying not to make a bulge.

Strictly speaking, backpacks were meant to hang on hooks on the wall, but Megan kept hers at her feet so that Trey could watch the proceedings through his hole. After lunch, Mrs.

Fitch showed a video about the animals of Oregon, including the huge rodent that was the official state animal—the beaver. Megan leaned down to whisper, "Hey, rodents rule!"

Then she jumped as a hand landed on her shoulder. Mrs. Fitch had sidled around to the back of the room just in time to hear Megan talking to her backpack.

"Megan!" was all she said, her bulgy eyes big and sorrowful behind the thick lenses. "Oh, Megan."

But as it turned out, having a teacher think you talk to backpacks was not the worst of Megan's problems that afternoon.

When Megan and Trey looked back at what happened that day, he quoted some lines of poetry from a course on The Mouse In Literature:

"'The best laid schemes o' mice an' men gang aft a-gley.'"

"Huh?" said Megan.

"It's about Scottish mice," said Trey. "It means that plans often go wrong."

"Tell me about it," Megan had said, because that afternoon their plans had indeed gone a-gley, and then some.

The house with the webcam had looked so innocent, set back from a silent street. As Megan walked there from school, she had no suspicions, and Trey made sure there was no room for suspicion in her mind. Riding on her shoulder, he talked nonstop about how pleased the Big Cheese was with her, and what fun they would have showing the Thumbtop to the Chief Engineer.

Actually, he was trying to do more than convince Megan that this adventure was okay. He was trying to convince himself. And he was having a hard time because deep down he thought his superiors had goofed. They shouldn't have ordered him to set up this webcam thing—not if it meant breaking a human law.

It was a question of trust.

If anything went wrong, Megan might never trust him again, and where would the Mouse Nation be then? Stuck in the Dark Ages, that's where; sneaking out to steal computer time at night for all eternity.

But for now he had to follow orders, and those orders were to get her inside the house.

"Here we are," he said, sounding as cheerful as he could. "This is it."

"A house?" she asked. "I thought we'd be going to a library or something. Not a house. Who lives here?"

"Some humans," he said, trying to sound as if it was no big

deal. "They're off in Florida. Aren't we lucky? Went away and left us their house, just like that."

They'd stopped on the sidewalk, and Megan showed no signs of wanting to go up to the front door.

"So it's mice in charge?" she asked. "Mice who said we could go in?"

"Well, duh," said Trey.

"But we can't! It's against the law."

"It's not against *mouse* law," he said, hoping he sounded soothing. "We do it all the time. And I'll bet you went in and out of people's houses on the island. Right?"

He climbed down her arm so he could see her face, and registered that it matched Not Convinced, No How, No Way on the Chart of Human Expressions.

"Look," he said, "I wish we didn't have to do it this way. I wish I could buy you a webcam. I wish we could find one in an empty barn or something. But I have orders to get you in here. The guys at Headquarters say they *have* to see inside your computer. You want to help them save the world, don't you? All that good stuff? And if I don't get you in there . . ."

"Then what?"

"They'll think I don't have my human under control. They might take me off the job. Send you some other Talking Mouse."

He looked so anxious that Megan relented. After all, she wouldn't hurt anything. And besides, the Mouse Nation needed her to do this, and she did believe in the nation, did believe it would be a power for good. And as long as no one saw her . . .

She walked up to the house, picked up the key that appeared at her feet, opened the door, and went in.

A guide mouse was sitting in the middle of the hallway. Megan's heart was pounding as she followed it deeper into the house, which had the sort of silence that tells you its humans are away, leaving only the occasional sound of a refrigerator turning itself off and on, and the faint ticking of a clock. It was one of those houses in which every surface is covered with ornaments, a house that doesn't have kids, and probably doesn't even like kids.

The mouse led Megan into a den where a computer sat on a spotless desk. She noticed a webcam above its screen, just like Uncle Fred's. Three mice were sitting next to the keyboard, saying "Hi!" (a simple wave of the right paw).

"Great setup, guys," said Trey. "Let's go."

Megan sat down to operate the computer. Hey, as long as

she was here, she might as well do what Trey wanted and get it over with, though her heart was still beating too loudly for comfort. Following Trey's directions, she clicked her way to a screen that showed five mice standing on a table in Silicon Valley.

"Computer engineers," said Trey, whispering now, very close to her ear. "Nerds. Very serious dudes. They can hear you, so watch what you say."

The Chief Engineer stepped forward and said something in MSL, starting with a wave of his right paw, and ending with a sharp twitch of his left ear.

"What did he say?" asked Megan.

"He said, 'Greetings, human, let's get started,'" translated Trey. "Typical engineer," he added in a whisper, hiding his mouth behind his paw. "No small talk."

No one noticed the boy in the green Oregon Ducks jacket as he hid his bike behind a bush and crept up to the window just as Megan sat down at the computer and started talking to it. Hidden by a climbing plant, he watched as she took a tiny screwdriver out of her backpack. Then he almost gave himself away with an "Aha!" as she pulled the tiny *thing* out of her backpack and loosened some screws. What was on the screen? Who was she talking to? No way to see from this window. He'd have to find some other way to solve the mystery. After a few minutes, he picked his bike out of the bush where he'd hidden it, and pedaled away with a huge sense of excitement. He was really on to something now.

It was going well. The Chief Engineer gave instructions in MSL, Trey translated, and Megan did what he asked, holding up the bits one by one as she explained how they fit together.

Trey watched Megan admiringly, thinking again that he had really lucked out with this human. Down in Silicon Valley, the engineers were also impressed, and when Megan had almost finished, the Chief Engineer said something in MSL.

"What was that?" asked Megan.

"He said you are smarter than he expected," said Trey. "For an immature human."

"*What?*" exclaimed Megan. She was about to explain that being young didn't make you dumb, when a mouse came running in from his watch post by the front door. He leaped onto the desk in front of her and gave an old-fashioned squeak, followed by some urgent gestures.

"Oh no! Human coming!" squeaked Trey. "Turn it off! Off! Everybody hide!"

Megan quickly clicked "Shut down" as Trey dived behind a big chair, and mice scattered in all directions.

She heard the sound of a key in the door. Panic spread upward, tingling through her body, making it hard to move. This is it, she managed to think. I'm going to jail.

Trey stuck his head around the corner of the chair.

"Move it!" he yipped, as loudly as he could. "Find a hole! Hide! The couch! The couch!"

There was a tiny space behind the couch. Megan quickly rolled over the back and squeezed herself down, just as the front door closed, and footsteps came down the hallway.

She held her breath as the feet went past the door of the den. Then came the sound of water gushing into something. Footsteps again, coming this way, into this room.

Megan heard the faint splosh of water being poured onto a houseplant. Two plants. Three.

An arm with a watering can appeared above her head, reaching for a plant on the windowsill behind the couch.

A woman's voice: "You're a thirsty little one. Lucky for you I came a day early!"

Megan held her breath as a few drops of water splashed onto her nose, but the woman never looked down. Soon Megan heard the heavy steps move back toward the door, and she felt it was safe to breathe—until the steps paused. Had the woman seen the Thumbtop parts spread over the desk? But then came the sound of a heavy person settling into a chair. And a man's voice. "For five thousand dollars, which is the *real* diamond?"

For ten minutes the woman watched the game show. Then came a commercial break, and Megan heard the chair creak as the woman got up and walked out of the room. Was she leaving? Alas, no. All she did was make a phone call, loud enough so Megan could hear everything—how her own TV was on the fritz, so she was watching at the Bellins' because she had the key, even though it wasn't her usual watering day. She didn't want to miss her game show *or* her soaps, so she'd be here till six.

Six! That would mean at least two more hours trapped behind this couch! Megan wondered what would happen if she made a break for it—if she ran past the woman to freedom. But she'd have to keep running all the way to Cleveland, because there probably weren't too many girls in the whole of Oregon with red hair standing straight up in front, and once the cops started looking for one, she'd be dead meat.

So there she lay. STUCK. And as the quiz show gave way to a soap opera, then another, Megan had plenty of time to think black thoughts about mice. How could they have blown it so badly?

At one point the woman went to the kitchen to fetch something, and Trey took the opportunity to scoot across to Megan's hiding place.

"Please forgive us," he whispered. "She never comes on Fridays! But someone should have known her TV was broken. Someone should have guessed she'd watch her shows here."

After the last soap opera sloshed to an end, the woman stayed on for some news headlines, so it was after six when she finally left. At last, Megan could scoop the Thumbtop bits into a plastic bag that she fetched from the kitchen, and get out of there.

A mouse was standing near the front door, droopy with misery. He sat up on his haunches just long enough to say something in MSL, then drooped back down again.

"He says his clan will never live down the disgrace," said Trey. "Do me a favor?" he whispered into Megan's ear before diving into the backpack. "Tell him you're not too mad at them?"

"It's okay," said Megan to the mouse. "I don't blame you."

She hurried out, hoping that just this once, Annie would be working late, and the house would be empty, and there'd be no awkward questions about vanishing for a whole afternoon.

chapter thirteen

It was worse than Megan had expected.

There was a police car in the driveway of her house. And her dad's car. And Annie's. And there was Joey on his bike, coming from the other direction.

Megan put down her backpack in the hallway, then went into the kitchen. A big cop was sitting at the table eating cookies, while her dad leaned against a counter, his arm around Annie.

"Here she is!" yelled the cop, standing up and scattering crumbs, a huge smile on his face. "You gave us all a real scare, young lady. Oh, don't you love it when missing kids turn up safe and sound? Anyhoo, I'll be on my way."

Which left Megan to face two very agitated people.

. . . .

When Megan had dumped her backpack in the hallway, Trey wriggled out and made his way inside the walls to the viewing slot by the refrigerator. Curly, Larry, and Julia were already there, and Trey gave Curly the whispered order to go keep watch over Megan's backpack. So it was Curly who saw Joey enter the house and crouch over the backpack and pull on the zipper of a pocket and take something out.

"Where *were* you?" Annie was saying, her voice pitched higher than usual. "I was home early today and I searched everywhere. The school, the library, even downtown. We thought you'd been kidnapped!"

"She's right," said her dad, wrapping his arms around his daughter. "We were scared to death."

Trey held his breath as he peered out. He could almost feel the pressure on Megan, almost feel the emotion spilling out of the adults. Would so much pressure make her break her promise to the Big Cheese? Make her tell these big humans what she'd actually been doing this afternoon?

"I wasn't far away," Megan said softly.

"But where?" asked her dad, stepping back to look her in the face. "You can trust us, Megan. I know you're having a few . . .

well, some problems. Like daydreaming in class and talking to bushes and talking to your backpack—your teacher called us about that. But we want to help you. Because we love you. Can you tell us what's going on?"

It was at this point that Curly shot into the viewing slot and tapped Trey on the back. He tried to say something—something about backpacks—but it was too dark for Trey to see the details, and it was too late anyway, because at that moment Joey came into the kitchen. With a plastic bag.

"Not a good time, pal," said Megan's dad.

"She was with me," said Joey, looking very pleased about something.

"Where? At your house?" exclaimed Annie, beaming now. "Why didn't you tell us, Megan?"

Megan stared at Joey, but there was no way she could guess what was going on behind that grin.

"We were at a *friend's* house, working on this . . . this *thing*," said Joey, waving the plastic bag. "Megan's thing. Trying to fix it."

"But you could have called!" said Megan's dad.

"I guess we were so busy we forgot," said Joey. "Right, Megan?"

"Well, please don't ever scare us like this again, Megan," said her dad, giving her another hug. "We were all ready to get your head examined, or ground you for life, so promise next time you'll call? One of you? What is that thing, anyway?"

"It's a . . ." Joey went on. "How would you describe it, Megan? Anyway, I've figured out how to fix it, and I've just remembered, we have the right sort of tools at home. So I'll work on it this evening. Okay?"

"No!" said Megan, walking toward him and reaching for the plastic bag. "It's mine. You can't . . ."

"But back at our friend's house, on *Spruce* Street, you said something different," he said slowly, holding the bag behind him and staring straight into her eyes. "Right after you'd finished with that webcam. And I'll give it back as soon as I've fixed it."

The mention of Spruce Street and webcams knocked all the fight out of Megan. She glanced at the viewing slot, hoping for help. Trey stepped forward as far as he dared and waved in a gesture that he hoped she'd recognize as, "It's cool." And in fact, all was not lost. He'd worked it out. Even if Joey had been looking through the window at the Spruce Street house, he couldn't have seen the mice on the screen.

Joey was leaving now, with a smile at Megan that didn't look totally unfriendly. Then Trey watched the remaining humans do a lot of hugging, with the big ones telling Megan that the reason they'd been so scared was that they loved her so much. And at that point, Trey rubbed his eyes and peered more intently at Megan, because something was happening that he'd never seen before. Water was coming out of her eyes and pouring down her face. Trey had read about "crying," and he'd seen it on videos, but he had no idea it could be so wet; and seeing tears on Megan's face gave him a twisting feeling inside that he wasn't used to.

Upstairs, Megan crashed onto her bed. Trey emerged from under the dresser and scrambled up to sit beside her, feeling terrible because her eyes were still leaking.

"I thought . . . I thought I could do what you said. I thought it would be safe," she said, in a throttled sort of voice. "And my dad . . . he was so nice and I sort of lied to him . . ." She didn't finish, but put her face into her pillow while her shoulders shook.

"Please, please forgive us," said Trey, patting her ear. "I'll never, ever, ever get you in a situation like that again, even if the boss orders me to do it. Cross my heart and hope to die."

She looked up as he crossed his paws over his chest, closed his eyes, and fell over backward on her pillow like a dead mouse.

"No more going into people's houses," she said.

"I promise," he said, still on his back but opening one eye.

He noticed there was still some leakage from her eyes, and he sat up to give some quick instructions to Julia in MSL. She ran off to the bathroom and came back pulling a sheet of toilet paper, which she dragged up onto the bed. Trey grabbed a corner of the paper between his front paws and started to dab at Megan's wet eyes.

He had meant simply to stop the leaking, but his dabbing did something better. It made her laugh, which seemed to be a great cure for leaky eyes. In a few minutes, she seemed almost back to normal. And she showed it by getting very, very mad.

"Joey!" she said. "It was good when he covered for me, but why was he spying on me? And why did he steal my Thumbtop? He's a rat!"

"Please," said Trey. "Don't insult our fellow rodents! Now, if you were to call him a dog, or a shark, or a rattlesnake . . . maybe a warthog. I've always thought there was something evil about warthogs."

"You don't seem mad at him!" said Megan. "You don't seem to *mind* that he's got the Thumbtop!"

"Oh, I'm mad," said Trey. "I mind. But being mad doesn't get things done. It doesn't help find solutions."

"Well, what does?" she asked.

"How about the power of thought?" he said. "Logical thought, starting with the simplest solution. He's a member of your clan, right? So he should listen if you appeal to his better nature. Isn't that what humans do?"

Megan thought about that. She didn't know Joey's regular nature well enough to know if he had a better one. But it was worth a shot.

chapter fourteen

The phone was in the kitchen, and so was Annie, which meant Megan had to tell her she needed to call Joey.

"Of course," said Annie. "Any time."

She clicked her way to the "Aunt Em" number on the phone and handed it to Megan as it rang—then looked a bit disappointed when Megan carried the handset out of earshot, taking it through the living room and out into the backyard.

From there, she could see a Joey-shaped shadow on the curtain of his room, holding the phone.

"Hi," she said. "I'm in our yard. Can you come down and talk?"

The Joey shadow reached for the curtains and pulled them open, revealing Joey himself, lit from behind as he peered down. Trey had climbed out of Megan's pocket to sit on her shoulder, but now he shrank back so the phone would hide him in the dusk.

"I can talk from here," said Joey. "Whazzup?"

"Thanks for saying I was with you," she began.

"Okay," he said. "But what were you doing? Who were you talking to on that webcam?"

"I can't tell you," she said. "I promised. I was just showing someone my computer."

"Computer!" he exclaimed. "So that's what it is! I thought it was just a phone or something. But a computer—that's a whole new ball game."

Megan could have kicked herself for telling him the truth about what was in that plastic bag.

"I want it back now," she said. "Please? Can you bring it down?"

But Joey was on a roll. "Hey, if it's a computer, all the more reason for me to put it back together, because I bet there's stuff in there that tells me what you've been doing—what sort of spying. Tell you what—here's the deal. If you tell me why you were in that house, I'll give it back. Otherwise, it's my *duty* to get the computer working again, don't you think? So I can find out what's in it? What sort of secrets?"

"But I never said you could take it!"

"And I never said you could go into that house! Are you in a gang or something? Like a bunch of hackers? Look, if you guys are planning a crime, I'll find out one way or another, so you may as well tell me now."

"I can't tell you," she said. "It's not a gang . . . just me. Please give it back. My uncle made it for me. I really, really need it. It means a lot to me."

"Means a lot to me too," he said. "Yeah, I'll give it back—just not yet. Okay?"

Megan didn't know what to say, partly because she had that feeling behind the eyes that means you might cry. Trey stroked her neck.

"Leave it," he whispered. "We'll get it back. We'll think of something."

Annie was calling.

"Okay," said Megan in a wobbly voice, and ended the call. She dropped Trey off at the bottom of the stairs then went into the kitchen to eat, although she really wasn't hungry, even for the leftover stew she'd helped to make.

Curly, Larry, and Julia had been sitting on Megan's windowsill watching the conversation in the dusk below them, and they could tell from the way Megan drooped that Joey had won that round.

They were not surprised when Trey rushed in from under the dresser, radiating a sense of urgency.

"Not good," he said, and told them of Joey's threat to put the Thumbtop back together and search its brain. "If he does put it back together, we all know what he'll find, don't we? He'll find mice, that's what."

Because they'd done something that he now realized was very dumb. They'd left the password on the computer, thinking it would be safe from prying eyes. Now everyone remembered what sites they'd visited when it had last been their turn to surf. Larry had been on his MouseBook page, writing his thoughts about the upcoming football game between Wisconsin and Ohio State. Julia was on MouseSpace chatting with a couple of friends, while Curly had been looking up Tillamook in the cheese section of Whiskerpedia, which has the answers to every question a mouse could dream up.

And Trey's virtual pawprints would be everywhere, with all his back-and-forth from Headquarters—including some references to the long-range plans of the Mouse Nation for the future of the world.

Everything was mouse, mouse, mouse.

Would Joey know how to bring the Thumbtop back to life? And if he did, could he make sense of what he found on it?

It was a risk Trey couldn't afford to take. At the very least, someone needed to keep watch while the computer was in Joey's care.

"Any guys in his house that you know of?" Trey asked the Cleveland Three. "Is there a clan we could e-mail, get them to watch Joey?"

"No mice there at all," said Julia. "That's the word on the street. The house is infested."

Meaning there was a cat.

Usually no clan would set up permanently in a house with a cat. At best, you could sprint in and out if you absolutely had to.

"Then it has to be one of us," said Trey. "Cat or no cat. Do I have a volunteer?"

The three mice all thought back to the last time they'd been asked to volunteer for a mission. That one had turned into the most uncomfortable upside-down ride in mouse history, and for a moment no one moved.

"Okay," said Trey. "Let's do it the hard way: Eeny, meeny, miny, mouse. Who's the guy for Joey's house? M-O-U-S-E spells . . ."

“I’ll go, I’ll go,” Curly interrupted, because he had a hunch he was going to be It, and he might as well look brave. Besides, who knew? It could even be fun.

For Megan, dinnertime was the worst since she’d arrived. Annie was so glad that Megan and Joey were hanging out together that she couldn’t stop asking questions. Did the two of them have a lot in common? Did Joey help Megan with her homework, maybe? Or play basketball with her? And just what had he borrowed from her that afternoon?

Megan’s answers were short: “Not a lot,” “No,” “Not yet,” and “That’s our secret.”

The word “secret” started Annie on a whole new string of questions.

Was there a secret club? Was it just the two of them, or were there others? Did they have a clubhouse? And a password? Annie had been in a club herself in fifth grade—the Secret Seven, no boys allowed.

“We were so bad. We’d borrow our moms’ makeup and jewelry . . .”

She was off on a long tale of rituals and secret signs and what fun it all was, especially with the lipsticks, while Megan worried about what might be happening right now to the *real* secrets on her Thumbtop, in that upstairs room across the fence.

Curly had been slow to get started because he had never been away from Larry and Julia in his whole life, and they were hesitant to let him go. Trey watched impatiently as they huddled around Curly with little pats and strokes. Yeah, yeah, yeah, he knew mice had this bond thing with other members of their clan. It was something he'd missed out on, being whisked off to the Talking Academy at such a young age. But this was ridiculous.

At last Curly pulled away and vanished under the dresser, then down inside the walls, and through a crack that led to the backyard. Larry and Julia stood on the windowsill, watching in the dim light. To the right, big pine trees blocked off the view, but to the left, past the scrubby grass of the yard, past some low bushes, beyond the corner where four fences met, stood Joey's house.

For what seemed like forever, the backyard was empty in the dusk, and the watchers strained their ears for the call of a bird of prey or the threatening yowl of a cat. But there was a blessed stillness out there, and at last they made out a tiny shape that darted across the grass and vanished in the long weeds near the fence. Then there was another agonizing pause until their sharp mouse eyes saw a brown-gray dot run around the edge of Joey's house, find a hole, and dive in.

The two mice stayed on the windowsill long after Curly had vanished into the house, and were still watching when a light came on upstairs. Yes, there was Joey, and there on a shelf above his desk they could just see their brown-gray dot. Then Joey yanked his curtains across, and now there was nothing to do but wait.

There are some events in the life of a mouse that he doesn't have to report to Headquarters. And there are other things that he'd better tell his boss about as soon as possible, or else.

Having the Thumbtop kidnapped by a young male falls into the second category, and late that night, with dread in his heart, Trey got Larry and Julia to help him crank up the big computer downstairs. Together they wrote the e-mail that was possibly going to get them all fired.

From: TM3@mousenet.org
To: Topmouse@mousenet.org
Subject: A Setback

I regret to tell you that the Thumbtop is temporarily out of our paws. We hope to retrieve it shortly.

Which was true. Of course they hoped to retrieve it. Who wouldn't hope? But that wasn't enough to satisfy the Big Cheese. He replied with one of those e-mails mice never want to get; the type of e-mail that can put a kink in your whiskers big-time:

From: Topmouse@mousenet.org
To: TM3@mousenet.org
Subject: Re: A Setback

We are most displeased with your news, and disappointed with your performance. I expected you to protect the Thumbtop above all else, and to value it more than your life.

"But you did your best, boss," said Larry.

"My best wasn't good enough, was it?" said Trey, trying to sound cheerful. He read on:

In your next communication, I expect you to give a full accounting of how this carelessness transpired, and what your plans are to remedy it.

Furthermore, the Chief Engineer had not finished his analysis of the computer when you broke off the webcam session. When you have retrieved the device, I expect you to complete your demonstration as soon as possible.

Yeah, right, thought Trey. If there was anything left to demonstrate after this night.

chapter fifteen

Megan woke to the sight of Larry and Julia huddled on the windowsill. No sign of Curly.

And Trey was pacing, pacing, as if he'd wear out his paws. He looked so worried that at one point Megan said, "It's not like it was your fault, exactly."

"But I'm in charge," he said. "That's how it works for mice. If you're in charge and something goes wrong, it *is* your fault. As far as the Big Cheese is concerned, *I* lost the Thumbtop."

"I'm sure we'll get it back," she said, trying to sound confident. Then she heard Annie calling, and went downstairs, away from the miasma of misery and anxiety and guilt that had engulfed her room.

. . . .

That Saturday, Annie wanted to bond with Megan by teaching her things she'd need to know when she grew up and had a house of her own, like how to use an old toothbrush to get the dirt out of cracks, and how to clean windows so they don't streak, and how to hunt dust bunnies so they don't fly away at the sight of you.

"I know it's *boring*, but your life will be much easier if you know the right way to do these things," Annie said. "I don't expect your mom had a chance to show you, on the island."

Which was true, though on this particular day Megan wouldn't have minded if she never learned.

While they worked, Annie kept asking about Joey. Did he and Megan have a regular meeting time for their secret club? What about food? Were they going to have *feasts* in their private place, wherever it was? It was hard to answer, of course, and for every question Megan dodged, Annie thought of three more. It was a huge relief when she decided that Megan was educated enough for one day, freeing her to sprint upstairs and see what Curly had found out.

Except that he wasn't back. Larry and Julia were still hunched on the windowsill, still gazing through light rain toward Joey's house. They didn't even turn their heads when Megan came in, and didn't want to eat the Cheerios she had smuggled up in her pocket.

"It's not good," Trey whispered. "They saw Joey leave an hour ago with his grandma."

"That's right," said Megan. "She's taking him to the mall to get shoes. Annie told me."

So where was Curly?

It was almost noon when Larry gave a squeak, and Megan and Trey hurried to the window. At first Megan couldn't see anything unusual, then a dead flower lurched to one side, a twig moved, and there was a slight swaying in a patch of weeds. Finally, a small shape sprinted across the grass to the safety of the house.

When Curly emerged from under the dresser, damp and tired, he scrambled up onto Megan's bed and flopped down in relief. The other three mice climbed up to be near him, and Megan lay down so her face was close.

"Whew!" said Curly in MSL (you wipe your forehead with your right paw). He would have been back much earlier, he told them, but for the cat. It was a real monster. When Joey went out, he left his bedroom door open, and the cat came in and sat on the floor and just kept watching Curly on his high shelf, licking its lips. Luckily, there was no way the cat could climb up, but no way Curly could climb down either until the cat fell asleep, and he could make a run for it.

"And the Thumbtop?" prompted Trey.

"So far so good," said Curly. "Joey tried to put it back together, but he didn't have a clue. No way he was going to make it work."

At one point Joey had called his dad and said that Megan had given him a puzzle to solve, and he'd described some of the parts. Megan *said* it was a computer, Joey reported, but when he told his dad the size of the keyboard, Curly could hear laughter coming from the phone, and Joey replied, "Sounds way too small, huh?"

When his dad couldn't help, Joey called his friend Spike. Could Spike come over tomorrow and help him? If it really was a computer, there'd be clues on it that could tell them what Megan was up to. Like maybe she was a—

Here Curly made a chopping motion, starting with both paws up near one ear and bringing them down sharply.

"A hacker?" asked Trey.

Curly made the quick nod that's the MSL sign for "yes" and explained that Joey was afraid that Megan and her mom might be hacking into computer networks, stealing secrets.

He went on with his story. Apparently, Spike was going to be busy today, so Joey arranged to show him the computer bits on Sunday, which was tomorrow, and maybe ask Spike's dad to have a look at it, because he knew all about computers.

Megan looked at Trey. Surely this was very bad news—the Thumbtop heading for a strange house? And to a strange dad, who might actually know how to fix it? But Trey surprised her one more time.

"Good work, Curly," he said cheerfully. "That gives us a whole night to rescue the Thumbtop. We'll run around to distract the cat, me and Julia, while you and Larry pull it out of there."

"But he put it in a drawer," said Curly. "It would take more than fifty guys to get it open." He looked sideways at Megan. "Or one human."

"No humans," said Trey. "Call me stupid, but I promised this one she wouldn't have to burgle. Right, Megan? We'll do it with mice. Easy peasy. I'll ask the commander to send over an army."

"That's one nasty cat," said Curly, not convinced. "Looked hungry, too. We could lose some guys."

"Unless we can get someone to keep it out of the way," said Julia, turning toward Megan, who was looking puzzled because Trey had stopped translating.

"Someone who can keep it out of our hair," said Larry, following Julia's gaze.

"Someone to keep it busy," said Curly, with one eye on Megan. "So it won't eat us."

"I wonder who?" said Trey, switching to human language as he also turned to look at Megan, so that now four sets of mouse eyes were fixed on her.

"You wonder who what?" she asked. "What have you guys been talking about? Why are you all looking at me like that?"

"We do need a little help," said Trey. "How would you like to cuddle a cute little kitty cat for a few minutes?" He almost made himself sick, talking about cats like that. "Just stroke it and pet it and talk to it, whatever humans do to cats? Keep it out of our way?"

"Now, wait just a minute," said Megan, sitting bolt upright on the bed. "Joey's cat? Where? In his house?"

"Oh, no, no, no, no, no!" said Trey, as if shocked at the thought. "You'd stay outside. Just hanging out in Joey's yard with the cute little kitty cat. There's no law against that, is there?"

Megan wasn't sure.

"Maybe there *is* a law," she said. "Maybe you *can* get busted for holding a cat without permission." She imagined that big old cop finding her under a bush at midnight with a strange cat, and her father's sad face as the cop dragged her home. "Sorry, guys. Is there some other way?"

To her surprise, Julia went into an urgent spasm of MSL.

"Just a moment," said Trey, and huddled on the pillow with the Cleveland mice in a conversation that to Megan was a blur of quickly moving mouse parts. She noticed one sign that involved paws sticking out at the top of the head like a goat's horns, which she later learned meant "You're kidding." The conversation ended with a sign from Trey, who pointed at his own mouth, then at Julia.

"Julia has something to tell you," he said finally, as the pillow circle broke up.

And with Trey translating, Julia told Megan what had happened last Sunday when she was out, and the young males had invaded her bedroom to look for the Thumbtop. Julia left nothing out: the footsteps on the stairs, the search of the bed, the rummaging in the dresser drawers.

Megan leaped up from the bed so vigorously that the springs almost bounced the mice right off.

"HE LOOKED IN MY DRESSER DRAWERS?" she yelled,

so loudly that the mice were glad the vacuum cleaner was going downstairs, and Annie wouldn't hear. "The rat! The warthog! Even my mom doesn't do that!"

The more she thought about Joey hunting for the Thumbtop in her dresser drawers, the madder she got. Now she wanted revenge in the worst way.

"I'll help you," she said. "I'll hold the cat. And you know what? I think you should all poop in *his* dresser drawers!"

"Pull-ease!" said Trey, pretending to be shocked, but delighted to see her so mad. "We would never do that. Even to Joey. Even to a warthog."

There wasn't much time to mount a raid, but when you have mice on your side, you don't need much time.

The most urgent job was to e-mail the Commander of the Greenfield Region and ask him to send over a mouse army. With no Thumbtop in the house, that meant using the computer in the kitchen, which wasn't easy because Annie showed no signs of leaving the kitchen unguarded. She had started to polish all her pots and pans, and it looked as though she might make the job last the whole afternoon.

At three o'clock, Trey led the Cleveland guys along a route

inside the walls to the garage, where they performed some miracles with string.

At three thirty, Megan went downstairs and asked Annie if she could send a couple of e-mails.

"Who to?" Annie asked with a smile.

"My mom," said Megan. "Maybe my uncle."

Annie washed her hands, booted up the computer, and then stood by as Megan checked her e-mail. There was a message from her mom, which she read quickly:

> Just heard from Red. Great that you have a step-cousin to hang out with.

Yeah, right, thought Megan. She clicked "Reply," and with Annie standing where she could read the screen if she really wanted to, Megan sent only:

> Thanks Mom. Things are okay. Annie's teaching me how to clean the house. I'll tell you more later.

"Finished?" asked Annie, eager to do battle with the next pot.

"Just one more," said Megan, then gave the MSL sign for "Go!" (It's a twitch of the left ear, or the left braid tossed back over the shoulder.) The effect was startling, as a mouse in the doorway relayed Megan's signal to the garage, causing a thunderous crash when Annie's old bike fell against a stepladder, which knocked over a box full of cans waiting to be recycled.

In the time it took for Annie to rush into the garage, pick up her fallen bike and the stepladder, and make loud guesses about raccoons or homeless people or earthquakes or perhaps some *child*, Megan quickly opened Trey's e-mail program, entered his password (Threester), and wrote:

> From: TM3@mousenet.org
> To: Greenfieldboss@mousenet.org
> Subject: Raid
>
> Bring 100 guys 269 Birch 1 a.m.

She had just hit "Send" when Annie came back muttering that she didn't think it was burglars, but it might be some sort of pest.

Megan couldn't resist. "No way it could be mice," she said.

"No way," Annie agreed. "This is a clean house. There's nothing here to attract mice, you can be sure of that!"

chapter sixteen

The house was quiet when Trey woke Megan with a gentle pat on the cheek. She'd gone to bed with her clothes on, so all she had to do was to put on her jacket and shoes and grab her backpack. Then, with two mice clinging to each braid, she tiptoed downstairs, let herself out, and ran across the damp grass.

There was an old wheelbarrow in the backyard. Megan trundled it against the fence and climbed in. Now she could reach the low branch of a tree and pull herself over the fence at the point where a corner of her yard touched a corner of Joey's.

"Yippee!" whispered Trey, as Megan jumped down on the other side, and the braid he was holding swung wide.

In a normal life, climbing into someone else's yard in the middle of the night is not something that you do often, if at all, and Megan felt little ripples of fear running up her body as she sprinted across Joey's yard to the side of the house.

Nothing could happen until she got control of the cat. She took a piece of tuna from a plastic bag in her backpack and pushed it through the cat flap in the kitchen door. Then she put a larger piece just outside the cat flap and stood over it with a dish towel. She only had to wait a couple of minutes before a big orange cat pushed its way through the flap.

And its world went dark as Megan dropped the towel over its head.

She grabbed the struggling cat and gently put it into the cardboard box she had brought along, with holes in it for breathing.

Then she almost screamed when one of her braids made a loud squeak right by her ear. It was Trey giving an old-fashioned mouse signal, the universal call to battle, and it brought about a stirring among the leaves and weeds at her feet, almost as if the ground itself were moving—a sea of mice flowing closer to the house.

While Megan held the cat flap open with her spare hand, Trey marched into the house at the head of his surging army, a wriggling river of brown-gray fur. Julie and Larry came last—Larry looking larger than usual with a shoelace rope wound around his middle. Between them, he and Julia pulled a plastic bag of old metal buttons and paper clips and watch springs that might just pass for parts of a Thumbtop if you didn't look closely.

Once inside the house, Curly showed Trey the gap under the kitchen counter that led to an easy climb to Joey's room.

"Follow me!" said Trey in MSL (it's the right front paw thrust forward). He led his army through the gap, up inside the wall to a crack in Joey's closet, then over a pile of sneakers and into the room. There the army halted in the dim light, looking to Trey for the next command.

For a moment, Trey felt like one of those generals he'd seen in movies at the Talking Academy. General Patton in World War II? Or better yet, Napoleon, because he was kind of short? Hey, he could get used to this.

First, Trey sent a scout mouse up onto the bed to verify that the human's eyes were tight shut. Then, finding the brightest patch of floor, he gave brisk orders in MSL. He assigned a team of ten mice to thread Larry's shoelace rope through the handle of the drawer where the Thumbtop lay. Next he ordered fifty mice to wriggle into position behind the drawer so they could push, while the other fifty pulled on the rope.

When everyone was ready, Trey gave the signal to push and pull—a squeak pitched so high that no human could hear it. He watched anxiously until he was sure the drawer was moving, millimeter by millimeter. And while it moved, he had time to work on the next task. He couldn't let Megan take the blame for this burglary, so he had to prove somehow that it was not she herself who had come to this room, but some more mysterious entity. He took a couple of mice off the pull line to check the doors and windows of the house—and yes, they were all securely bolted on the inside.

Then he discovered another way to get Megan off the hook, and he almost laughed out loud. By the dim glow of the lights on Joey's sleeping game system, he spotted a worksheet of sixth grade algebra. Honors algebra. Way beyond anything a fifth grader could do, especially one who'd had problems with wet math books.

Quickly, Trey told the captain what he needed, and the captain hunted up his four best math mice and pulled them off the pushing and pulling lines. These guys were good. In no time they had solved the algebra problems in their heads and checked off the correct answers (not easy, but you can do it if two mice grip a pencil low down and two others hold it higher up and move it around).

While this was happening, Trey had time to look around the room. That's when he saw something that made his whiskers tingle, something that could solve all his problems in one go.

It was a corkboard. Pinned to it was a ticket to an Oregon Ducks football game at Stanford University, at the top end of Silicon Valley. Near the ticket, Joey had pinned a map of the Great America amusement park—right in the middle of Silicon Valley. Right next to the headquarters of the Mouse Nation.

Wow.

For Megan, time was passing so slowly that she was afraid it had stopped altogether. At first things had gone quite well. The cat had tried a couple of yowls but she'd rocked its box in her arms until it quieted down. But then the rain started. Her jeans were soon wet, and rain trickled down her neck, and the cat was starting to yowl again and scrabble around in its box, which was getting wetter by the minute, and softer, and more likely to burst from the struggles inside.

"Nice kitty, good kitty," she whispered, rocking the soggy box. It wouldn't hold out for long at this rate, and already a furry foot was sticking out. Megan rocked harder, and to her surprise, the cat began to purr. Maybe it liked wearing wet cardboard. Maybe it just liked her. She thought back fondly to Tiger, the cat she'd had when she was small. It was kind of neat to hug a cat again,

even one in a wet box. But how long could she keep him quiet?

After what felt like an hour, Trey pushed his way out through the cat flap, and Megan could guess from the way he walked that things had gone well.

"We've got it!" he whispered. "They're bringing it out now."

A team of four mice pushed through the cat flap, pulling a plastic bag behind them. Then came the full flood of the mouse army, pouring out of the house, running to safety as the cat smelled mouse, and the wet box wriggled and hissed.

As soon as the last mice had scuttled away, and her own mouse team was safely on her shoulders, Megan opened up the box and watched the cat run back into the house. Then she put the bag of Thumbtop parts into her backpack and clambered over the fence.

Back in Megan's room, Curly, Larry, and Julia felt so exhilarated after the raid that they played a little Chase My Tail, which is a game that giddy young mice play when they are happy—spinning faster and faster as they try to catch their own tails. Even Trey joined in for a moment to work off some of his excitement.

Megan couldn't have chased her tail even if she had one. She was way too tired, and wanted only to get into bed, but Trey begged her to stay awake just a little longer and put the Thumbtop together. The sooner the Big Cheese knew they'd got it back, the better for all concerned.

It didn't take long, and soon Megan, like Joey, was just a bump in the bed, softly rising and falling in sleep.

Trey watched the bump for a moment. He was so proud of her. She might not be a mouse, but she was the next best thing. This was a human to be cherished. This was a human who had earned her rest.

When the three Cleveland guys finally wore themselves out and went to sleep, Trey sat down for some serious Thumbtop time. First he e-mailed the clans that lived with Joey's friends Spike and Dustin, with some specific questions. When he got replies, he wrote to his boss:

From: TM3@mousenet.org
To: Topmouse@mousenet.org
Subject: Success

We have retrieved the Thumbtop, so we can now arrange for the Chief Engineer to complete his study of it. There will be no need to set up another webcam session, because I have found a way for Miss Megan to bring the computer to Headquarters in person.

He went on to explain what he had seen in Joey's room. The ticket to a football game. The map of Great America. And how these things could work together for the glory of the Mouse Nation and the future of the planet.

chapter seventeen

Megan woke up that Sunday morning to see Trey smiling at her with a grin so wide it showed all his teeth.

"Good morning," he said. "Very, very good morning. After a very, very good night."

"It was good, wasn't it, getting the Thumbtop back."

"That too, but I mean *after* you went to sleep." He did a pirouette. "We've been making plans, me and the Big Cheese."

"Oh?"

"He'll tell you about them himself. He wanted to talk to you earlier, but when I told him you were asleep, he said he'd wait. Do you know the last time that guy waited for someone to wake up? Probably never. He must think you're the greatest thing since sliced cheese."

Which was nice, but what could he want from her now?

Megan waited while Trey set up an IM conversation on the Thumbtop.

"Here we go," he said, as the first words from the Big Cheese unrolled on the screen. Megan picked up her magnifying glass and read:

> Congratulations, Miss Megan. It will be a joy to welcome you to our world.

"I'm glad to be in your world," she wrote, assuming that he meant the world of knowing about mice, or something.

"I mean it literally," came from the Big Cheese. "You will be the first human ever to visit us at our Headquarters, here in California."

Which was definitely not what Megan expected. She looked urgently at Trey, and could see that he was still very pleased with himself.

"Where did that come from?" she asked. "What makes him think I could ever . . . Doesn't he know anything about human kids? We can't just go where we want. It's impossible!"

"Tell him that," said Trey, with a knowing grin. "Try telling the Big Cheese something is impossible. See where that gets you."

Megan picked out the words, "Sorry, it's impossible."

And that brought a quick mouse lecture, as Trey had known it would. She should know by now, wrote the Big Cheese, that the word "impossible" did not exist in the mouse vocabulary. Megan would bring the Thumbtop to Headquarters so the engineers could study it in detail and finalize their plans for its mass production. Meanwhile, he and Megan would discuss the alliance between their species, and make plans for a glorious future. The power of his whole nation would be at her disposal for Operation Mouse Magic—the plan that would bring her to California. And he looked forward to her arrival on Sunday, October 26th, at 10:30 in the morning.

He signed off, leaving Megan's head whirling. How had her adventure in the night with a wet cat led to this? She gaped at Trey, half expecting him to say that she was right and the Big Cheese was wrong and the idea of getting her to Headquarters was the lamest mouse joke he'd ever heard.

But Trey was in the middle of a pirouette. When he came out of it, he said, "It will happen, because—"

Feet were running upstairs, and Trey dived into the bed as Annie knocked and opened the door without waiting. She was wearing the clingy dress and tightly pulled back hairdo that went with Sunday brunch.

"Oh dear," she said. "You are so not ready. Didn't you hear me call?"

"Sorry," said Megan.

"It's a brunch day, remember? I have to go there now—why don't you walk over later? It's only six blocks and the rain has almost stopped."

Under the covers, Megan felt a sharp jab.

"I have stuff to do," she said.

"With Joey?" asked Annie brightly.

"No—just homework," said Megan.

"Well, if I see Joey at the restaurant, I'll send him over, shall I? Maybe he can help."

Joey! Megan *really* didn't want to think about Joey. Any moment now, he might come roaring over in a towering rage, after finding the Thumbtop gone. She remembered from Julia's story that he had a key to this house, which made her feel very vulnerable. Maybe she *should* walk over to the restaurant, to be among adults. But Joey might be there too. He could be anywhere. For the rest of her time in Oregon, he'd be close by. As she listened to Annie's car pull away, she started to wish that they'd never retrieved the Thumbtop, that she'd just let Joey keep it.

That's when Trey dropped his bombshell.

"Speaking of Joey," he began. "He's the one who'll take you to California, of course, though he doesn't know it yet."

"Joey!" Megan yelled. "No *way*! He wouldn't take me to the corner store. He probably hates me by now. And even if he didn't, there's no way he *could* take me there. It's not like he can drive!"

"Doesn't have to drive," said Trey. "He's getting a ride. He's going to a big football game down there, then to Great America. And he'll take you because we'll spook him into it, with Operation Mouse Magic."

He told her what he'd seen in Joey's room. First, there was the football ticket for the Oregon Ducks' game against Stanford. More important was the map of Great America, the park so close to Headquarters that you could almost slip away to visit the Big Cheese between rides. Spike's dad would be driving, and Trey had checked with the clan in Spike's house—it was a big car with plenty of room for Megan as well as Joey and his two friends.

"As for the mouse magic," Trey continued, "he'll probably be halfway spooked as soon as he finds the Thumbtop's missing. He'll know there's no way *you* could have got into that house—we checked, and all the doors and windows were bolted. And did I tell you we did his algebra homework for him? Honors algebra? No offence, but no way you could have done that."

"No way," agreed Megan weakly.

"So we've softened him up for some really good magic. We'll spook him so bad that he will be putty in your hands. He'll be afraid that if he doesn't take you to Silicon Valley you'll turn him into a toad. Or maybe a warthog."

Trey had hoped that Megan would show a little more enthusiasm for scaring the you-know-what out of Joey. After all, hadn't he been the one to declare war? By searching her room? Spying on her? Taking her Thumbtop? Refusing to give it back even when she asked nicely?

But instead of "Great idea, Trey, let's get started!" she said, "Isn't there some other way I could get to Headquarters? Maybe Annie could take me to Great America, or my dad."

"Not going to happen," he said. "Even if they did have time to take you, d'you think they'd let you out of their sight for one minute so you could get over to Headquarters? It's got to be Joey. And it's important, remember? To help us get Thumbtops? Cement your alliance with the Big Cheese? Two species working for the future of the planet? Yadda yadda yadda?"

Megan flopped back in the bed.

"I just don't think spooking Joey will work," she said. "It'll only make him hate me more."

"Tell you what," said Trey. "Let's have a trial run. Joey will come after you today, right? As soon as he looks closely at the bag of junk we left for him. Then you can try a little practice spooking. See how it goes."

"You mean I should let him think I'm a witch or something?"

"You got it."

Megan sighed. She certainly couldn't tell Joey the truth about last night, and magic might just protect her from his anger. At least for today.

It was hard, waiting for Joey. Larry was on watch in the big front bedroom, and even though she trusted him, Megan found herself going in every so often to peer at the street too, watching for a bike.

On one of these visits, Larry made some urgent signs, pointing to the driveway. Megan swiveled her head and saw a car. Annie's car! She turned to run back to her room while Larry dived for cover, but it was too late—Annie blocked the bedroom doorway.

"Megan!" she exclaimed, and to Megan's surprise looked hugely pleased. "You didn't come in to play with my makeup, did you?"

Megan nodded, because what else could she do?

"Sit down," Annie said, still smiling. "I'll show you how to do it properly."

She gave a running commentary as she worked. "A little of this blusher on the cheekbone . . . that looks good . . . a hint of blue on the eyelids, see how I put it on? And darkening your lashes, that's always important for people with your coloring."

Megan watched herself in the mirror and wondered how she could get Annie to stop, partly because it was so weird seeing herself change, and partly because she was desperate to get Annie out of there in case Joey arrived. Because if Joey turned up now, before she'd done any spooking, wouldn't he tell Annie the truth? And if Annie believed she'd broken into his house—and that other house too, because Joey would surely tell Annie what he'd seen on Spruce Street—wouldn't Megan be more or less grounded for life? With no chance whatsoever of getting to Headquarters?

"There!" said Annie finally, standing up. "Aren't you beautiful! Now, won't you come back to the restaurant with me so I can show you off?"

"Sorry," said Megan. "I really have a lot to do."

"Oh well," said Annie. "Enjoy your new face while you do your homework. Gotta run!"

She grabbed the coat she'd come back to fetch, and left. Megan headed toward the bathroom to wash her face, but Trey caught up with her just in time to stop her.

"Leave it!" he said. "Don't wash it off! It's wonderful. It makes you look so, well . . ."

"Scary?" asked Megan.

"I was going to say grown-up," he said. "Gives you authority. But scary too. I'll grant you that."

It was late morning when Larry finally came running in from his guard post, making urgent signs.

"Joey's here!" said Trey. "Think magic!"

The mice dived under the dresser, leaving Megan sitting on her bed, her heart beating so strongly she was sure Joey would hear it.

The front door opened, then feet on the stairs, two at a time, and her bedroom door was thrust open wide as Joey stormed in, his hair darkened by rain.

"Hey!" Megan said, with a smile that she hoped looked normal and friendly; though with the face she was now wearing, "normal" was perhaps not the right word. And Joey did sort of stop dead when he saw her.

"What the . . . ?" he exclaimed. But the new face only slowed him for an instant.

"You really are a burglar," he said, scowling down at her as she sat on her bed trying to look serene. "It's not just that house on Spruce Street. You broke into my room and took that computer thing last night—left me this junk."

He held out the plastic bag and Megan could see the paper clip she'd put in it yesterday, plus some metal buttons and hooks and eyes from Annie's sewing kit.

"I left what?" asked Megan, trying to sound calm.

"This bag of junk. And when I showed it to Spike's dad and said it was a computer, he thought I was crazy because . . . *look* at it. And *you* must have put it in my room."

"How could I have?" she asked. "I happen to know your doors and windows were all locked on the inside."

Had he gone a little pale?

"*Someone* got in," he said, speaking more softly than before. "*Someone* took your stupid computer. Who else could it have been?"

That was a good place to start on the magic. "I've never been near your room," she said. "I've never even been in your house. But it could have been my friends."

Joey gaped at her. "Friends? What friends? Dustin's sister Caitlin—she's in your class. Says you don't have any friends."

Now! thought Trey, under the dresser. He's primed and ready. Spook!

His human came through. And she was good.

"They're not the sort of friends anyone knows about," she said. "My friends are different. They have special powers. For instance, they can go through walls. Some walls, anyway."

He gaped again. "You mean like *imaginary* friends?"

"Oh no, no, no," she said. "Not imaginary at all. My friends are real. You could touch them if you ever caught them."

Joey was looking around the room nervously now, as if he was starting to believe her.

"And they're good at math," said Megan. "Did you check your algebra homework?"

Joey was speechless for a moment. "I thought . . . I sort of thought I'd done it in my sleep," he mumbled.

"Ha!" Megan said, sounding very confident now. "Like that's going to happen."

Joey turned away from her with a groan, and found himself

facing the map of St. Hilda Island. It was mostly blank because there were so few people on it, but one corner seemed to catch Joey's eye—the part labeled "Witch's Cove."

"Is it . . . Are you and your mom . . . You're not . . . ?"

Megan saw where his eyes were pointing, and helped him out.

"Are we witches?" she asked. "I guess that's for us to know and you to find out."

Which seemed to be the last straw for Joey. Looking as if he'd rather be anywhere else, he flung the bag of bits on the floor and ran at top speed down the stairs.

When he'd gone, Trey came bounding out of hiding, yelling, "Yay! That worked like gangbusters—couldn't have been better. We're off and running. Off and spooking. He's so scared of you now . . ."

He'd expected at least a pirouette out of Megan, but she had gone off to the bathroom, her expression hard to read under the makeup.

When she came back, her face scrubbed pink and shiny, she flopped facedown on the bed. Trey jumped up beside her.

"As I was saying," he said into her left ear, "he's so scared of you now, the rest will be easy. I'll tell the Big Cheese it's all systems go for Operation Mouse Magic. We'll think up some great spells. Spells that will scare the . . . Scary spells. Aren't you pleased with yourself?"

With her face in her pillow, Megan mumbled something. Julia jumped up and leaned in near her right ear to listen.

"Miss Megan isn't pleased with herself," she told Trey in MSL. "She doesn't want to frighten Mr. Joey. She doesn't want him to hate her."

Trey leaned a little closer to the left ear and made his voice as gentle and persuasive as possible.

"It's just a few good spells," he pleaded. "We won't hurt him. Just scare him enough to get him under our control, so he'll do anything to make the spells stop."

"What sort of spells?" Megan mumbled into her pillow.

"Well, Curly and Larry have been thinking some up," said Trey. "How about this one? Curly saw it in a movie. We can put some dye on Joey's hairbrush so he gets a green streak. Or maybe tie all his shoelaces together, really tight. Stuff like that. And here's one of Larry's—we'll loosen the top of the saltshaker . . ." His voice started to trail off as Megan's nose stayed firmly in her pillow. "So it all dumps out on Joey's spaghetti," Trey finished flatly.

Megan sat up. "Didn't you see his face? He was so scared! And all those things will frighten him more, like he's being haunted. How would you feel if someone kept casting spells like that? Would you ask that person to go to California with you? It's just not the way you get *humans* to do things for you!"

Trey looked as if someone had let the air out of him.

"Well, I can't think of any other way to get you to Silicon Valley," he said. "Can you? And I have orders. Now that the Big Cheese is expecting you, I *have* to deliver you, or else!"

Megan gazed at him. Was this going to be like that terrible afternoon on Spruce Street all over again? Mice just not getting it right, where humans were concerned?

The front door opened again, and this time it was her dad, calling, "Hey, Megan, I'm home! Brought you some lunch!"

For once, Megan was glad for an excuse to leave the world of mice.

And Trey was left gazing into the widening gap that seemed to be opening between his species and the only human they had.

chapter eighteen

"Your lunch, *mon petit chou*," said Megan's dad, handing her a couple of his takeout boxes. "It means 'my little cabbage', but French people love their little cabbages, so that's okay. Annie went off to the mall with some old school friends, but we can do something much more important—watch my Seattle Seahawks."

Megan fetched a fork and joined him in the living room. He was lying on one of the two couches, clicking the remote to find his football game.

"Ah, this is what Sunday afternoons used to be like," he said. "And now I can't even watch a whole game. It's a hard life, kiddo."

Megan was hungry, and the egg thing and the pastry thing in the boxes tasted great.

"These are really good, dad," she said. "Red Magic strikes again."

He twisted his neck around to look at her. "Wait a minute. Where's that face I heard about? Annie told me she'd made you up to look like a million dollars!"

"Sorry," she said. "Not my thing."

"Just like your mother," he said, with a grin. "She was never crazy about makeup. Okay by me if you wait a few years. Like ten."

When she'd finished eating, Megan stretched out on the second couch, her head near her dad's. And as they watched the game, she almost forgot about makeup and mice and Thumbtops and mouse magic.

Until her dad said, "What's eating Joey? Saw him pedaling up the street, going like a bat out of hell."

"Really?" said Megan.

"He's a good kid," said her dad. "We're so glad you two are getting on well. But he did not look like a happy camper."

Then he suddenly sat bolt upright and roared: "He! Could! Go! All! The! Way!" and Megan thought he meant Joey until she saw that a Seattle player had scooted halfway up the field before he fumbled the ball, causing Megan's dad and probably tens of thousands of other dads all over the Northwest to flop back into their horizontal positions with a groan.

"Poor old Joe," Red continued, as if he hadn't been interrupted. "That whole family has problems. Grandma's getting

frail, and her house needs work—the roof leaks, and she can't afford to fix it. Jake used to pay for that sort of thing, but, well, you know about his business problems. And now he's in even worse shape because he's just not that good at selling those Tick-Tock things and he's afraid he'll be fired. We know what happens then, don't we."

"We do?"

"He might have to pull his money out of the restaurant. Then we'd all be toast."

"Toast?"

"Kaput. Dead meat. Belly up. Flipping burgers at Mickey D's. Living on Annie's salary. But I shouldn't be telling you all this."

Megan suddenly remembered the conversation in the restaurant—was it only three days ago? So much had happened since then that she'd clean forgotten her promise to fix it.

Now she said, "I told you I can help, remember?"

Her dad laughed. "Of course. Forgive me, but I'd forgotten. You and your MBA. Yeah, right. That'll be the day."

True, Megan hadn't even consulted yet with the *M* part of her Mouse Business Assistance team, but mice really could do anything, right?

"Wanna bet?" she asked. "Wanna bet I can't do it?"

"Seems like a pretty safe bet to me," he said with another laugh, "even if you are the smartest ten-year-old in Oregon, which I don't doubt for a minute."

"How much?" she asked.

They settled on fifty dollars, which Megan figured would be enough to pay her expenses on the trip to California. And now she was sure that the trip was going to happen, because her dad had given her a great idea—the perfect way to use mouse magic. Now she had a plan that couldn't fail.

. . . .

"I've got it, I've got it," she said, bursting into her room when her dad had to leave soon after halftime.

"I get it—you've got it," said Trey. "What is it?"

"Mice can do anything, right?"

"That's what we all say," Trey replied, delighted that her mood had changed. He'd had a rough couple of hours with Julia, who'd been giving him a bad time for not understanding young females. "With enough mice and a place to stand, you can move the world. That's a quote from an old Greek dude, Archimedes. Except he probably didn't say 'mice.'"

"Can they mend roofs? Help people sell things? Fix restaurants so they make money?"

"Er," said Trey, thinking maybe even Archimedes might have allowed for some exceptions to his rule.

But Megan wasn't stopping for any exceptions.

"If we do those things," she said, "we'll save Joey's family. We can still use mouse magic but it will be good magic and he'll be so pleased that he'll want to help. Maybe he'll even stop hating me."

She told them what her dad had said about Jake's problems selling Tick-Tocks, and Aunt Em's roof, and how bad it would be for Joey, as well as everyone else, if the restaurant failed.

"But even if we do all that good stuff," said Trey, "it'll still look like magic. Won't Joey be spooked?"

"Maybe—but he's going to be pleased too, isn't he? And we can even give him some warning so it won't seem so spooky."

"Whatever works," said Trey, pulling the Thumbtop toward him. "I'll tell them at Headquarters. Gentler magic: Operation Mouse Magic (with Kindness)."

If Megan could have seen inside Joey's head, she would have found that the last thing he expected from her was kindness. He was well and truly spooked.

But as he biked around town in the drizzle, not going anywhere in particular, his fears slowly calmed down, and he started to get mad. He HATED being so mystified. He HATED the way Megan had made him feel like such a wuss, up there in her room. He HATED the fact that the world where logic worked was slipping out of his control.

What had he done to deserve this? Well, yeah, so he'd led the search of her room last week. Yeah, yeah, so he'd been spying on her a bit, like on Spruce Street. And then he *did* take her computer thing from her backpack. But hadn't he saved her butt by telling Annie and Red she had been with him? When she'd really been breaking into a house, for some reason? Didn't she have any gratitude?

That last thought was the one that stuck in his head, and helped his outrage win out over his fear. He wouldn't just sit and take it like a helpless victim. He'd organize his own magic, something that would freak *Megan* out. After riding a few more blocks, he decided on a course of action that would put him back in command of the situation. For one day, at least, she'd be under *his* control.

And the person who could help him was Dustin's sister Caitlin. He turned his bike toward Dustin's house.

"So what's she like?" Joey asked. "In school?"

"Bit weird," said Caitlin. "She doesn't say much. Doesn't have any real friends that I can see. Sometimes she goes all goody-goody, as if she's, you know, *better* than us? Like rescuing a mouse in the classroom. Oh, and I saw her taking old water bottles out of the trash and putting them in the recycle bin. Yuck! She really needs to lighten up."

"Let's help her do that," said Joey.

"Good thinking," said Dustin.

It didn't take long to think up a plot. Caitlin fetched a pad of yellow sticky notes, and they took turns thinking up messages to write on them, like:

RECYCLE
BY ORDER OF MEGAN MILLER

and

TURN OFF THE LIGHTS
BY ORDER OF MEGAN MILLER

and

EAT YOUR VEGETABLES
BY ORDER OF MEGAN MILLER

And one for Megan's desk that mystified Dustin and Caitlin, but that Joey explained was a private joke:

NOW WHO'S GOT
SPECIAL POWERS?
—JF

Caitlin promised to get to school extra early and stick the notes in the right places, such as next to light switches, and by the trash bins, and in the cafeteria.

But none of them reckoned with the mice in Dustin's house. They'd eavesdropped on the kids with alarm, and while their host family was eating dinner, these brave mice dashed into the den to e-mail news of the plot to Trey.

"Uh-uh," said Trey, when he read the message. "You want the good news or the bad news?"

"How about the bad news first?" said Megan.

He pushed the Thumbtop toward her, and she read the e-mail through her magnifying glass.

"Hey, it's sort of a compliment, isn't it, saying I take those things seriously, like recycling?" she said. Then she noticed that Julia was making a sign—holding one paw out as if to stop traffic.

"She's saying, 'No way,'" translated Trey, as Julia went into a long speech. "If it was mice, they'd *hate* someone new telling them how to behave. And from what she's seen in movies, she thinks it's probably the same for kids."

And of course Julia was right. New kids didn't stick their necks out like that.

"So people will think I'm a total dork if those notes go up," said Megan sadly.

"Don't worry," said Trey. "No way we'll let them go up. That's the good news. And in fact I have an idea for a counterplot.

Nothing too unkind," he added quickly, seeing Megan's expression. "Just some gentle mouse magic to show that we can out-magic Joey any time."

It took less than an hour to carry out the counterplot. Megan fetched some yellow sticky notes from the kitchen and wrote things like "Oh, Caitlin!" or "Boo!" or "Surprise!" on ten of them. Then they took turns thinking up messages for Joey that would remind him of Megan's powers, while leaving everyone else mildly puzzled.

Like this one suggested by Julia:

Ask JOEY FISHER
To fix your computer

and from Larry:

What's happening on Spruce Street?
Ask JOEY FISHER

And Curly came up with:

Having trouble with algebra?
Ask JOEY FISHER

When they had finished, Megan put the two stacks of notes in plastic bags to keep them dry. With Trey in her pocket, she walked to Pine Street, where Dustin and Caitlin lived, and hid the Caitlin notes under a bush. Then she walked a few blocks to the middle school and stashed the Joey notes behind a fence.

Sometime in the night, the little plastic bags vanished.

When Joey got to his school the next morning, he noticed that some of the kids were giving him strange looks. Then he became aware of little notes stuck around the school—notes about Joey Fisher.

Many of them in places that were locked up tight each night.

"Whazzup?" asked some of his friends.

And although the other sixth-grade kids thought the notes were kind of cool, and even some seventh and eighth graders looked at him with new respect, Joey was severely spooked. Worse than spooked—he felt flattened like a bug on a windshield. And it didn't help when Dustin called after school to say that all of Caitlin's Megan notes had been switched in the night for other messages, and he told Joey his head hurt after Caitlin, who was a great softball pitcher, had flung a shoe at it, because (as she said) who else but Dustin could have made the switch?

chapter Nineteen

"Now we've got him," said Trey. "We've really got him. The fish is on the line. Let's strike now—with a devastating attack of kindness."

Megan had just gotten home from school, and with Trey on her shoulder, she was looking out past the pine fronds at Joey's house. Through his window, they could dimly see a shape moving around, a restless-looking shape, its hand sometimes going up to run through its hair. Not a happy camper.

"Let's do it," said Megan. She picked up the Thumbtop and wrote:

From: Meganbug2@gmail.com
To: Joeyfish98@aol.com
Subject: Those Notes

Hi. I hope you liked our notes. Yours were funny,

> but you see why we had to change them. To make up for that, my friends are going to do very, very nice things for your family.
>
> Don't worry. Nothing bad will happen.
>
> But don't tell ANYONE.
>
> My friends are everywhere. They will KNOW.

She hit "Send" and got back to her homework until Curly, who was on windowsill duty, gave a yip.

Joey must have read his e-mail, because there he was at his window, gazing over at Megan's house. Was he a little pale? Hard to say. Megan waved at him, hoping to look nonthreatening. And knowing what nice surprises were coming his way, she couldn't help grinning like a Cheshire cat.

For the rest of the week, Joey kept his distance, and all Megan saw of him was an occasional glimpse of a green jacket on a bike, shadowing her from a block or two away.

She, meanwhile, was very busy as e-mails buzzed back and forth between Greenfield and the Operation Mouse Magic (with Kindness) task force in Silicon Valley, and between the task force and the rest of the world.

. . . .

After a couple of days, Joey relaxed a bit. Nothing weird had happened and maybe nothing was going to happen. At least nothing spooky. He was more and more convinced that there was a logical reason behind the things Megan had done. She must be a spy of some sort. Those two years on an island? That could be a cover-up for when she and her mom got their spy training, like learning how to go into locked houses and doing stunts with sticky notes. When she broke into that house on Spruce Street? Must have been talking to her handler. And the tiny computer? You could hide that sucker in your socks—perfect for spies. All that talk about magic and friends who can go through locked doors was just to distract him from the real truth.

Who was she spying *for*? Hard to say—but maybe those good deeds she was promising would give him some clues.

But when the first good deed happened—in Tallahassee, Florida—it was so weird that it blew him away completely, and for a while left him feeling spooked all over again.

Operation Mouse Magic (with Kindness) started with an e-mail from Megan:

From: Meganbug2@gmail.com
To: Joefish98@aol.com
Subject: My Powers

Your dad's going to be a superstar. Remember, don't tell him, OR ELSE.

It so happened (as mice knew) that Jacob Joseph Fisher, usually known as Jake, was flying to Tallahassee, Florida, to sell Tick-Tock-Clicks. It also happened that a teenager called J.J. Fisher had just won a huge singing contest on television, and, for a couple of weeks at least, he was one of the most famous people in America.

Before Jake arrived at the Tallahassee airport, little notes appeared on the desks of reporters and television producers and radio DJs (with tooth marks if you looked close) announcing that the great J.J. Fisher was coming to town.

When Jake flew in, he was greeted by a huge sign saying, TALLAHASSEE WELCOMES J.J. FISHER! Reporters and television cameras and teenage girls fought for position as everyone yelled, "J.J.!" "Where is he?" "Where's J.J. Fisher?"

Joey got an e-mail from his dad describing what happened next.

I said, "My name's J.J. Fisher," and they all said, "You!" like I was pond scum, and the teenagers looked as if I'd murdered their J.J., but as long as the news guys were there, they did funny stories about the mix-up, so I got to show them the Tick-Tock-Clicks. And guess what? One of the big TV stations here wants me on their morning show, and they'll all be using Tick-Tocks to take pictures of each other. Fame at last!

And there was an e-mail from Megan. Just one word:

See?

For about ten minutes, Joey was spooked. Very spooked indeed. Then he got his brain working again and decided that, hey, if Megan and her mom really were spies, there was no reason why they wouldn't have contacts in Tallahassee. Maybe they knew some guys who worked in television there, for instance. But what sort of spy network could it be?

He decided to write down his thoughts in the hope that it would clear his brain, so he set up a document on his computer labeled "Megan Spy." It began with questions:

1. Are Megan and her mom working for a foreign power?
2. Are they stealing industrial secrets for some big company?
3. Are they in a terror group like maybe for the environment?

His dad had told him about one environmental group that sometimes set things on fire or blew stuff up. He couldn't imagine Megan doing that, even to protect sheep or whatever, but it was possible. And if that was the case, shouldn't someone tell the FBI? Or Homeland Security?

But there were two reasons not to do that yet. One was that Megan had threatened all sort of dire things if he told—and he did believe that her friends, whoever they were, were watching him, and maybe even tapping his phone and reading his e-mail.

And the other reason was that he still had no hard evidence.

He decided to keep notes about every single thing Megan had done, so that if he did turn her in to Homeland Security, he'd have some backup.

He made a chart on his computer:

Actions of Megan Miller	
What She Did	Explanation
Entered house at 590 Spruce Street to use webcam	
Took objects from locked house at 269 Birch Street	
Took stationery from backpack at 753 Pine Street	
Entered Fairlawn school to display notes	
Entered Garfield Middle School to display notes	
Spread false information in Tallahassee, Florida	

He was almost eager now for Megan's next stunt (or whatever it was), because it might give him more clues.

And he only had to wait two days. Once again, the stunt (or whatever it was) started with an e-mail:

> Now it's your grandma's turn for all the fixings.
> Remember, not a word, or else!

All the fixings? That sounded scary. Joey didn't want his grandma fixed. He liked her just the way she was. But he couldn't really warn her because . . . well, because. So all he said before he went to school was, "Remember to lock the doors." Which got him a puzzled look because she always did keep them locked.

Here's what happened:

Mice in nearby Eugene had sneaked onto the computer of a local charity and added the name "Emily Fisher" to a certain document. When Joey came home from school, he found a truck parked in front of the house, and three men were examining the roof.

His grandma was at the front door, beaming with pleasure.

"Can you believe it, Joey?" she said. "These kind people do house repairs for seniors in Lane County. Free! I never even heard of them, but they say my name was at the top of their list."

Joey's first thought was that perhaps Annie had set it up, but when Annie herself came by, you could tell from her squawks of delight and amazement that she had not.

And when Joey checked his e-mail, there was a one-word message from Megan:

See?

Joey was blown away. She was good. He entered *Fixed roof at 269 Birch Street* on his chart, but there was still nothing he could put in the *Explanation* column.

He had to admit that he had absolutely no clue how Megan was doing this—or why. Two good deeds, so far. Would there be a third? He sort of wanted one and sort of didn't—until the opportunity for a third good deed actually turned up. And when it did, Joey and his grandma both needed it desperately.

It was the cat.

Aunt Em's cat had shown no apparent ill effects from its time in a wet box. But who knows what goes on in the brains of cats? When the roof guys went to work on Aunt Em's house, they cleared some junk out of her attic.

Including boxes.

Cardboard boxes.

Deep in the cat brain, two and two slotted together and made *YIKES*. And the cat took off.

Joey's e-mail to Megan was anguished.

To: Meganbug2@gmail.com
From: Joeyfish98@aol.com
Subject: A Favor

Grandma's cat ran away and she's so worried. Please can your friends find it?

And he included a description. Big cat. Sort of orange color. White paws (as if Megan didn't know).

"Trey," said Megan. "This should be right up your street. An animal in distress."

Trey ran over and peered at the e-mail. Then he turned away and pretended to stick a paw down his throat in the sign for "Barf."

Megan reached out to tickle him behind an ear. "You know you can do it with two paws tied behind your back."

Which was true, of course. Mice keep track of the movement of cats, so the Commander of the Greenfield Region had already heard that an orange-colored monster had appeared at a house on the other side of town, doing the "Take me in and love me" routine that mice despise (rub against legs, purr, purr, look hungry). A member of the clan in that house had made his way next door to report the invasion, so the commander was able to give Trey the information he needed in twenty seconds flat.

With a speed that knocked his socks off, Joey got an e-mail telling him the name and telephone number of the people who had the cat. An e-mail that left him profoundly spooked.

chapter twenty

The day after Aunt Em got her cat back, an e-mail was waiting for Joey after school.

I hope you've enjoyed our good deeds. Now I want to ask a favor. Wave if you can come around here about 4.

Feeling a bit foolish, Joey waved in the direction of Megan's window, even though there was nothing there except the tiny stuffed toy he'd seen on the windowsill that first night.

Megan was sitting at the kitchen table, with her friends tucked into their viewing slot, when Joey arrived. She was glad to see he looked much less terrified than the last time they'd talked face-to-face, up in her room.

She fetched him a can of Coke and sat down opposite him.

"How's it going?" she asked, because that's what Annie often said to get a conversation started.

He laughed. "You know how it's going—you've been doing really weird stuff."

"But good stuff, right? How's your dad, by the way?"

"Fine, fine," said Joey, as if his mind wasn't on the answer. "He got some sort of award for selling all those Tick-Tocks. In Florida." He stopped and ran his hands through his hair. "Can you tell me how you did it?"

Megan shrugged. "Just my friends," she said, as if it was no big deal. "Friends with special powers who do my bidding."

"But friends in Florida? Friends in Eugene? Friends in Dustin's house and where you found the cat?"

"Why not?" she said. "They're everywhere. Everywhere in the world, pretty much."

"Are they all spies?" he asked.

"Spies!" she exclaimed, with a look of genuine astonishment. "Why d'you keep asking me about spies?"

He put his head down on the table with a sort of "AAARGHHH" sound, but soon sat up again, and Megan was glad to see he was smiling.

"Can you at least tell me a bit more about these—er—friends?"

he asked. "Are you the only person they do things for?"

"I'm the only one so far, but they want to help all humans. They want to help us run the planet because—"

"So they're not *human*?" he interrupted, leaning forward as if he were on to something big.

"How could they be?" she said. "No humans can do what my friends do."

She watched closely to see if she'd spooked him again, but he looked more interested than spooked, his eyes wide.

"Is it something to do with your computer thing?" he asked, taking a sip of Coke.

"Sort of. I'm not allowed to tell you, exactly. But I can tell you what favor I want." She couldn't help grinning now, because she knew it would sound so weird. "I want you to take me to the Ducks game at Stanford. And then to Great America."

Joey's Coke shot out in a fine brown spray.

"You want WHAT?" he shouted.

"I want to see the football game at Stanford and then go to Great America with you the next day," Megan repeated patiently, trying to sound as if it were the most normal request in the world as she fetched a paper towel to mop up the Coke. "I know you're going. Spike's dad is driving, and there's room for me in the car. Don't ask how I know."

Joey gazed at her in silence for a moment.

"Friends, huh?" he asked.

Megan shrugged.

He ran his hands through his hair again, then stood up and went over to the phone.

"If I set it up with Spike, will you tell me what's going on?"

"I hope so, sometime," she said.

"And if I don't set it up?"

"No way I can ever tell you."

He paused, and she could see excitement building on his face, as if he wanted this strange adventure to continue.

"I'll ask," he said, as he started punching numbers on the phone. "Just one thing: why do you want to go? I mean, what do I tell Spike? That it's something to do with friends who aren't human?"

She laughed. "Tell him I want to see the Ducks beat Stanford. Doesn't everybody? And I've always wanted to go to Great America. What other reasons could I have?"

When Spike answered, Megan listened anxiously in case Joey tipped him off about the weirdness of the situation. But Joey played it straight, asking if Megan could come to the Stanford game.

Then he held the phone away from his ear because Spike

had become quite loud—loud enough for Megan to hear that he was yelling, "The sheep-girl? You want to bring the sheep-girl? Ba-a-aaa!"

Megan forced herself to smile. "I heard that!" she said.

Joey threw her an apologetic look, and glued the telephone tight to his ear so no more sheep sounds could escape. Now all Megan heard was Joey's side of the conversation as he told Spike that Megan was really okay, and she really wanted to see the Stanford game and Great America. Then there was a pause, and Joey repeated the part about the game and Great America to someone else.

When he put down the phone, he smiled at Megan and said, "Spike's dad says it's fine with him." Then he added, "Sorry about the sheep bit."

"That's okay," she said. "You get used to it. You get used to a lot of stuff when you have special powers."

Joey stood up and started to head for the door, until Megan stopped him with something else to blow his mind.

"Oh, and there's one other thing."

"What is it?" he asked, suspicious again.

"You can help me save my dad's restaurant. Remember? You were there when I promised to do it."

Joey groaned and sat down again. "Don't tell me! Your friends who aren't human all have MBAs and know everything about restaurants and—"

"Well, duh," she said.

"Really?" he asked, focusing his eyes on her.

She just smiled. "But there are some things they can't do—like anything in public," she said. "No way they can be seen, so they'd like your help with something."

She handed him a couple of attachments she'd printed up

from an e-mail sent by her Mouse Business Assistance team in Silicon Valley. It looked so official that Joey's jaw dropped.

"A survey, huh?"

"Right," she said. "It's to find out how many people from Greenfield would go to the restaurant if it was, you know, green."

Joey looked at the list of questions in his hand. "You want me to go to every house in Greenfield?" he asked.

"'Course not," said Megan. "It's a scientific sample. My MBA team picked the names with a computer."

He still hesitated.

"It'll help your dad too, right?" she said. "And your college fund. Deal?"

"Deal," he said with a grin, and picked up the blank forms and the list of houses to take them to.

The MBA Task Force was indeed now going at full speed, with mouse teams doing intense research at some of the most famous restaurants in America. And these teams sent daily e-mails to MBA central with tips on how a restaurant can be fresh and delicious and profitable all at the same time.

The task force left one big job for Megan—collecting case

histories about green restaurants from the back issues of magazines.

And Annie helped. She was waiting one day when Megan came home from school.

"I'm taking the afternoon off," she said. "Getting my hair done. Do you want to come with me and get rid of those braids finally?"

Megan was even less inclined to lose her braids than the last time, of course, because they made such good handles for mice. But she could use the ride.

"I really need to go to the library," she said. "I have to do some research."

Annie sighed. "Okay," she said. "The library it is. But you can't keep putting me off forever, young woman. One of these days we'll get you spruced up!"

Megan ran upstairs to collect Trey, because after his time in the Main Library of San Francisco he knew libraries like the back of his paw, and could help her find what she needed. As she came into her bedroom, Julia, who'd been on kitchen watch, shot out from beneath the dresser with ears and paws and tail going at a full screech of MSL.

"It's a book," Trey translated, looking up from the Thumbtop. "A library book you had in Cleveland. Julia was halfway through when you took it back. Something about a mouse with a name that sounds like Desperate. Couldn't tell exactly from her signs."

"Despereaux," said Megan, who had loved that book before she'd met real mice. "Fine, I'll get it out for her."

Then Curly and Larry asked for books too—so when Annie picked Megan up from the library later that afternoon, she exclaimed, "*What* a strange girl you are!" Because Megan had checked out *The Tale of Despereaux*, *The Boy's Book of Magic Tricks* (for Curly), and, for Larry, *The College Football Yearbook*.

Annie didn't see the stack of articles from back issues of magazines that Megan had copied and tucked under her jacket—articles with titles like "From Greasy Spoon to Green Star," and "Out with the French, in with the Fresh," and "Restaurants—the Green Revolution."

They were still some way from home when they saw Joey. He'd parked his bike on the sidewalk and was walking up to a front door.

"What the . . ." exclaimed Annie. "Does he think it's Halloween already? Is he trick-or-treating or what?"

"He's working for me," said Megan. "He's doing a survey."

Annie almost drove into a lamppost as she swiveled to look at Megan.

"A survey? What survey?"

Megan shrugged as if the answer was obvious. "To see what sort of restaurants people like best," she said. "To see if they'll come to Dad's restaurant when he starts cooking food from—you know—near here."

"Ha!" said Annie. "You're really *serious* about that project? That's so sweet, but really, Megan, my dear, restaurants are so complicated. . . . Yes, your dad has some problems now, but I'm sure it's nothing to do with where the food comes from!"

"Wanna bet?" said Megan.

Annie laughed. "Like how much?"

"Well, not money," said Megan, because she was down to her last two bucks after paying for the copying at the library. "How about this: if I'm wrong and people want the restaurant to stay the way it is, you can cut off my braids. And if I'm right and they want the food to be fresh and local, you'll . . ." She thought for a minute. "You won't use any makeup for a week!"

Annie laughed and patted her cheek, as if to reassure her makeup that it was safe. "It's a deal," she said.

Megan tugged fondly on her braids, because she knew how the survey would come out. Not that it was rigged, exactly, but mice don't like surprises. Megan's MBA team had already secretly surveyed families in Greenfield and other places like it, by asking mice to eavesdrop on their host families. And the reports were clear. There was not a lot of hankering for classical French food out there. People really did want food that was grown locally—fresh and delicious. The braids were safe.

chapter twenty-one

The braids were indeed safe.

As Joey found out, the people of Greenfield were fine with French food once in a while, but mostly they wanted Oregon food, from a menu they understood.

"So now what?" asked Joey, watching Megan skim through his survey.

"Now we make a presentation," she said. "Can you come with me to explain your report?"

"Okay, I guess," he said. "But I think you're going to need much more than that survey."

"I have much more than that," said Megan, thinking of the pile of papers that had been growing in her bedroom as her MBA team e-mailed the results of its research. "My friends have been busy."

. . . .

On the day when Megan and Joey were due to make their presentation, Trey insisted on coming along to the restaurant. Megan hung her jacket in a strategic spot so he could watch the proceedings from a pocket. He listened closely as Megan told her dad how other restaurants made deals with local farmers for their best and freshest food, and found ways to cook it so the natural flavor came through, and set prices so that people could afford to eat there. And still made a profit.

It seemed to be working. As Trey watched, Red Miller's face went through a great many of the expressions on the mouse chart. First came Fond Indulgence, of the sort you might see (according to the charts) on a parent whose kid does something cute. This was followed in almost dizzying succession by Intense Interest, then Amazement, then Excitement, and finally, Astonishment, after Joey read out the results of his survey.

Annie ran off to the restaurant bathroom laughing, her hands to her face. She came back a few minutes later wearing her natural skin, with a few really cute freckles now showing on her nose.

"What the—?" asked her husband.

"We had a bet," said Annie, and explained how very wrong she had been.

"Well, I've always said you look great without makeup," said Red.

"Yes, you have always said that," said Annie, sitting down with a sigh. "And that's what you'll get. For a whole week, right, Megan?"

"That's right," said Megan, going over to tickle her stepmother's cheek with a triumphant braid.

Of course Megan's dad wanted to know a whole lot about where all this wonderful information had come from, and of course Megan was prepared, because the head of her MBA team in Silicon Valley had coached her. For every question starting with "How on earth . . . ?" or "Where the heck . . . ?" Megan had an answer, with the names of magazines or professional journals or Web sites where her dad could check.

There were some facts he couldn't check, of course. Those were the facts that brave mice had gathered firsthand from restaurants in Berkeley, California, and Boulder, Colorado, and Santa Fe, New Mexico—famous restaurants where the food was fresh and local, and you had to reserve months ahead, and the owners made a bundle.

Her dad did have one theory about where some of *that* information might have come from.

"I guess your mom knows people in that world, people who are, well, green," he said. "She helped you, right?"

"Megan doesn't need help," said Joey, grinning at her. "Didn't you know she has special powers?"

Of course the adults laughed, not believing a word. "All I can say is, keep those special powers coming," said Red, "and your daddy will be a rich man."

"Rich enough to pay my fee?" asked Megan.

He laughed again and fetched fifty dollars from the till.

"You've earned it," he said. "What are you going to buy?"

Which gave her an excellent opening to bring up the trip to California. She'd been afraid that Annie and her dad wouldn't let her go, but she needn't have worried. They were delighted, of course—it was wonderful that she and Joey got on so well. Wonderful that she was such a fan of the Oregon Ducks. Great team.

. . . .

Back on Cherry Street, Trey himself led Curly, Larry, and Julia in a game of Chase My Tail, while Megan grinned at them.

Trey was overjoyed because, in spite of a few problems along the way, the trip to California was going to happen. Megan was glad about that, of course—and about everything else that was going right, such as the fact that her dad was proud of her, and Joey didn't seem to hate her anymore.

And indeed, in the weeks before they were due to head south, Joey even invited her to play basketball a couple of times. She wasn't as good as he was, but she got off some great shots, including one from about twenty feet that made Dustin ask, "Where did that come from?"

"Just Megan's special powers," said Joey.

"Or dumb luck," mumbled Spike, who'd never scored from that far away in his life.

Then there was that evening at the restaurant.

Her dad had closed it for a week while he made deals with local farmers and ranchers, and practiced new, green recipes. On the evening in question, Megan and Annie were having dinner there, trying out his new way of cooking free-range chicken.

"I should have done this sooner," said her dad, putting some roasted vegetables on her plate next to the chicken. "If it doesn't make me rich, please tell me again how it's saving the planet!"

She reminded him how his green restaurant wouldn't waste tons of gasoline to bring in food from distant places, with long-distance trucks sending out clouds of greenhouse gas to warm up the planet. The food wouldn't need tons of fertilizer and pesticides, washing into streams and lakes to hurt fish.

They were expecting Joey and his grandma to try the new chicken, and when they arrived, it was with a surprise in tow.

"Jake!" exclaimed Annie as she ran to greet him.

"Can't stay long," he said. "I'm on the red-eye to Dallas. But hey, always time for some Red Magic. And time for cousins." He reached over and squeezed Megan's shoulder.

"Sit, sit," said Megan's dad. "And eat, eat. All I ask is your honest opinion."

"What are you doing to me, Red?" asked Jake, pretending to be appalled as he looked at his plate. "Whatever happened to those velvety sauces, those lighter-than-air soufflés, those meltingly delicious . . . I mean this looks like chicken."

"It is," said Red. "Eat."

With a sigh, Jake ate. And asked for more. And ate again. "It's awesome," he admitted. "You know, I'd forgotten chicken could taste this good. And these vegetables. Man, I think you're on to something here. Let's hope it works."

"For you and me and Joey's college fund, right?" said Red.

"Speaking of which, I got a raise," said Jake, running his hand through his dusty-yellow hair, the way Joey sometimes did. "Because my last sales trip was so great. And the boss says he might give me time to work on my blobs. Finally. Then who knows? Once I get them right, maybe he'll put blobs on all his Tick-Tocks to charge them up from the sun. Save the planet."

He turned to Megan. "Hey, did your uncle tell you we've been e-mailing back and forth? He has some great ideas for my blobs. Thinks they're groovy, he said. Oh, and he told me about that little computer he made for you. I'd love to see it."

"A computer?" asked Annie. "You have your own computer? I'm not sure I approve of that. Why didn't you tell me?"

"I didn't tell you because . . ." Megan said, going a little red. "Because it's really too small for humans."

She pulled the Thumbtop out of her pocket and passed it to Jake.

"That is indeed seriously small," he said admiringly, turning it over in his hands.

"If it's too small for humans," asked Annie, peering at the Thumbtop, "who could use it? Fairies? Pixies?"

Megan shrugged. "Maybe mice," she said, and everyone

laughed. Especially Joey, who almost did that Coke-spray thing again through his nose.

Soon the restaurant was ready to reopen as Red Goes Green, but there was one problem: how to let people know it had changed?

"Wish we could afford an advertising agency," said Megan's dad.

They couldn't—but they didn't need one, because if anyone can publicize a restaurant quickly and efficiently, it's mice.

Little notes turned up on the desks of food critics at the Eugene *Register-Guard* and the Salem *Statesman Journal*, and the Portland *Oregonian*. These critics had not been very complimentary about Chez Red when it opened, saying things like "Another French restaurant? Who needs it?" or "Good but old-fashioned," or "Same old same old."

Now the little notes announced the change of name to Red Goes Green, and invited the critics to take another look.

They did—and as soon as they got back to their offices they wrote rave reviews, saying things like "Natural flavor comes soaring through."

And the telephone at the restaurant rang like crazy as people clamored for reservations.

"I think this is the turning point!" said Annie. She had rushed home from the bank to throw some food in front of Megan before racing over to the restaurant. "It's a lot of work, but we're going to make it! And it's all thanks to you and that research."

Megan noticed that although the week of the bet was over, most of Annie's makeup had stayed off, and there wasn't even enough now to totally hide the freckles.

Annie wasn't the only person who thought Megan had done a great job. Her mom wrote:

> Hey, just heard from your dad. TERRIFIC job getting him greened up like that! He thinks you're the greatest thing since sliced bread. Good on you, mate, as they say in Australia.

Megan replied:

> Cheese. The greatest thing since sliced cheese. That's what we say in Oregon.

chapter twenty-two

"How many mice did it take to get us here?" asked Megan.

It was Saturday night, a couple of hours after the football game in which the Oregon Ducks had beaten the Stanford Cardinal to a pulp. Megan was outside Spike's uncle's house in the nearby hills with Trey on her shoulder, gazing down at the lights of Silicon Valley. Straight ahead and a little to the right they could see different colored lights, some of them in the shape of Ferris wheels and roller coasters: the lights of Great America. And just beyond those lights they could make out the dark place where tomorrow Megan would find Headquarters, ground zero for the Mouse Nation.

"How many guys did it take to get us here?" Trey repeated. "Let's do a mouse count. There were three big clans in restaurants hunting up all that information. That's a couple hundred. Greenfield guys, finding the cat. Then there were the dudes at the newspapers, for those reviews. That could be another thirty. Twenty-five or so in Eugene for the grandma thing. And another few hundred in Florida working that J.J. stunt."

"And there'll be hundreds more down there, I suppose," said Megan, gazing into the valley.

"Thousands," said Trey. "And who knows what they're plotting."

"Plotting?" she said. "You mean like planning? Planning how to make all those Thumbtops?"

"That too," said Trey, in a flat sort of voice.

"Well, what else?" asked Megan, starting to worry. "You don't think they'd, like, *kidnap* me or anything, do you?"

"No, *you'll* be safe," he said. "Trust me, you're the best thing to come their way since cheese crackers. But they might just have a little surprise for *moi*."

"Like what?" she asked.

"Well, in his last e-mail, the Big Cheese thanked me for my services," he said. "Almost like my job was over. A couple more talking mice graduated just after I did, and they'll need practice. Can't blame them if they want a turn as your interpreter."

"No way!" Megan exclaimed, forgetting to keep her voice down (though Joey and Dustin and Spike were yelling so loudly as they watched a replay of the Ducks game that it didn't matter). "I don't want another interpreter! I want *you*. We're friends. Hey, let's not even go to Headquarters if they want to split us up!"

"We have to go," he said. "I promised. It's a mouse thing: we keep our promises. Look, I could be wrong."

"You'd better be," said Megan, reaching up to give him a gentle back rub.

After breakfast, Spike's dad dropped Megan and the three boys at Great America, and then went off to play golf.

Great America looked tame enough as they came through the gate. There was a carousel for little kids, and flowers, and palm trees. But beyond the palm trees, monster rides rattled and roared. And beyond *them* was that other world.

Joey was saying, "Okay, guys. How about that Vortex thing first?"

Megan wished she could go along, even if it meant being turned upside down by some monster ride. But she knew what she had to do.

"You go," she said. "I'll meet you back here at three."

The boys stopped abruptly and stared at her. This was plainly something they hadn't expected.

"What, are you afraid of going on the big rides with us?" asked Dustin.

"No way," said Megan. "I'll do stuff that's just as scary."

Which was true, of course.

"My dad told us to keep together!" said Spike. "Joey, she's your cousin. . . ."

"Step-cousin," said Joey, with a half smile. "Step-*second*-cousin. And Megan . . . well, Megan sort of does her own thing."

Spike didn't need much persuading. Indeed, he and Dustin looked quite relieved not to be saddled with a fifth-grade girl whose hair stuck up in front. As they all ran off toward a towering ride, Megan looked at their disappearing backs and wondered if she'd ever see them again—if she was insane to leave the company of humans and dive into an alien world.

Inside her pocket, Trey felt her stillness and sensed her nervousness. In fact, he'd expected it, and thumped out a message with his feet: Thump thump thump THUMP, thump THUMP! "Charge!"

Megan got it and checked the map she'd picked up at the gate. Yes, that's where she had to go, between a big roller coaster and a water ride. That's where she'd find a certain stretch of fence with a gate in it. And on the other side of that gate would be the headquarters of a whole other nation.

The big metal gate, when she found it, had the sort of combination lock where you punch in a code. Megan entered the numbers that Headquarters had e-mailed to Trey. There was a click and the gate opened, and Megan found herself in an empty parking lot at the back of an abandoned office building.

Trey climbed out of her pocket and onto her shoulder. "So far so good," he said. "Look! Over there. That's the door we want."

It was an ordinary-looking door, and there was a key on the ground in front of it. Megan fitted the key into the lock, and the door swung open to let her into the headquarters of the Mouse Nation.

It was just a normal office building except that it was deep in dust, and cobwebs hung from the ceiling.

"Are you sure this is the right place?" Megan whispered, reaching up to touch Trey for reassurance.

"What did you expect, the Magic Kingdom?" Trey whispered back. "This is it. Trust me. I've seen it on our Web site. They call this corridor Main Street."

As Megan's eyes got used to the half dark, she saw that paths had been cleared through the dust by mouse feet, and a lone mouse was sitting in the middle of Main Street, waiting.

"Looks like our guide," said Trey, as the mouse turned and walked slowly down the corridor ahead of them. They passed offices full of working mice, and as Megan followed, she was aware of a strange sound–the soft, rhythmic thumping of rear feet as dozens of dangling mice landed on keyboards.

The guide mouse stopped at the door of a room with a huge table down the middle. Except for cobwebs on the ceiling, this room was spotlessly clean, and the shining surface of the table reflected the ranks of mice that were sitting on it, gazing at the door, waiting.

In the center of the group was a mouse with a chain of office around his neck, sitting upright on a matchbox, which made him a little taller than the rest. Fifteen other mice were arrayed in a semicircle behind him, each wearing a piece of red thread around the neck.

"That's the Mouse Council," whispered Trey. "And the Big Cheese."

"Should I say hi?" she whispered back.

"No, no," he said. "Not unless he says it first. He likes things formal."

And the setup looked very formal indeed. To one side of the Mouse Council stood a group of twenty smaller mice in four rows. As Megan sat down on the chair that had been placed for her at the head of the table, these young mice began to sway together and wave their paws, ears, and tails in unison.

"It's the Youth Chorus," said Trey. "They've written a song for you." He translated:

Welcome Miss Megan
We're all on your side.
You've brought us the Thumbtop
Our joy and our pride.

With work and with luck
And with heart and with soul
We'll soon have a Thumbtop
In *every mousehole.*

"Now say it was great," Trey whispered.

"That was great," Megan said, her voice booming off the walls and ceiling, too loud for this silent world. The mice on the table looked up at her as if they expected something more.

"I'm sorry I don't have a song for you," she went on. "But I've brought this."

She reached into her pocket and fished out the Thumbtop. Did she hear a sharp intake of mouse breath? The members of the Mouse Council leaned forward to get a better view as she opened the lid of the computer and pushed it across the table.

The Big Cheese came down from his matchbox and ran his paws over the keys.

"It is excellent," he said in MSL, as Trey translated. "Let us hope we have a million or more by this time next year."

Megan laughed, thinking the Big Cheese had made a mouse joke. But he looked up at her sharply and said, "Do not underestimate us. We have learned enough about the computer to know how it can be mass-produced, with a little human help. Our engineers will now study it in greater detail so we can finalize those plans."

He waved a paw, and a couple of mice pushed the Thumbtop to the edge of the table. There, a team formed a mouse rope: as one wrapped his front paws tightly around the Thumbtop, another dangled him from the table by his tail, and so on until there were mice reaching all the way down to the floor. In a matter of seconds, the Thumbtop was scuttling rapidly out the door.

"Neat, huh?" whispered Trey. "Those guys must be from the gymnastics team."

"Wait!" whispered Megan. "When do I get it back?"

But the Big Cheese was talking again, as Trey translated his words about interspecies collaboration, and untold future benefits to mice and humans.

Then Trey stopped.

"What's he saying?" Megan whispered. "What's happening?"

Trey didn't answer immediately, but leaned against her neck.

"I was right," he whispered, when the Big Cheese had finished talking.

"Right about *what*?"

"Mouse rotation," he said sadly. "The boss just said what a great job I did, blah blah blah, yadda yadda yadda. And they want to give another mouse a chance to work with a real human. I'll go to the training department."

"No!" Megan said, out loud. Every mouse head in the room swiveled in her direction, but she didn't care. "I want Trey to stay with me. I need him."

The Big Cheese made a dismissive sign with his paw.

"Miss Megan," he said, slowing down his gestures as if he were speaking to someone very young, "you need *a* talking mouse. You do not need *this* talking mouse. Talking Mouse Three, or Trey, as you call him, will be most useful to us in training, where he can give our young mice practice in understanding spoken language, as well as a firsthand report on your world. Talking Mouse Five will take his turn as your interpreter."

"Sorry, kid," whispered Trey, when he'd finished translating. "Once his mind is made up . . . Hey, maybe you'll like Five. He's, well, he's different, but he's okay deep down. I'll e-mail, and we'll meet again sometime. I'm sure of it."

With one last pat of Megan's ear, Trey climbed down to the floor. A group of ten escort mice formed up around him, and he was marched out of the room with only one glance back over his shoulder.

And before he was even out of sight, Megan felt strange mouse feet climbing up her arm.

"Greetings, madam," came a voice with a British accent. "Allow me to introduce myself. I am Talking Mouse Five, but you may use my preferred appellation of Sir Quentin. While your previous interpreter immersed himself in popular culture, I acquired my verbal facility with the assistance of classic television dramas from Great Britain. I think you will find my conversation appropriate, nay, even improving, for a young lady of the human persuasion."

chapter twenty-three

What a difference a mouse makes.

With Trey on her shoulder, Megan had felt quite safe in the headquarters of the Mouse Nation, reassured by his soft weight and the feel of his feet on her shoulder. The feet that were on her shoulder now just felt creepy, making her all too aware that she was in the world of an alien species.

Without Trey to guide her, should she just leave? *Could* she leave if she wanted to? There were bars on the windows, and when she had entered Headquarters, the door had slammed shut behind her. Could she even open it from this side? That question led to a deep fear, like a cold hand twisting her guts, because no human on the planet knew where she was. She could hear distant screaming from Great America, but if *she* screamed, there was no way anyone would hear her.

What would her mother do in this situation? The only advice that Megan could remember right now was, *When you're in a tight spot, head for the hills.* But that wasn't a whole lot of use when you were stuck in the world's biggest mousehole, without a hill in sight.

She remembered another piece of advice from her mom: *Take three deep breaths, because it can't hurt and it might help.* And it did help. After her breaths, Megan felt calm enough to notice that the Big Cheese was finishing one last speech. Then, as he led the Mouse Council down from the table and out of the room, Megan was aware of a spate of words coming from her shoulder.

"My master wishes to convey," Sir Quentin was saying, "that your initial endeavor will be to peruse, and ultimately to sign, a treaty between our two illustrious species. He has withdrawn temporarily, that you may ponder this document in peace, but will return for the ceremonial signing."

Megan noticed that two mice were pulling a piece of paper across the tabletop toward her.

"Where's Trey?" she asked. "I need him."

"Have no fear, madam," said Sir Quentin. "The mouse to whom you refer will be more than adequately replaced by my humble self, since my linguistic abilities match, nay, exceed those of my colleague. In other words, as he might put it in the modern vernacular, heh-heh, I talk good. Now, may I draw your attention to the treaty that will assure peaceful coexistence between our two species?"

Megan told herself to concentrate as she gazed at the sheet of paper that had landed in front of her. It read:

Historic Treaty Between the Species

I, Megan Miller, a human being, hereby declare that my species (Homo sapiens) will live in peace with the mouse (Mus domesticus), and we will cease all efforts to harass and persecute that species.

Human beings will also assist the Mouse Nation to manufacture sufficient computers of appropriate size to meet the needs of said Nation for purposes of communication, education, and planetary adjustment as agreed between the parties aforementioned.

Signed, on behalf of humans:

____________________ Date: __________

(Megan Miller)

"I can't sign that!" said Megan.

"Rest assured, madam, that a writing implement will be

provided," said Sir Quentin. "You'll get a pen."

"That's not the point," she said. "There's no way I can speak for all humans!"

"For good or ill," he said, "you are the only human we have."

She read through the treaty again, and started to get mad. She'd never seen a treaty before, but she knew that they were meant to have something for *both* sides.

"Look at it!" she said. "It says *we* have to leave *you* in peace. *We* have to help *you* make Thumbtops. But mice don't have to do anything for us!"

"An interesting point," said Sir Quentin, "and one that is worthy of debate. However . . . Yikes!"

The "Yikes" came as Megan stood up so quickly that Sir Quentin had to grab a braid.

"I'm not waiting for any debate," she said, angry enough so that she was no longer afraid. "I'm not waiting for anything. We're going to look for Trey."

"Oh madam, I beg you!" wailed Sir Quentin. "I am instructed to keep you here until the treaty is signed. Any deviation from the program, any transgression of the rules, will reflect badly upon my person!"

His voice was squeaky now with fear, but Megan didn't

let that slow her down as she marched off to look for the one mouse among the thousands in this place who was her friend.

As she walked down the corridor, she heard the sound of an old bicycle horn like the one in Uncle Fred's garage, which went "oo-OO-oo" if a human squeezed its rubber bulb (or a mouse jumped on it).

"Madam, our alarm system has been activated!" squeaked Sir Quentin. "That authorizes our armed forces to take extreme measures."

"What are they going to do?" asked Megan. "Hit me with an atom bomb?"

There was no sign of any bomb—just panic, as some mice rushed out of offices to look, and others ran into offices to hide. A platoon of armed guards formed in front of her, made up of six rows of mice carrying toothpicks, but Megan stepped over the top, unscathed.

"Oh madam, where . . . I beseech you . . . pray desist," came the twittering from her shoulder. "Madam, I beg you . . . There are parts of this nation which even I am forbidden to penetrate. If it is thought that I am complicit in your unauthorized explorations, I will be, as they say, dead meat!"

She got the message, but she wasn't about to stop.

"Then tell me where I can find Trey," she said. "Where's the Training Department?"

"To tell you that, madam," Sir Quentin said, "would be more than my poor life is worth."

He sat silent on her shoulder as she stuck her head into different offices, trying to guess which department was which. At any other time she would have been fascinated by the research that was going on, because these mice plainly had their paws on every aspect of human life. In one office, computer screens showed pictures of American senators; in another, facts about business; in yet another, charts on climate change; and finally one with maps of the world.

A mouse in this office turned and said something that looked sharp and angry.

"We have violated yet another rule, madam," said Sir Quentin. "Entry into this department is authorized only for mice with security clearance, which I, alas, do not possess."

"Then take me to Training!" she said.

"Very well," he said miserably. "Although you may be sure I will be punished for my pains. Take the second turning to the right, and the third door on the left."

Then he hunkered down on her shoulder as if trying to be invisible.

• • • • • • • • • • • • • • • • •

The members of the Mouse Council had withdrawn to the council chamber, where the sound of the alarm shook them profoundly. A few were afraid that it might mean something they all dreaded—a visit from the pest control guys of Santa Clara County. But the Big Cheese guessed the truth, even before a messenger mouse rushed in with the news that their human was on the loose, and rampaging about.

"Should we pursue her?" asked the Director of Mouse Safety.

"Absolutely not," said the Big Cheese. "My guess is that she will be brought to us, and when that occurs, we must appear, above all, calm. We must show this human that we are in complete control."

When Trey was led out of the conference room, he was aware of feelings that were not very mouse. For once in his life, he had really, really wanted to disobey. And it wasn't just that he'd much rather hang out with Megan and the Cleveland dudes in Oregon than be stuck here teaching, for crying out loud. There was more. The thought of never seeing Megan again gave him a most unpleasant feeling—maybe a bit like the way Larry and

Julia had felt when they'd thought Curly was gone forever.

But if his bosses said he would be sent to the Training Department, that's where he would have to go. The bottom line is that you obey. Not that he had any choice, because the mice who'd escorted him out of the conference room stuck to him like lint.

Rows of young mice were waiting for him in the classroom, and he had just started to tell them about his first view of Megan, and how humungous a human really is close up, when he heard the "oo-OO-oo" of the bicycle horn alarm, thunderously loud in that silent place. The young mice scattered, as the squeak of sneakers could be heard in the hallway, and Megan's voice saying, "Take me to Training," and the frightened twitter of Sir Quentin's reply.

Trey felt a surge of relief as Megan appeared in the doorway. He couldn't run to her—that would have been altogether too much defiance of the Big Cheese's orders. But hey, as a very large mammal, Megan could do anything she liked. And who was he, one poor mouse, to resist?

What Megan saw when Sir Quentin brought her into the room was a mouse (with a piece missing from one ear) sitting on a matchbox under the eye of the ten trembling escort mice. Behind Trey was a notice reading:

Today's Talk:
Life Among the Humans
Speaker: Talking Mouse Three

The rest of the room was empty except for one piece of poop, where a frightened young mouse couldn't hold it, and a few small tails sticking out from beneath the ragged drapes that covered the window.

"Trey!" said Megan, as she walked toward him.

"Don't touch me, lady," he said, looking over at the escort mice to make sure they were paying attention.

Megan bent down and scooped him up.

"Got you!" she said, with a wink that only Trey could see. "And you can't wriggle free, no matter how hard you try!"

She picked Sir Quentin off her shoulder with her free hand and put him down at the front of the classroom. "Don't worry, students!" she said, turning to the curtains. "I have brought another talking mouse to teach this class! It was really nice meeting you, Sir Quentin."

"Do I understand," he said, "that I am to assume the role

of my young colleague in providing instruction for these youngsters?"

"You got it," said Megan. "I have other plans for this . . . this little *pest*."

With both hands now firmly around Trey, who was making a good show of wriggling to get free, she marched out of the room. From the corridor, she could hear Sir Quentin saying: "Young mice, pray cease to conceal yourselves from the human gaze! Emerge, that I may enlighten you on the joys of immersion in the great dramas from television's golden age. . . ."

Megan leaned against the wall, trying not to laugh—which wasn't easy, with her hands around a mouse who was himself shaking with laughter. But they both felt less like laughing when they saw that regiments of mice were marching toward them from both ends of the corridor, in columns wide enough to stretch from wall to wall, and deep enough so there was no way Megan could step over the top. Soon she was completely surrounded, and she was afraid that the mice in front might actually climb up her pants to attack.

"EEEK!" she said.

"This could be bad," whispered Trey.

"So what do I do?" she whispered out of the corner of her mouth.

"Tell them I'm a hostage!" Trey suggested.

She glared down at the attacking mice.

"Stay off me or the mouse gets it!" she said loudly. The mice backed off slightly. "Now what?" she whispered. "Should we just leave and go back to Great America?"

"No, no, no, not without permission," he whispered back. "Besides, we have work to do, right? Thumbtops for all? Two species, one planet, yadda yadda yadda?"

Megan thought quickly. Yes, even if things had gotten a little weird, she still owed it to her species to get the most help she could out of the Mouse Nation. But there was no way she wanted to be stuck with Sir Quentin as her interpreter.

"They can't make you stay here!" she whispered, as the front row of mice inched closer, their front paws barely an inch from her shoes.

"So let's make sure they don't," he said. "Let's go find the Big Cheese and get him to sort things out. Face it, right now they need you more than you need them!"

That gave Megan the chance to say something she had always wanted to, something from the movies Uncle Fred loved to watch. Holding Trey above the heads of the mouse army, she said, "Take me to your leader!"

There was a moment of confusion, then the army parted

to let her through. A platoon of nervous-looking guide mice led her up one corridor and down another, until they reached a sign that read:

MOUSE COUNCIL

No Unauthorized Mice Past This Point

"Thanks, guys," said Megan. "You may be unauthorized, but I'm not."

And she sailed into the Council Chamber.

chapter twenty-four

You had to hand it to the Mouse Council.

They held their ground when the human burst in. Indeed, it was a picture of serenity. All fifteen members of the council, and their boss, were sitting on the coffee table in the middle of the room, having their mid-morning snack. Small piles of Grape-Nuts were arranged in bottle caps in front of each mouse, while waiter mice hovered behind them pulling plastic bags of Grape-Nuts, ready to serve second helpings.

The Big Cheese calmly signaled the waiters to clear the table, and patted his ear in the sign that means, "I'm listening."

"I need Trey to stay with me," Megan began.

She sat on the floor to bring herself closer to mouse level as she told them just how well Trey had done his job in Oregon. It was Trey who had led the rescue of the Thumbtop from Joey,

and coordinated Operation Mouse Magic (with Kindness) and arranged her ride down here to Silicon Valley.

"We would expect that degree of efficiency from Trey, as you call him," said the Big Cheese, which Trey himself translated. "He is, after all, a mouse."

He sat back and waited to see what she would say next. In the silence, Megan became aware of the faint screams from Great America, and the thump of mouse feet on computer keys from nearby offices. But mostly she was aware of the waiting mice.

"There's something else," she said, a bit more loudly than she had intended. "Trey is my friend."

The Big Cheese made the paw-to-mouth sign that means "laughing out loud."

"The dog," he said, with distaste, "is frequently described as man's best friend, indicating that when humans claim friendship with a member of another species, it is because they *own* that animal. Mice have *bonds*. There is the bond of the clan, the bond of the region, the bond of the nation. But friendship between members of different clans—let alone different species—that does not seem useful."

That gave Megan a flash of inspiration.

"Friendship *can* be useful," she said. "When humans are friends—when they like the same things and they like being together—they make a good team. And it's the same for humans and mice. Trey and I make a great team."

She had pushed the right button. The members of the Mouse Council looked at each other and nodded. Friendship might not make much sense in their world, but teams certainly did. The Big Cheese turned around and conferred quickly with his advisers.

"If we allow TM3 to remain with you," he said, looking around to make sure his council was in agreement, "will you then sign the treaty between our species?"

"I don't mind signing a treaty, but not that one," she said.

"It's all for mice. It doesn't say what mice will do for humans."

The Big Cheese silently cursed the lawyer mice who had drawn up the treaty. In spite of all their education, hanging out in the best law firm in Silicon Valley, had they got it wrong?

"I understand your concerns," he said. "May I suggest that *you* write a treaty on behalf of your species? Spell out exactly what humans want from mice. Ask for whatever you wish—the sun, the moon, or the stars—remembering that for us the word *impossible* does not exist."

The sun, the moon, or the stars? On behalf of the whole human race?

"Wouldn't it be better if my uncle wrote the treaty?" she asked. "He'd probably do it better than I could."

The Big Cheese smiled. "There is a human saying that I believe we can adapt to this situation. 'Better a human in the hand than two in a bush.' You, madam, are the human we have in our hand, and I know your intellect to be more than adequate for the task, especially with Trey on your team."

Megan took a moment to think, and in the silence she could again hear the scream crescendo that wafted over the fence each time one of the big roller coasters of Great America turned its riders upside down and inside out. All those humans on that side of the fence, and on this side, one kid trying to guess what those humans wanted most in the world, or what they needed, or both. What *would* they ask for in her place?

Megan thought of her mom chasing wombats around a hot desert, and then she got it, of course. She knew absolutely what to put in the treaty.

She smiled at the anxious mouse faces turned her way, waiting for her answer.

"Okay, I'm ready," she said. "We'll do it. Me and Trey."

"You and Trey," said the Big Cheese. "A team. I like that."

They followed a guide mouse down a dusty corridor. The "all clear" signal had sounded (three quick bleats on the horn), and this time as they passed offices full of working mice, the occupants looked up and waved.

The guide mouse led them to a closet full of office supplies left over from when humans worked here. Megan helped herself to a pad of yellow paper and a pencil, and followed their guide to the old company lunchroom. Two dilapidated vending machines leaned against the wall, their doors hanging open. One was still full of soda. The candy machine next to it was almost empty, and the guide mouse said something that looked apologetic.

"She hopes you like coconut bars," said Trey. "The guys have eaten all the others, but mice don't do coconut."

Megan wasn't crazy about coconut either, but she was hungry, so she helped herself to a couple of bars and a soda. Then she sat at one of the tables and wrote:

Treaty Between Mice and Humans

"Let's start with what mice want," she said, with her mouth full.

"Well, of course we'd like humans to ban traps and poison and cats," said Trey. "But that's not going to happen. Let's stick to what you guys can really deliver."

"Like helping mice make Thumbtops?"

"You got it. Oh, and we don't want you telling everyone about us."

Megan chewed on her pencil, which tasted almost as good as old coconut, then wrote out two things that humans could do for mice:

* Humans will help the Mouse Nation make Thumbtops.
* No human will ever tell other humans the secrets of the Mouse Nation unless the Mouse Nation gives permission.

"Okay?" she asked.

"Works for me," said Trey. "Now I guess you get a couple for humans."

"The first one is obvious," she said, and wrote out:

* Mice will never hurt humans or mess up human computers.

"Good," said Trey, scooping up a piece of coconut, sniffing it, then throwing it down in disgust. "Now one more. The biggie. The sun, the moon, or the stars. And you know what? I think I can guess what it's going to be."

Megan smiled at him and started to write, and as the final item of the treaty emerged, Trey did a slow pirouette, because it was exactly what he'd expected.

The guide mouse brought them back to the conference room, where the Mouse Council was again arrayed in a semicircle on the shiny surface of the table, with the Big Cheese at the center. Although you couldn't tell it from his stillness, the leader of the second most powerful species on the planet was nervous. This whole day had been such a test of his leadership! And yes, he had made some mistakes. Like that first treaty—that was a nonstarter. But what about this new one? Had it been smart to allow a human—and a young one, at that—to write it?

When Megan came in, the Big Cheese patted his ear, meaning he was listening. She sat down and read her treaty:

Treaty Between Mice and Humans

* Humans will help the Mouse Nation get Thumbtops.
* No human will ever tell other humans the secrets of the Mouse Nation unless the Mouse Nation gives permission.
* Mice will never hurt humans or mess up human computers.
* Mice will help humans stop climate change and save the planet.

When she had finished reading, there was stillness. Had she insulted the Mouse Council? Did they hate her treaty? Had she asked for too much? Then came a sound so soft she wouldn't have noticed it at all if she hadn't seen it happening. Sixteen pairs of mouse paws were clapping.

"Excellent," said the Big Cheese. He looked at her with

admiration. "Your requests on behalf of humans make perfect sense. Some of us"—he glared at the Director of Technology, who took a step backward—"some of us thought you might ask for something for yourself, such as money, or candy, or help with your homework. I knew better. Climate change is indeed the most urgent question facing the planet, for all species. We know that many humans choose to ignore the evidence, but we mice have studied the subject in depth. And like virtually all *human* climate scientists, we recognize the truth: that it is humans who are responsible for climate change, and only humans can slow it down. Are you with me so far?"

"Absolutely," said Megan, because it was exactly what her mom would say.

"At present there is not much we mice can do to help," the Big Cheese went on. "But once we have the technology—once we have adequate computer power—we can work wonders. Don't ask me how!" He raised a paw as if to stop a question. "It is our habit never to divulge a plan until it is completely ready to go. But we can give it a name. Let us call it Operation Cool It."

While he was talking, a mouse team had typed the new treaty into a computer. Now they printed two copies, with space for the signatures of Megan, the Big Cheese (under his formal title of Chief Executive Mouse), and all fifteen members of the Mouse Council. Finally there was a space for the signature of a witness.

A group of carrier mice brought in an ink pad, formed a mouse rope, and lifted it to the tabletop.

"I could have done that for them," whispered Megan.

"That would be no fun," Trey whispered back. "We like to do things for ourselves. Hadn't you noticed?"

Megan signed both copies of the treaty and added the date, while the members of the Mouse Council each pressed a paw onto the ink pad and then onto the treaty to make their mark. Finally, Trey put his pawprint on the "witness" line. Everyone stood back to admire the treaty, while attendants went from mouse to mouse with tissue to wipe the ink off their paws.

A mouse team brought in the Thumbtop, mouse-roped it up to the tabletop, and parked it in front of Megan.

"Now that our engineers have had time to study this computer," said the Big Cheese, "we are ready to approach the human who can help us in its production."

"Uncle Fred!" exclaimed Megan, suddenly awash in relief at the prospect of telling her uncle everything. "Can I call him? Or e-mail him from here right now?"

"No, no, no, no, no!" said the Big Cheese. "Not yet! You

yourself probably had doubts about us in the beginning. You may even have considered reporting us to the authorities. Am I right?"

Megan nodded, remembering that first day when she had indeed thought of blowing the whistle.

"A full-grown human," the Big Cheese went on, "even one with an adventurous spirit, could harbor graver doubts. And if he informs the authorities, he is more likely than a child to be believed. Thus he must be approached with the greatest of care."

He had a point. Megan's exhilaration went down a notch. Yes, Uncle Fred might be overjoyed to learn about the Mouse Nation, as if one of his favorite science fiction movies had come to life. But then again he might not. He might even think that the evolution of mice was more like one of his horror movies, where some creature has grown powerful enough to pose a threat to mankind, and has to be zapped.

"We are already making plans for our approach," the Big Cheese was saying. "Our Wall Street branch will take the lead, but we will need your help in bringing your uncle to New York in a couple of weeks."

Megan gaped at him. Getting Uncle Fred to New York in a couple of weeks? Did the Big Cheese think that she could perform miracles? That she was a mouse? There was no way she could get *herself* to New York in two weeks, let alone an uncle.

The Big Cheese seemed to read her mind once again. "You may think that it will be difficult to arrange such a trip," he said. "But, my dear Miss Megan, young humans do it all the time at no cost, accompanied by a relative who may well be an uncle. We will show you how."

A mouse standing by the computer in the corner clicked it to start a presentation. It was all about pets doing tricks on television. There was a ferret who pushed buttons on telephones; a dog who moved chess pieces around with its nose; two parrots who sang "God Bless America" in harmony; and a pig that had learned a clunky hula dance. Each animal came with at least one kid and one adult.

"You see?" said the Big Cheese, rather smugly. "First, you and Trey will prepare a performance. An animal act, if you will. You will then be invited to perform your act on television in New York, and will bring your uncle as your adult protector." He gave a mouse laugh, paw to mouth. "You might say that we will set a trap for the uncle. A nice soft trap."

"Easy peasy," whispered Trey, and sounded as if he meant it.

chapter twenty-five

It was so strange to be a human among humans again. After the silence and order of the Mouse Nation, Great America was overwhelming in its noise and brightness.

Megan blinked at the hordes of happy people who had no clue how their planet had changed. Would they ever know? Would they look back to this time as the turning point when global warming began to slow down? Would anyone ever tell them how it came about?

She needed time to sort through everything that had happened. She was also hungry, in spite of the coconut bars, so she bought a hot dog and carried it to a bench half hidden by some bushes, away from the crowds.

"Do you really think it will happen?" she asked, as Trey climbed out of her pocket and onto her knee.

Trey took the piece of bun that she handed to him. "Do I

think *what* will happen?" he asked, with his mouth full. "The trip to New York? Thumbtops all around? Fixing climate change? Or all of the above?"

He was feeling remarkably good about himself and his whole species. The fact that he'd delivered Megan safely to headquarters gave him a glow of pride; and when you added the extra facts that he'd kept his job, and that their two species were now linked in a binding treaty, things had gone great. Better than great.

"Let's start with the trip to New York," said Megan.

"Absolutely, it will happen," he said. "But there's nothing we can do about it right now. We're in Great America, woman! And we don't have long. Let's take a ride on that . . ."

Then Trey went completely still, except for the claws that dug into Megan's leg as his eyes focused on something behind her. She turned to follow his gaze, and found herself looking into the blue eyes of Joey, round with surprise, set in a face that was as white as cream cheese.

As Joey told Megan later, he'd worried about her after she'd gone off on her own that morning because he'd be the one in trouble if anything happened to her. Throughout the day he'd watched out for that flash of red hair sticking straight up above a blue jacket, especially when he went on high rides that let him survey the whole park.

He was at the top of a ride called the Drop Tower when he finally saw the red hair/blue jacket combination. He kept his eyes on the hair as the ride dropped him to earth, then ran to the spot where he had last seen it. And there was Megan sitting on a bench eating a hot dog.

And there was the mouse—sitting on her knee, its lips moving as if it was talking.

Joey took a step closer just as the big roller coaster nearby came to a halt, and it was quiet enough to hear a voice that was perfectly timed with the movement of the mouse's lips.

That was when the mouse saw him, and Megan turned to look, and for a moment Joey couldn't move. Then he freaked out and turned and ran, as Megan leaped up from the bench and ran after him with Trey clinging to a braid.

As she was running, Trey hissed in her ear, "Talk to him! He mustn't tell *anyone*!" because there was no doubt about it—Joey had heard at least half a sentence. Then Trey dived into Megan's pocket for a bumpy ride as she sprinted through the crowds. By the time she caught up with Joey, he had joined Dustin and Spike near the front of the line for the Demon.

"You found her!" said Spike.

"Hey dude, you gonna barf?" asked Dustin, gazing anxiously at Joey's white face.

"I'm okay," said Joey, throwing a terrified look in Megan's direction. Then at the very last moment, before it was their turn to get on the Demon, he wheeled away and sat on a bench.

And there he stayed while Spike and Dustin and Megan rode the Demon, and Trey dug his claws into the lining of Megan's pocket as they spun in spirals and whirls and figure eights, and he had no clue whether he was up or down, except for brief moments when he could glimpse the ground and the kid in the Oregon Ducks jacket, white-faced with his new secret.

"Talk to him!" Trey had said. That was easy for him to say, but there was no chance to talk when they came down from the Demon, because Joey had already run ahead to the front gate, where Spike's dad was waiting for them.

There was no chance as they started on the long drive north, because when Spike's dad saw Joey's white face, he made him sit in front.

When night began to fall, and the car was dark enough, Trey

wriggled up to Megan's shoulder and whispered, "We'll stop to eat. Talk to him then."

But when they pulled off the road for hamburgers halfway home, Joey stuck close to his friends, and there was no way Megan could get at him. For the rest of the trip, all four kids slept, and by the time Megan was rolled out of the car, Joey had already been dropped off.

Her dad more or less carried her up to bed, and she pretended to be half asleep so he wouldn't stick around to talk. As soon as he had turned off the light and closed the door, Trey jumped up on the windowsill and peered out toward Joey's house, while Megan kneeled on the bed so she could look out too.

Curly, Larry, and Julia climbed up to join Trey on the windowsill.

"What's wrong, boss?" asked Larry. "Did the Ducks lose?"

"Did something bad happen at Headquarters?" asked Julia.

"Nothing like that," whispered Trey. "It's Joey."

He told them what had happened in the park.

Through the tracery of pine branches, they could see the looming shape of Joey's house, and a light in the bedroom, where Joey himself was sitting with his back to them.

"He's on his computer," said Trey, remembering the layout

of the room. "He's probably e-mailing his dad."

"D'you think his dad will believe him?" asked Megan. "An e-mail about a talking mouse?"

"Who knows?" Trey replied. "It's not worth the risk. He might have seen you coming back through that gate from Headquarters. If someone tells the cops to check there . . ."

He sort of slumped, and the other mice went into a comfort huddle around him as they gazed through the dark at the boy who now had so much power over their species.

Megan reached up to stroke Trey, but the mice on the windowsill were so closely packed together that they formed a solid mass of fur, and she found all four of them under her hand. She felt terrible because it was her fault. She should never have talked to Trey in public. The entire Mouse Nation had trusted her, and she had let them down. And she had let her own species down too, because now that she'd broken the terms of the treaty, the mice wouldn't have to keep their side of the bargain. And if their nation was destroyed . . . She couldn't bear to think about it.

As they watched, Joey stood up and ran his hands through his hair, as if he hadn't quite decided what to do next. Then he pulled the curtain across, and a minute later, he turned off his light.

"Could you see the screen?" asked Megan. "Could you tell if he sent an e-mail?"

"No," said Trey. "It's too far, even for us."

"Well, we have to find out," said Megan. "Maybe I should go over right now. I could throw some dirt at his window—get him to come down."

"You think he wouldn't yell?" said Trey. "And wake up the whole street? He's way too jumpy. Someone has to sneak into his room and see what he wrote."

"I'm not sneaking into his room!" said Megan.

Trey turned around and smiled, his first smile since Great America. "Who said it had to be a human?" he asked. "Curly's an old hand at this game. Right, Curly?"

"Right," said Curly. But he was thinking about that cat, and didn't sound very enthusiastic.

This was the first time Curly had made the crossing to Joey's house in the dead of night, the first time when the safety of the entire Mouse Nation depended on him, the first time under a full moon, which made him an easy target for owls.

As the others stood huddled at Megan's window, gazing down at the too-bright patch of backyard, Joey's house looked impossibly far. They wished that both houses were set in a jungle, instead of on blank patches of moonlit grass, where even at top speed a mouse would be exposed to danger.

At last they saw Curly leave the shadow of their house and make his run for it, a faint black dot sprinting across the grass to the fence. Then nothing. And there was nothing for them to do but wait, just like the last time.

Joey's house felt very familiar to Curly now as he made his way through the kitchen, with the smell of cat sending ripples of fear running through him. He could just make out the shape of the cat itself in its basket as he tiptoed past, its tail twitching slightly as if dreaming of mice. But it stayed asleep as Curly got safely past and sprinted for the familiar hole that led behind the kitchen cabinets, up inside the walls to Joey's closet, then over the pile of sneakers and into his room.

Joey was a silent lump in the bed. Curly could make out the shape of the computer he had been using before he fell asleep, and it was asleep, too. But what had it been doing before that? Had it been sending e-mails? Might news of a talking mouse already be buzzing around the world in e-mails and tweets and Facebook pages and blogs?

Curly hopped up on the desk, then reached out and pushed the space bar, waking the computer from its sleep.

The light! The light from the screen! Would it wake Joey up? Curly hid behind the monitor, just in case, but there was no movement from the bed. Curly emerged and looked at the screen.

Joey had started an e-mail:

From: Joeyfish98@aol.com
To: Jakefish68@aol.com
Subject: Guess What

Hey Dad you won't believe this but

Later, Curly realized that he should have headed straight home to report that, yes, Joey had started an e-mail, but, no, he hadn't sent it. Then Trey would have decided what to do next. But Curly wanted to take matters into his own paws.

Joey had been spooked by their mouse magic, right? Well, he'd show Joey a little mouse magic of his own by adding something to the message—like the warning that Megan had put in her e-mails to Joey: "Don't tell ANYONE. My friends are everywhere. They will KNOW."

But that would be way too much for one mouse. The most

he could do on his own was probably "SHHHH," which should get the point across.

He hit the caps lock key and reached over it to click the *S*, then ran around to lean on the *H* until it repeated six times, which he hoped would be enough to persuade Joey to keep quiet. He was concentrating on this task so intently that he didn't hear the rustling of bedclothes behind him, didn't see the dark shape rise up from the bed, wasn't aware that anything was wrong until he suddenly found himself inside a glass that had been brought down sharply on the desk to trap him. He spun around, feeling nothing now but the slippery walls of the glass, just able to see by the screen's light the shape of Joey's face looming above him.

"Got you, little mouse!" said Joey, his voice muffled to Curly's ears. "And you're not getting out till you tell me what's going on! I know you can talk, remember? I heard you!"

Curly's view changed to a huge ear distorted by the glass, as Joey bent down to listen.

The ear vanished, and the view of Joey went fuzzy again as the muffled voice said, "Please talk to me! I promise I won't hurt you. Please, little mouse!"

Curly felt panic rising. He had been in tight places before, but never imprisoned like this, never trapped in a glass, never mistaken for a talking mouse. Quickly, he tried to remember what he had been taught in his Surviving Humans course. Rule One was that you should never let humans see how smart you are, but should always follow the procedure for WWAWMD, which stands for "What Would A Wild Mouse Do?" Right now, no one had to tell Curly how to behave like a wild mouse, because he couldn't help it. Instinct had taken over, and he began scrabbling wildly at the glass walls of his prison.

Then Joey switched on the light, and that helped Curly to calm down and *think* as he gazed at the familiar freckled face, distorted by the curve of the glass.

"Megan sent you over to spy on me, right?" Joey asked.

Curly was tempted to start a dialogue by pointing toward

his mouth and shaking his head, meaning no, he wasn't the magic mouse who could talk, but he forced himself to keep acting wild, to keep scrabbling. And there really was a sense of panic building up in him. A glass is no place for a mouse, and Curly knew there was a danger that he might run out of air.

Luckily, Joey knew that too. He fetched a plastic container from his grandma's kitchen and punched some holes in the lid for air. There was plenty of room for Curly and some torn-up paper to sleep on, and a handful of Cheerios.

"You'll stay right there," Joey said, "until someone tells me the truth about what's going on!"

And as his prisoner, Curly didn't have any choice.

chapter twenty-six

Megan woke up to a sight that was familiar from the last time Curly had gone alone to Joey's house: a huddle of anxious mice on the windowsill.

"He's not back!" she said, reading their body language.

Then suddenly all three of them sat bolt upright.

"Look!" said Trey. "Oh, look!"

Megan kneeled on her bed and peered out. There was Joey at his window, looking her way. In his hands was a plastic container with something dark inside—a dark shape that moved.

With their sharp eyes, the mice could see more than a dark shape.

"It's a mouse," Trey confirmed sadly.

Julia said something that looked urgent. Larry joined in with a couple of quick gestures, which included a clawing motion with the left paw.

"Julia's terrified that Joey will hurt Curly," Trey interpreted. "She's saying, 'Please please please get him back.' And Larry thinks Joey might feed Curly to the cat."

"No way," said Megan. "Joey's not cruel, I'm sure of it. I bet he'll give Curly back if I ask."

She dressed as fast as she could and ran down to the kitchen to telephone Joey, but Annie was using the phone, which left Megan with only one choice—to sprint through the backyard and climb over the fence. She ran to the front of Joey's house, meaning to ring the bell, but was just in time to see his bike disappearing down the street as he pedaled off to school, his backpack bulging.

Annie had seen Megan run into the yard and was waiting for her as she climbed back over the fence.

"Well, that's one way to get dirty before school," she said. "What on earth were you doing?"

"I just wanted to talk to Joey," said Megan miserably. "He has something of mine."

And she thought of that "something," and how scared he must be.

It was a bad, bad day for everyone.

Larry and Julia, of course, were basket cases. Trey was

feeling terrible, as his worries piled up on top of each other like a teetering stack of blocks. There were worries about Curly, and worries about how Trey had betrayed his nation by letting Joey hear him talk, and worries about the trip to New York, and worries about his job, and worries about Operation Cool It, and the planet, and the future of man and mouse. The trouble was that until he knew what was happening to Curly, and what Joey had in mind, Trey couldn't do a thing about any of his other worries. And for a mouse who thrived on action, this was torture.

For Megan, of course, the day was full of anguish. Had she been right when she assured the mice that Joey wouldn't hurt Curly? How well did she know him, anyway? Was he perhaps so spooked by her mouse magic that he wanted revenge? And could he take out his revenge on a mouse?

At lunchtime she found herself running the four blocks from Fairlawn to Garfield Middle School, hoping to pick Joey out from the crowd, hoping to persuade him to give Curly back. But his school looked so big and noisy, and there were so many boys in green Oregon Ducks jackets, she gave up.

For Joey, the day was not great either. As he pedaled to school with the hard corner of the plastic container pushing into his back, he realized that taking the mouse with him was a dumb move. He'd wanted to show it to Dustin and Spike, but now it occurred to him that there was no way they'd believe it could talk unless he could get it to say something, which seemed unlikely. And the news might whiz around the school that Joey Fisher had lost it.

Then there was the problem of Megan's special powers. If he told anyone that this mouse could talk, she'd surely find out, because her mysterious friends must be watching every move he made, somehow, and listening to every word. Some of his fear of her was coming back—the fear he'd felt when she'd first started spooking him. He'd coped with that fear, of course, by deciding that there had to be a scientific explanation behind her stunts. But there was no scientific explanation for a mouse that talked.

There was no scientific explanation for a mouse that could write *SHHHHHH* on his computer.

It had to be witchcraft—had to be magic of some sort. But who could believe in that?

He left the mouse container under his gym shorts in his locker, coming back between classes to lift a corner of the shorts and whisper, "Dude, you wanna talk?"

But all he got was a burst of WWAWMD, as Curly scrabbled at the plastic walls of his prison.

. . . .

When the school day ended at Fairlawn, Joey was standing on the other side of the street, waiting.

"Hey! There's Joey Fisher!" Caitlin said in an admiring voice. Megan watched her take off across the road with two of her friends. The three of them surrounded Joey and peered into the plastic container he was holding, then jumped back with soft "EEEK"s and giggles, and ran back to where Megan was standing.

"It's just a creepy old mouse," said Caitlin, with a grin. "Joey wants to show it to *you*, for some reason."

Megan felt her heart beating strongly as she hurried across the street. Joey didn't say anything, but held out the container so she could look through the lid at the creature inside.

"Curly!" she said, and reached out.

Joey kept both his hands firmly around the container and pulled it back a little.

"Curly?" he said, with a little smile. "That's a real dumb name for a mouse."

"Please," she said. "Can I have him back? Look, he's so scared!"

Curly was still in his WWAWMD mode, scrabbling around as if he was frantic to get out.

"You can have him back as soon as you tell me what's going

on," said Joey gravely. "Like how did you get this mouse to talk? And to write? He was writing on my computer when I caught him. And what does he have to do with . . . with all those stunts you did?"

Megan's first instinct was to tell Joey the truth, because more than anything, she wanted Curly out of that container. But as she looked through the plastic, she saw Curly put a paw to his lips, signaling for silence. She felt a rush of love for him, because, like all mice, he was plainly putting the welfare of his species above his own.

And she told Joey how it would have to be.

"I can't tell you anything," she said. "Not now, anyway, because it's not just me. It's a whole team, and I have to get permission."

"A team?" he asked, with the beginning of a smile. "Like a team of witches? Or a bunch of black cats or something?"

"Sort of," she said.

"Really?" he said, not smiling now.

"I said sort of," she said, meaning that if you changed cats to mice and black to brownish gray, he'd be about right.

"Okay," he said slowly. "How long will it take to get permission from your witches or whatever? So you can get your mouse back?"

Megan thought about the Big Cheese and his warnings about the danger of telling other humans the biggest secret in the universe. Was there any way he'd give her permission to tell Joey? Just to save one mouse out of millions?

Looking down at Curly, she knew she had to give it her best shot. "Come to my house in about an hour," she said.

And she noticed Curly holding his paws together above his head in a sign of triumph. She had done the right thing.

On Cherry Street, panic had been building all day.

When Megan arrived, it didn't help, because she was in such a state herself that she found it hard to talk straight.

"Curly . . . I've seen Curly . . . Joey won't give him back unless . . . well, he says Curly was writing on his computer and he wants to know how. He wants to know everything and he'll be here"—she looked at the clock—"at quarter past four. What can we tell him?"

"Nothing," said Trey. "We can't tell him anything. You know that. It's in the treaty, remember?"

"But we have to get Curly back!" she wailed, remembering the brave face peering up at her from the plastic prison.

"So?" said Trey. "He's only one guy." Megan noticed that

Larry and Julia were nodding in agreement, even though they looked totally miserable. The good of the Mouse Nation came first, way ahead of the interests of an individual mouse.

Julia said something that Trey translated: "Will Joey be kind to Curly if we don't get him back? Will Curly be his pet?"

Megan sat down at the table and picked Julia up to stroke her gently.

"I think he'll be kind," said Megan. "Let's hope so." As she stroked Julia, she felt a soft trembling against her arm. Larry had come over to lean on her for comfort, so she picked him up for a stroke too.

As if the stroking had activated his brain, Larry suddenly wriggled free and ran to the middle of the table, where he faced Megan and said, "We can take him! If Julia climbs up to bite his ear, and I bite his hand, and Trey—"

Trey stopped translating at this point. "You kidding, big guy?" he said. "Joey going to the doctor with mouse bites? From mice that might have diseases? That's the best way to get everyone on the block wiped out."

"You got a better idea?" asked Larry.

Megan remembered something her mother had said when a man with a gun claimed he owned half of St. Hilda, and wouldn't let her pass. There was only one cop on the island, and he was the guy's brother-in-law, so he wasn't likely to help. In the end, Susie Miller had walked over to the man's house.

"I found a way to tame him, Meggy!" she had said when she came back, triumphant. "I told him I needed his help. He was so flattered, he turned into a pussycat."

Megan told the mice that story (except for the pussycat part).

"Let's tell the Big Cheese we need Joey's help," she said. "And it's true. It's going to be hard, getting to New York. I'll bet Joey *can* help."

Trey was looking at the clock. "It's worth a try," he said, because for once he was all out of ideas. "Let's roll."

They used the big computer so that everyone could see what was happening. Megan typed as Trey dictated the most difficult message of his life:

From: TM3@mousenet.org
To: Topmouse@mousenet.org
Subject: Our Team

As we prepare to lure Miss Megan's uncle to New York, I suggest adding a member of her clan to our team. As you know, Joey Fisher was of great help in delivering Miss Megan to Headquarters. I would

> like his help with the next phase of Operation Thumbtop. Of course we would have to tell him about the history and goals of our nation, but I feel confident that those secrets will be safe with him.

Trey paused. "Now comes the hard part," he said. He thought for a moment, then dictated:

> P.S.: Mr. Joey is already aware of some of our powers, through an accidental overhearing for which I take full responsibility. However, I remember that you once said, "There is no disaster that mice cannot turn to the advantage of themselves and their nation." I believe that to be true in this case.

Megan was about to send the message when she looked at the clock. Only thirty minutes to go.

She added:

> P.P.S.: Joey will be here in half an hour. Please give us your answer before then.

She looked around at her friends, took a deep breath, and hit "Send."

chapter twenty-seven

Trey's e-mail was posted on the big screen in the council chambers, and the effect was much as Trey had feared. MSL signs for "Treachery!" and "Fire him!" and "After all we've done for him!" and "We're doomed!" fluttered up from the group.

When it came right down to it, however, there was only one voice that mattered. And curiously, the Big Cheese didn't look too unhappy.

"Remind me where this young male fits on Miss Megan's kinship chart," he said.

The computer team dangled and clicked its way to a chart they'd put together weeks ago, when Megan first became important to their nation. They brought up Joseph J. Fisher (occupation: child), son of Jacob J. Fisher (occupation: inventor/salesman), Megan's father's second wife's first cousin.

The Director of Technology cleared his throat (in MSL, it's a swipe across the throat with the tip of the tail).

"Yes?" said the Big Cheese.

"You may recall that, at your request, we investigated the parent Jacob," said the director. "The clan at his old place of work in Greenfield provided us with details about his main invention."

"Ah yes," said his boss. "The solar blob. An interesting development, and one that could prove valuable to us. Indeed, Trey's accidental treachery could turn out to be of benefit to our nation, enabling us to kill two cats with one stone. Tell him that he is reprimanded for his carelessness, but he has my permission to proceed."

When Joey brought Curly to Cherry Street fourteen minutes after four, he couldn't suppress a soft "EEEK" as he saw three mice on the kitchen table.

"These guys won't hurt you," said Megan. "They're my friends. No mouse magic."

She noticed Joey was shaking a little as he sat down, keeping both hands on the container in front of him. Inside, Curly pressed his nose against the wall of his prison as Larry and Julia ran up to nuzzle him through the plastic.

"Please let him out," said Megan. "We have permission to talk to you, and we'll tell you everything."

But Joey kept one hand on the lid of the container.

"Your friends. All this time—they're *mice*? Just *mice*?" He almost laughed.

That was too much for Trey. "*Just* mice?" he echoed. "A billion brains, all of us smart, all working together?" He walked forward to stand in front of Joey. "We've met, remember? In Great

America. You wasted your time trying to get *this* guy to talk," he said, pointing to Curly. "He's plenty smart, but I'm the only talking mouse in Oregon. And I am authorized to welcome you to our world."

Megan watched Joey anxiously.

"No way," he said weakly. He put his head down on the table, his hair squashed up against the container. "Not possible. No way," he repeated, his voice muffled now.

"Way," said Trey. "You guys evolved. Why not us? The difference is we did it fast and we did it in secret. In fact, you're only the second human to know. How does that feel?"

Not too good, apparently, because when Joey sat up, Megan could see that he'd gone a little pale. But to everyone's relief, he pried the lid off the plastic container and watched as Curly leaped out to celebrate his freedom. First he ran to each mouse in turn to rub noses, then rushed up Megan's arm to nuzzle her ear. When he came down, he ran over to Joey and made a little bow to show there were no hard feelings.

"Sorry I had to lock you up," said Joey, reaching out to stroke Curly gently on the head. "I wasn't going to hurt you. But Megan, you see why I had to keep him prisoner, don't you? It was the only way to get *you* to talk."

"Yes, I understand," she said. "And I'll talk. But first, you'd better watch this."

She reached over to the keyboard of the big computer and started the presentation that had turned her own world upside down not so long ago.

There is no easy way to learn about the Mouse Nation, because no human mind is programmed to believe that such a thing can exist. Joey had one advantage. He already knew that some mice, at least, are smart. But it still blew his mind to learn just how far and how fast they had evolved. Then came the most mind-blowing bit of all—Megan's picture, with the slogan:

The Thumbtop
Made by humans, meant for mice.
Coming soon to a mousehole near you.

"*Your* computer!" he exclaimed. "So *that's* what it's about. They want your computer in every mousehole?"

"Why not?" replied Megan. "It's the only computer that fits."

She began to explain how mice would use Thumbtops for the good of the planet, but Joey wasn't listening.

"*Every* mousehole?" he said. "No way! That's millions of Thumbtops, maybe billions. And if they're all in a network . . ."

He jumped up and paced around the kitchen, running a hand nervously through his hair. "It's just . . . Megan, we have to talk."

He headed outside, and Megan followed him to the driveway. As if he needed more time for his thoughts to settle, Joey shot a few baskets while Megan sat on the steps and watched. Today, Joey's aim was terrible. After the ball had clanged off the hoop a couple of times, he stopped even pretending to shoot, and came to stand in front of her, the ball under one arm.

"This could be one of the most important things that's ever happened in the history of the world," he said gravely.

"I know it," said Megan.

"It's so cool, hearing a mouse talk," he said. "But think how dangerous it could be if they *all* get computers. Man, that's really scary! They could hack into *our* computers and make them all crash. All our networks. Then *nothing* would work–like banks or airlines or hospitals. Businesses. Even the army. We'd all be in trouble, our whole civilization."

"That's what I thought too," she said, "until I got to know mice better. They've promised not to do any of that stuff, and

I believe them, because they need our civilization to do well. Look, it's all here, in this treaty."

She had brought her copy of the treaty outside, and she pointed to the bit that said:

- Mice will never hurt humans or mess up human computers.

She started to explain how she had written the treaty at Headquarters yesterday, but Joey wasn't listening because he had read on to the next item in the treaty, and laughed.

"It says here they'll help stop climate change," he said. "C'mon now, Megan, there's no way, is there? I mean, what can they do to the climate? Little *mice*?"

"Why not?" she asked. "It's worth trying, isn't it? Humans aren't doing such a great job. And mice really can do anything. They proved it. Like my mom. They found her in the outback when I thought she was missing. And your dad . . ."

Joey slapped his forehead. "Mice?" he exclaimed. "*Mice* did that J.J. thing in Florida?"

"Of course," said Megan. "And your grandma's roof, and the cat, and the research for the restaurant, and getting those reviews . . ."

"Stop it!" he said, laughing now.

"And those notes in your school," Megan added. "They had fun doing that."

"So *that's* how . . ." he began, then was quiet for a moment as he let it all sink in. "Okay," he said finally, walking up and down as he bounced his ball. "Okay. So mice are really smart. And let's suppose they're on our side, for now. Let's suppose they really can do something about climate change. But what happens if they decide not to stick to your treaty? Suppose some evil mouse takes over and they declare war on us? They really could end our civilization, right? And it would be all our fault. Two kids in Oregon." He sat down on the steps and put his head in his hands. "Megan, we have to tell someone. Maybe not the FBI, but at least an adult, like my dad or your dad."

Megan took a quick glance at the kitchen window, where four anxious mouse faces were gazing out.

"We will tell an adult," she said. "Quite soon. My uncle Fred. The mice need him to help them make Thumbtops. Will you promise to keep the secret till then? Until my uncle knows?"

She could almost see the thoughts chasing each other across his face. It still looked partly scared and partly worried, but she could also see the beginning of a huge excitement as he came to grips with the biggest secret in the history of the world.

"Okay," he said. "Deal. I won't tell anyone. At least for now."

Megan jumped to her feet and couldn't help spinning into a slow pirouette of triumph. Then she made the thumbs-up sign to the mice in the window, and led Joey back into the kitchen.

When Joey sat down at the table, Trey, Julia, and Larry patted his hand in welcome, while Curly ran up his arm to perch on his shoulder. Joey flinched for a second, then, to Megan's relief, reached up and tickled Curly behind the ears.

"Welcome aboard," said Trey. "Someone wants to talk to you—someone very important. It's the Big Cheese."

"The big *who*?" asked Joey.

"Cheese," said Trey patiently. "Our fearless leader. The most important mouse on the planet, that's all."

Joey watched the computer screen as it revealed a scene that was now very familiar to Megan. The Big Cheese was sitting on the polished surface of the conference table, with his Mouse Council arranged behind him.

Megan noticed that Joey looked impressed—and that he almost fell off his chair at the Big Cheese's first words, translated in a rather gloomy voice by Sir Quentin.

"Welcome to our nation, Mr. Joseph. Pray, ready yourself for a journey to New York."

chapter twenty-eight

"EEEEEK!!!"

It was the loudest EEEEEK ever to ring out on Cherry Street, maybe the loudest in the history of Oregon.

Annie had come home to find her kitchen table covered with mice, while Megan and Joey seemed to be watching some sort of mouse movie on the computer.

Even though they were deafened by the EEEEEK, everyone stayed fairly cool.

Trey stayed cool enough to realize that it was better to be a pet mouse than to scuttle away like a pest. He gave the TMWNR sign, which means "This Mouse Will Not Run" (you wrap your tail once around your body, trapping your feet). Curly, Larry, and Julia got the message and, with a little trembling, stood their ground.

Megan was cool enough to tap out "Have to go now" to the Big Cheese in Silicon Valley, and log off.

And Joey was coolest of all. He simply told Annie the truth.

"These are very smart mice," he said. "And we're going to make a video with them."

"It's a video about mice using my computer," said Megan.

"I'll borrow Dustin's camera," said Joey. "We'll train a mouse to surf the Web and do e-mail. That is," he added, seeing a warning look from Megan, "he'll *pretend* to do all those things."

Annie was still busy with small EEEKs.

"But in my *kitchen*? On my *table*?" she squeaked, hoisting up her skirt as if afraid a mouse might run up it. "And they're not even pretty mice. They look like, well, *pests*!"

Julia glared at Annie, and Megan quickly picked her up and stroked her. This was no time for a mouse to act insulted.

"Don't worry, Annie," said Joey, in his most soothing voice. "These guys are special. They're smart and they're clean."

"Joey can't keep them at his house because of the cat," said Megan. "So they can live in my room. It will be great having pets, with you and Dad out so much of the time."

"Well, pets, yes," said Annie. "But wouldn't you rather have a cute little puppy or a kitten?"

"Dogs and cats aren't smart enough to use the computer," said Megan.

"Besides," said Joey, "their paws are way too big."

Annie was softening. "But what will they live in?" she said. "They can't run loose all over the house!"

"Maybe we can buy a cage," said Joey.

"Well, there is an old birdcage in the garage," Annie said reluctantly. "You're welcome to it, Megan. As long as it stays in your room."

"So that is how I came to be a pet," Trey wrote to the Big Cheese that night.

It felt strange, describing himself with that word, even though his captivity was purely symbolic because the bars on the birdcage were quite far apart, and mice had no trouble squeezing through. Right now, Larry was practicing going in and out, while Curly and Julia took turns swinging from the bird perch.

Trey's e-mail continued:

> There are some advantages to the status of "pet." The adult female bought us some "mouse food," which is actually delicious.

He paused for a bite of the mouse food, then finished his e-mail:

> Of course it is as a "pet" that I will appear in the video that should bring us and our humans to New York. As I had predicted, Mr. Joey will be of great help in making it all happen.

Joey was indeed so useful that Megan wondered how she would ever have done this part of Operation Thumbtop without him. He arrived the next afternoon with Dustin's camera, all ready to shoot the *Mouse Uses Computer* video that would win them their trip to New York.

They started with a rehearsal, as Trey walked up to the Thumbtop and began tapping away at the keyboard.

"There's a problem," said Joey, looking through the viewfinder. "You can't really see what he's doing. His paws are too low down."

"And there's another problem," said Megan. She had noticed that Curly, Larry, and Julia all had the droopy look of mice who felt left out. She whispered to Joey, "Any way we can use the other three?"

They solved both problems by finding a role for everybody.

Larry became a mouse desk when Megan strapped the Thumbtop to his back with a piece of Velcro from Annie's sewing kit. Now everyone could see Trey's paws as he sat upright to tap at the keys. For Curly and Julia, Megan wrote out some signs on strips of paper and glued the ends to big wooden matchsticks, so they could carry one sign between them.

After some more rehearsals, everyone was ready, and with a few stops and starts, Joey shot the video. First, Curly and Julia ran by with a sign saying "Mouse Uses Computer." Then Larry walked into the shot with the Thumbtop strapped to his back, and crouched down still as a rock as Trey strode up with a bit of a swagger and pushed the space bar to wake up the computer.

Curly and Julia ran by again with a sign reading "Time to Surf" as Trey tapped his way to a page called Cheeses of the World. When the sign read "Mouse Mail," Trey pretended to read his e-mail, and for "Playtime," he brought up the solitaire game that Uncle Fred had installed, and made a couple of moves.

"Now what?" asked Megan.

"I'll edit the shots together," said Joey, who'd helped his dad with editing in the old days. "Maybe put in some music."

While he uploaded the video to the computer so he could edit it, Megan made popcorn and put four little piles of it on the kitchen table for the mice. Not that there was time to eat much, because the video only lasted a couple of minutes.

"It's great!" said Megan, because it really did look professional. "But now what?"

"Now we put it on the Internet," said Joey, with his mouth full of popcorn.

"Where, on YouTube?" asked Megan.

"No, because then everyone will see it, and it won't be news anymore," said Joey. "I know another site where we can put it. Then we can tell the TV people where to find it."

"But which TV people?" she asked.

"That part's easy," said Trey, with a pirouette. He was feeling great about himself after seeing the video. "Our guys are everywhere, remember? The dudes at the TV networks will know the best humans to contact."

He sent off a few e-mails, and in half an hour he had a reply from the captain of New York Clan 463,877, which hung out at the offices of ABS—a TV network with a morning show that often included pet tricks.

Joey uploaded the video onto the Internet, and Megan sent off an e-mail to tell the people at ABS where they could find it.

And now there was nothing to do but wait.

Three days after they'd e-mailed the TV network about the *Mouse Uses Computer* video, Megan came home from school to find Annie in the kitchen, an excited pink color in her cheeks.

"I just got a phone call from some television people!" she said. "ABS in New York. About that video. I gave them Joey's number because that's who they want to put on TV—the kid who made the video."

"But . . ." Megan began.

"And he'll need an adult to go with him," Annie was saying. "His grandma isn't up to it, and Jake's got some sort of trade show, so I guess it'll have to be me. Not that it's a good time for me, with the restaurant so busy, but New York is so great in November–skating at Rockefeller Center, the smell of roasting chestnuts."

As she talked, Megan glanced at the gap beside the refrigerator, where a mouse in the half dark looked up at her and shrugged as if to say there wasn't a whole lot he could do about the situation right now. Megan picked up the telephone and hit the button for Joey's number, but it was busy.

So now what? She ran upstairs, and a moment later Trey emerged from under the dresser.

"Don't worry!" he said. "Joey will handle it. I'm sure he will. He has to."

Larry was on lookout duty in the big front bedroom when Joey's bike came whizzing down the street. Megan ran downstairs just as he burst into the kitchen.

"It's all happening!" he said, grinning from ear to ear. "I've been talking to the ABS guys. I told them Megan's uncle invented the Thumbtop, so that's who they want–me and Megan and her uncle."

"Oh," said Annie, a little sadly. "Not me? I'm off the hook?"

"Yes," said Joey. "Sorry."

"Maybe another time," said Megan, reaching out to give Annie a pat.

Joey took a different approach. "Someone has to help us handle the mice," he said. "You wouldn't want to do that, would you?"

"Absolutely not," said Annie, sounding more like herself again. "Besides, I *really* have to stay here and help with the restaurant. In fact, I should be there now."

She went out, leaving Joey and Megan to give each other high fives, while the four mice emerged from the space beside the refrigerator to slap each other's paws.

"Hey," said Joey, "maybe you'd better warn your uncle before the TV people get to him."

But they were too late, because at that moment the phone rang. Megan picked it up, and it was Uncle Fred, except that he was laughing almost too hard to speak.

"*Mice!*" he said, when he could finally talk. "ABS just called," (more laughter). "They want me on *TV* talking about *mice* using our *Thumbtop*? They said you and that cousin of yours set this up. What do I know about mice using Thumbtops?" Another deep belly laugh.

When there was a long enough pause, Megan explained that she and Joey would show off their trained mice. All Uncle Fred had to do was to talk about how he invented the Thumbtop.

"What the hey?" he said. "Let's do it. Who am I to turn down a trip to New York? And all that free advertising? Maybe someone with big bucks will see the show and want to invest." Then he laughed some more, as if he really didn't expect that to happen.

chapter twenty-nine

It was cold when Megan climbed into her dad's car for the drive to the airport, carrying the old birdcage and its cargo of mice. There was frost on the branches of the big dark trees, and the lawn was bristly and white.

Joey was waiting in front of his house, hopping from foot to foot around his duffel bag to keep warm.

"I just got an e-mail from Dad," he said. "He's stuck at a big trade show in Virginia, but he'll be watching on TV."

"So will just about everyone in Greenfield," said Megan's dad. "Now, if you guys could just remember to mention the restaurant . . ."

At first, the check-in woman at the airport wanted the mice to travel in the baggage hold, but Joey pointed out they were TV stars, and the TV company would not be happy if their stars freaked out from traveling as baggage. So they stayed with Megan, who undid her braids so the mice could hide behind her hair as she brought them out of their cage one by one to gaze down at their planet from the shelter of her hair.

Curly, Larry, and Julia went first, and marveled at what they saw. This was way better than crossing the country upside down in a shoe or a boot. Trey went last, climbing onto Megan's shoulder after they changed planes in Denver.

"Look at that, will you? You can almost see the greenhouse gas," he whispered, gazing down on the Denver suburbs. And they didn't look good as a smoggy haze enveloped the land, and the highways were clogged with cars.

"You think your guys can really change all that?" Megan asked.

"Why not?" Trey replied. "I don't know how we'll do it, but we will. Trust me: we've got our best brains working on Operation Cool It. Nothing left to chance."

The flight attendant came around to close the window shades so everyone could watch the movie, and as Trey ducked back behind Megan's hair, she continued his thought in her head. Nothing left to chance—except for the most important part, that's all. Except for Uncle Fred. That's where chance would come in big-time. Because if he didn't want to help . . . She could hardly bear to think about it. If he didn't want to help, all bets would be off. And the planet would be out of luck.

Uncle Fred was waiting at Kennedy Airport, though Megan hardly recognized him at first because he'd trimmed his beard for the occasion. He gave Megan a huge hug. Then he shook Joey's hand.

"Welcome to the family," he said. "A cousin of Megan's is a cousin of mine. That's what I told your dad. Did I tell you, Megan? Jake and I have been e-mailing a lot about our inventions. Quite a guy."

With Uncle Fred was a uniformed driver, who hustled them all into a white limo for the ride to their hotel.

"This is nuts," said Uncle Fred. He couldn't stop grinning. "But hey, if they want to put me in a limo and pay my bill in a big hotel, and give the Thumbtop all that free publicity, who am I to complain?"

"You can thank my mice," said Megan, holding the cage up near his face.

"EEEK!" he said, but with a laugh. "Did it have to be mice? Couldn't you have trained a dog or a cat?"

"People keep asking that," said Joey.

"They're not smart enough and their paws are way too big," said Megan, leaning against her uncle. She hadn't realized how much she'd missed him.

As they drove from the airport into Manhattan, she felt excitement building up steadily. This was her first time in New York, and although she'd seen these skyscrapers in movies, it was quite different to be in among them, craning her neck as the limo sped them to a big hotel near Central Park.

• • • • • • • • • • • • • • • • •

Their rooms were high up, looking south at an array of lights and bustle and the promise of adventure. All four mice climbed onto Megan's shoulders and gazed with her at the city, enraptured by the sight.

For Megan, this felt a bit like the night when she and Trey had stood in the hills above Silicon Valley, looking down at the patch of blackness that concealed the Mouse Nation. As on that night, she had the tingly feeling that comes from knowing that somewhere down there is a secret world of living, thinking beings, creatures with enormous power.

"I think our guys are off thataway," said Trey, as if reading her mind. He pointed at some lights in the far distance. "Past Wall Street, which is that second bunch of skyscrapers."

Megan peered down toward the far tip of Manhattan.

"Wow," she said, pressing her nose to the window.

"Yes, wow," said Trey. "We've come a long way, kiddo, and we're almost there."

A limo came at six o'clock the next morning to take them to the television studio. While the humans went off to the makeup department, the mouse cage was parked in the Pet Holding

Area. That's what the humans called it: the local clan called it the zoo, because of the parade of animals that came through. Until now, their favorite TV stars had been the mouse-eating animals, like cats or snakes or birds of prey, because the younger mice loved to tease them, going as close to the claws or fangs or beaks as they dared.

But nothing could beat these guests, especially that talking mouse everyone had read about on the Web site: the guy who had Made Contact.

The studio clan had even written a song for the occasion, and as soon as the humans were out of the way, the six young mice who made up the Youth Chorus lurched into action:

We welcome thee,
Oh TM3,
And Forties, Two, Eight, Seven.
With Thumbtops we'll
Soon hope to feel
The joys of mousely heaven.

"Thank you, thank you," said Trey, using human language because it was still so rare in a mouse that it would give these guys something to tell their grandchildren about.

"Oh, man, it's good to have someone here we can respect," said the captain. "You wouldn't believe what we've seen go through here—snakes, cats, a mongoose. . . ."

"Got any tips for us?" asked Trey. "Any suggestions for this TV thing?"

"Sure," said the captain, and gave the visitors some helpful hints. They should remember that the active camera was the one with the red light on it. And there was one move that always worked well—a sudden turn of the head to look into the lens, which inevitably produced a human chorus of, "It's like he knows he's on TV!"

"Honey, your hair is a challenge," said the woman who was getting Megan ready to go on TV.

"Sorry," said Megan, wondering if maybe they'd decide not to put her on the show after all because of the way the front part of her hair still stuck straight up, looking weirder than ever now that the top part was long enough to bend over a bit. But the woman went to work with some sort of goop and smoothed it all down.

"There you go, pumpkin," she said. "It's good for half an hour if you stay out of the wind."

Megan was afraid the half hour might be up before they even went on TV, as the three humans and four mice waited in the Green Room.

"Hey, it's really happening," said Uncle Fred, who didn't seem in the least bit nervous. "Just think of all those millions of people who'll be watching—what a chance for us, huh, Megan? To tell the world about our Thumbtop? Or anything else, come to that."

Millions of people! Millions of people all staring at her? When she went red just talking to twenty-seven fifth graders?

"Forget the millions," said Uncle Fred, guessing what was going through her mind. "Just pretend you're talking to one person. That's what I did when I was on TV in Cleveland, talking about my ant-zapper."

A woman came to shepherd them onto the set, and led them to a couch facing two very famous hosts. Megan was all too aware of the cameras arrayed around them, waiting to suck them up and send them into millions of homes—to millions of people.

No, Megan told herself, not millions of people, one person. Think of one person. For some reason, the face of Brandon, the alpha male from school, swam into her consciousness—someone who wouldn't believe a word she said unless she put it very, very well.

And that helped. As the hosts introduced them all in turn, Megan waved at the camera and said "Hi" to Brandon.

Next, the cameras showed her and Joey fastening the Thumbtop to Larry's back while Uncle Fred told the hosts what a challenge it had been to make it so small. Then the cameras focused on the mice as they performed their act, with Curly and Julia running by with their signs as Trey surfed and e-mailed and played solitaire, remembering to make a few mistakes so people wouldn't guess how ridiculously smart he really was.

And at one point he spun his head around sharply to look straight into the camera with the red light, as the two hosts said in unison, "It's as if he knows he's on TV!"

Then it was time for the kids to talk. First, Joey described how they had trained the mice for the movie, which wasn't hard because these guys were so smart.

"And Megan?" asked the woman host, with a bright smile.

"I helped my uncle invent the Thumbtop," she said. "And it could be very important for the climate, right?" she added for Brandon's benefit. "Because it uses much less power than most computers."

"Seriously," said the male host. "Does it work for humans as well as mice?"

"It works for me!" said Megan. "I'll show you." She unfastened the Thumbtop from Larry's back and used a toothpick to tap out some words on it. "Can you read that?" she asked.

The camera zoomed in to the tiny screen, which read:

Great for mice and kids.

"Well," said the male host, "it looks like a winner. When will these computers be in the stores?"

"Who knows?" said Uncle Fred. "So far, this is the only one." Then he looked straight into the camera. "If there's a company out there that wants to make a deal, let's talk!"

Everyone laughed one more time.

A commercial started, and they were hustled off the set. On a TV screen in the hallway, Megan could see the two hosts chatting to each other while the commercials were on.

"How about those mice?" the woman was saying.

"How about that little computer?" said the man. "I'd really like one for my kid."

And all over America, as people ate their breakfasts, they muttered, "How about those mice?" or "How about that little computer?"

In Greenfield, Megan's dad and Annie gave each other high fives and said, "How about those kids?"

But in the lobby of the television building, where people often came in to watch the shows, a man in a suit rumpled from his night on a train was speechless.

chapter thirty

When the TV segment was over, the rumpled man in the lobby of the ABS building found a place to wait. It was just beyond the banks of elevators, a great place to lurk if you wanted to pounce out and surprise three humans and four mice who'd be coming down.

And surprise them he certainly did.

"Jake Fisher!" yelled Uncle Fred, giving him a bear hug. "Jakefish, my e-mail buddy! You look so much like Joey I'd have known you anywhere!"

When he'd untangled himself, Jake turned and held out his arms to the two kids, but they hung back for a few seconds, as if too astonished at the sight of him to move.

"Dad!" said Joey finally. "How did you get here?"

"Night train," said his dad. "I suddenly got more free time

than I expected, so now I can show you New York. Maybe the American Museum of Natural History first, or a boat trip around the island? Then we can go skating at Rockefeller Center. How does that grab you?"

Not too well, apparently. Joey sneaked a look at Megan, who was busy sneaking a look at him, and both looks meant that this development could spell danger for the Mouse Nation and its nice soft trap for Uncle Fred. Because no matter how the nation had decided to close its nice soft trap, surely an extra human would gum up the works.

"EEEK," Jake said, looking down at the cage that Megan was carrying. "Did it have to be mice? Couldn't you have used a cute little puppy or a . . ."

"Their paws are too big," said Joey, recovering enough to grin.

"And mice are special," said Megan, as she hauled Trey out of the cage. She brought him up near her face, pretending to kiss him, turning so the adults wouldn't see that she was whispering the urgent question, "Now what?"

She held him near her ear just long enough to hear his reply. "Thumbtop, quick."

As she put him back into the cage, she slid in the Thumbtop beside him. And when she climbed into the cab that took them back to the hotel, she put the cage at her feet, making sure that her legs blocked the view of a mouse sending urgent e-mails.

Meanwhile, Jake was explaining why he was in New York.

"It's like this," he said. "The boss and I were at a big trade show in Virginia, selling Tick-Tocks. And I said I thought we'd get more orders if they'd been fitted with solar blobs. Remember, Fred? I e-mailed you a couple of weeks ago about that. How the boss had said I could get back to research on my blobs?"

"Of course I remember," said Uncle Fred. "I got all excited. Your blobs could be great for those things, and a lot else."

"You betcha," said Jake. "But yesterday the boss went back on his word. Said he'd changed his mind, and that I'd be more useful to him on the road. Selling. So we had an argument. He said, 'Do I take it that Tick-Tock-Clicks are not your top priority?' And I said, 'You got that right.' So he fired me and here I am."

"Oh man, that's one dumb boss," said Uncle Fred.

"You got *fired*?" said Joey.

Jake reached out and rumpled his hair. "Don't worry about it, kiddo. I'll find something better. When one door closes—you know how that goes."

"Wish we could be partners, partner," said Uncle Fred.

"Those blobs of yours—they could really be something. But right now . . ."

"Right now's not a good time for inventors, is it?" said Jake. "No money around. But hey, maybe I can learn to cook. Then I could work at your dad's place, huh, Megan? Now that he's doing so well. But we don't have to think about that now. We're in New York, guys! So what's it going to be? The museum first? Or the sightseeing boat?"

Or getting an uncle into a nice soft trap? Where did that fit in?

"A message for you, sir," the desk clerk told Uncle Fred when they got back to the hotel. "I believe it was a British gentleman on the telephone."

The message for Uncle Fred was simple. "Please check your e-mail for a communication from Nation Productions."

"Groovy!" said Uncle Fred, beaming as they all rode up in the elevator. "They must have seen the show. Maybe someone really does want to invest in the Thumbtop."

Jake hovered in the doorway while Megan and Joey followed Uncle Fred into his room, and watched while he opened his laptop to check his mail.

"Here it is," he said. "Take a look. How about that!"

Megan and Joey peered over his shoulder to read:

From: Natprod@mousenet.org
To: Fbarnesinvent@gmail.com
Subject: Miniature Computer

We were impressed by the demonstration of the small computer and would like to explore the possibility of collaborating with you in a project that could prove fruitful for all concerned. Please meet with us at 2 p.m. today. Our offices are located at 597 Springle Street in Manhattan.

Uncle Fred was grinning from ear to ear, though he tried to sound cool. "Well, it's worth looking into, I guess," he said. "You kids don't have to come. You could go off with Jake—have fun at the museum or something."

"I have to come with you, Uncle Fred," said Megan. "I helped you invent the Thumbtop, remember? So I should be in on the business deals."

"Me too because I . . ." Joey began, until Megan gave him a look.

He changed course. "I'll do something with Dad," he said,

though he didn't sound enthusiastic, and Megan could guess how much he hated to miss whatever the mice had planned.

"Okay, Megan," Uncle Fred was saying. "You can come with me—but let's not expect too much. When those Nation people see just how hard it is for their fat fingers to use a Thumbtop, they might not be quite so interested."

Behind Uncle Fred's back, Megan made the MSL sign for "laughing out loud," but Joey wasn't into laughing right now. He was watching his dad, whose phone had just buzzed with an incoming text. And Jake was gazing at the screen as if he didn't quite believe what it was telling him.

"Joey!" he said. "What did I say? One door closes and another one opens? How's this for a new door." He handed over his phone. "Read it out loud."

Joey read:

> We have been informed of your blob technology, and also that you are in need of employment. We would like to explore the possibility of collaborating with you in a project that could prove fruitful for all concerned. Please meet with us at 2 p.m. today. Our offices are located at . . .

Joey stopped reading.

"Go on," said his dad.

Joey gulped. "At 597 Springle Street. And it's from Nation Productions."

"Wow," said Uncle Fred. "No kidding! The same firm! How cool is that? So maybe we *can* be partners, partner."

"Maybe we can," said Jake, grinning. "I guess those Nation guys must have been at the television building? Heard us talking."

Megan looked at Joey and saw the same expression on his face that must have been on hers. It was WOW. And relief. And huge admiration for a species that could do anything.

She glanced at the cage and saw that Trey had clasped two paws above his head while doing a pirouette—not just the sign for triumph, but double triumph.

After a nap and some lunch, it was time to go to Springle Street. Jake had ironed his suit so he no longer looked rumpled, and Uncle Fred had stuffed himself into a suit too.

"Bet you didn't know I even *had* a suit, Megan," he said as he walked somewhat stiffly to the elevator. "I bought it for your mom's wedding. How long ago was that—twelve years? It still fits if I don't button it up. And if I don't breathe," he added, shaking the suit from the inside with his rumbling laugh.

As they got into the elevator, Jake noticed that Megan was carrying the old birdcage.

"Hey, do those mice go everywhere with you?" he asked.

"Not to business meetings, they don't!" said Uncle Fred, noticing them too. "We'll wait while you take them back to your room."

"These mice are special!" said Megan. "We wouldn't be here without them."

"And they're a business asset, right?" said Joey. "They could be useful for commercials and things."

"Okay, okay," said Uncle Fred, chuckling. "As long as those Nation guys don't go all EEEKy on us when they see the cage," he added, causing Joey and Megan that special pain you get when a laugh bubbles up inside you and you absolutely have to swallow it back down.

On the cab ride, Jake and Uncle Fred were talking a mile a minute, trying to guess how Nation Productions had tracked them down, and whether they'd want to market the Thumbtop and the solar blobs as one package, and just how much money there might be in it for each of them.

Trey half listened, but most of his mind was on what would really happen in the next couple of hours. Yes, he had faith that his leaders in the Mouse Nation could do anything, more or less. But two adult males in one soft trap?

True, both of these humans were cool. But would they *stay* cool when they found out that their species wasn't the only one on this planet that could think and plan and use computers? Or would one or both of them freak out? And a full-grown human freaking out—even in a part of town so desolate that an extra EEEK or two wouldn't attract attention—would that mean the end of the adventure? And a huge danger to the Mouse Nation?

Curly, Larry, and Julia weren't exactly helping to calm his nerves, because they were almost too excited to stay in their role as pets. Yeah, yeah, yeah, Trey could understand. These guys from Cleveland had been watching the uncle all their lives—adoring him, actually, as mice often do adore the humans at the center of their world. Soon, if all went well, they'd be able to communicate with him, mouse to man—and they were giddy with the thought. Larry was hopeless. He'd long since memorized every single statistic about the uncle's glory days playing football for Ohio State, and now he had such a bad case of hero worship that he would have wriggled out of the cage to jump on the uncle's knee if Trey hadn't given him a warning nip on the tail.

chapter thirty-one

The cab drove past Wall Street and almost to the far tip of Manhattan. Then it pulled onto a street full of empty office buildings that were plainly ready to be torn down. There was no one about.

"This is it," said the driver, stopping in front of a building that had some of its windows boarded up. "This is 597."

Uncle Fred looked as if he wanted to head back to the hotel. "Maybe I copied the address down wrong," he said.

"No, this is what they gave me too," said Jake, checking his phone.

And Megan pointed to something. "Look!" she said.

It was a printed sheet of paper taped to the door of 597, very low down.

Nation Productions, Inc., it read. **Walk in**.

Uncle Fred paid the cab driver. After he drove away, it was very, very quiet. The door of 597 opened into an entryway that looked as if it hadn't been swept for a year. Shafts of light came through a gap in the window boards and lit up some broken chairs that were stacked in a corner.

"How could it be . . . ?" Uncle Fred began.

"Maybe it's a start-up," said Jake. "Just moved in."

"Look! Another sign," said Joey. "At the bottom of the stairs."

Like the sign outside, this one was also low down. It read, **Nation Productions, Inc. Walk up to Room 202.**

Jake started up the stairs with Joey, but Uncle Fred hung back.

"Come on, Uncle Fred," said Megan. "We'll protect you. Me and my attack mice."

That got a laugh out of him as he started up the dusty stairs, but it was a weak one.

On the second floor, Jake and Joey were waiting for them.

"This is weird," whispered Jake. "Doesn't seem to be anyone around."

All the office doors were shut except the one labeled 202, which stood half open.

"Psst!" said Trey, from the cage.

Megan held it high so she could hear him whisper. "We're coming out. We don't want these guys to think we're prisoners."

She stood still while the mice wriggled out between the bars. Trey, Larry, and Julia ran up her arm to ride on her shoulders. Curly hopped over to Joey's shoulder, to ride on him.

"Megan!" hissed Uncle Fred, making it to the top of the stairs. "Put those mice away!"

At that point, Larry lost it. He took off in a great leap onto Uncle Fred's broad shoulder, with the result that their entrance into Room 202 was just as EEEKy as Uncle Fred had feared, with the difference that *he* was emitting the EEEK.

It didn't seem to matter, because there was no one there. Just two mice that looked like stuffed toys standing next to a computer keyboard on a spotless desk (and a wall of grayish-brown fur packed under a bookcase, if you looked closely).

"Hey, where is everybody?" asked Uncle Fred, and Megan was glad to see he didn't seem to mind having Larry on his shoulder, after the first EEEK.

Jake noticed that the two toy mice had each raised a paw in a stiff salute. "Oh, that's cute," he said. "See that? They must be robots—programmed to greet us."

"Okay, gentlemen," said Uncle Fred. "Nice gimmick!"

"Where d'you think they are?" asked Jake. "Maybe watching us on a camera somewhere?"

"Like up in the ceiling?" suggested Uncle Fred. He gazed upward as he said, "You can come in now!"

"Look," said Megan. "On the computer."

One of the mice had brought a paw down stiffly on the "Return" button, causing some words to pop up on the monitor:

Starting Soon
A Proposal for Collaboration
With Mr. Fred Barnes
And Mr. Jake Fisher
In a Movie

"A movie!" exclaimed Jake.

"Hey, works for me!" said Uncle Fred. "Not sure where the Thumbtop fits in, but blobs are always good for movies, right, Jake? *The Blob that Ate Chicago*?"

He laughed as he sat down in one of the large chairs that faced the computer, wriggling around to get comfortable, much as he did at home before watching one of his favorite DVDs. Jake sat on the other chair as the mouse by the keyboard clicked again and up came a title:

Birth of a Mouse Nation

"Great—it's science fiction," whispered Uncle Fred. "Could use a better title, though, don't you think? Something with a bit more oomph, like *Mice on the Rampage*."

"How about *Rodents Rule*?" suggested Jake. "Or *M-Force*?"

"Good ones," said Uncle Fred. "We can help these people."

He leaned forward as the computer began the presentation that was already familiar to Megan and Joey, showing how mice had learned to read and write and use computers.

Megan watched the two men anxiously. At any moment, one of them would surely realize they weren't seeing fiction at all, but a documentary.

"Great idea for a movie!" Jake was saying. "Mice learning to run computers. It's a bit far-fetched, of course."

"Hey, it's science fiction, remember," said Uncle Fred. "I love it. Anything goes."

The presentation reached the scenes showing how hard it was for mice to borrow computer time from humans. And Megan held her breath because she knew what must be coming next—the part about the Thumbtop, the part that would surely tell Uncle Fred and Jake the truth about what they were watching.

And indeed, the Thumbtop did come next. It was a new picture, taken off a television screen that morning, with Trey at the computer in the foreground and the two famous hosts looking on. Then the screen filled with the words:

We need
A FEW MILLION THUMBTOPS.
Thank you, Mr. Barnes
Thank you, Mr. Fisher

Jake gave a little yelp of laughter. "A few million Thumbtops?"

"Yes, why do you need millions?" asked Uncle Fred, tipping his head back and talking to the ceiling as if a camera up there would carry his words to the humans in charge. "Why millions when you can make one Thumbtop *look* like millions in a movie?"

Megan decided it was time to help him out. "What if it isn't a movie, Uncle Fred?" she asked.

"Okay, so maybe it's for TV," he said. "Same deal."

The computer presentation had ended. In its place, two mice appeared on the monitor. One of them had a tiny chain of office around its neck, and the other kept bowing in a courtly sort of way. Just in case there was any doubt about their importance, a caption along the bottom of the screen read:

His Excellency, the Chief Executive Mouse
Interpreter: Sir Quentin

"Greetings," said Sir Quentin, coming out of a particularly deep bow. The webcam zoomed in so everyone could see his lips moving as he said, "My master wishes to convey his warmest regards to Miss Megan's illustrious relatives. I bid you welcome to the Mouse Nation, Mr. Fisher, Mr. Barnes."

But the humans' brains were still stuck deeply into movie-making.

"These people are *good*," said Uncle Fred. "That must be the prototype of the mice they'll use. It's great animation!"

"Isn't it, though," said Jake. "Best I've seen."

"I am gratified that you consider my demeanor to be animated," said Sir Quentin. "I do indeed constantly strive to present a lively visage to the world. However, if by 'animation' you mean some type of technological deception, I can assure you that my master and I are as mammalian, as veridical, as organic as you are yourself. In the words of the great bard, 'If you cut us, do we not bleed? If you tickle us, do we not laugh? If you pull our whiskers, do we not squeak?' That's from Shakespeare," he added helpfully. "Slightly adapted for mice."

"What the . . ." said Jake. He looked frozen for a moment, then put his head in his hands. "No, I . . . It can't . . . They're not . . ."

Joey moved over to stand behind his dad's chair, and put his arms around his neck.

Now there was absolute silence in the room, and silence from Silicon Valley, where Megan could imagine the whole Mouse Council holding its breath.

Larry couldn't stand the tension, and rushed down Uncle Fred's stomach and onto his knee, turning to look up at him imploringly.

Slowly, Uncle Fred reached out to stroke him.

"Work with me, Megan," he said softly. "Will you please? In this movie—just how do you think it happens, mice evolving like that? How could the movie be made, well, realistic?"

"I guess it would show how mice have always been smart," said Megan, "like it said in the presentation. They just didn't know they were smart until computers came along."

"And then what?" he asked softly, as if he were in a trance.

On the monitor, Megan could see the Big Cheese totally still, as if barely breathing.

"They'd need tiny computers, wouldn't they," she said, feeling that she and her uncle were sharing the same trance. "Computers that are small enough for mouseholes."

"So the movie we'd make," Uncle Fred continued, looking at Megan, not blinking, "it would start with a bunch of mice on a mission, looking for the world's smallest computer."

"Every mouse in America, probably," said Megan.

"I wonder where they'd find one," he said.

"Maybe somewhere like Cleveland," said Megan.

"Okay, Cleveland. Or Toledo. Or Pittsburgh. Somewhere like that. And who's invented this computer?"

Megan couldn't keep a grin from starting.

"How about a big guy and his niece?"

"That would work," he said, still gazing into her eyes, still not blinking. "That would work for the movie. Big guy with a beard, maybe."

"Then she takes it away to Oregon," said Megan, talking faster now. "The niece, that is."

"And then?"

"Maybe a mouse wakes her up in the middle of the night," said Megan. "A talking mouse. She's scared at first, but then he becomes her best friend."

"But it's not just the *girl* the mice would be after, is it?" Uncle Fred continued, his voice softer than ever. "They'd need the uncle, of course. They'd need him to help them get computers. Millions of computers."

There was silence again, until Joey asked, "And what would the uncle say?"

"The uncle in the movie?" asked Uncle Fred. "That uncle? He'd be blown away, of course. He'd be totally gobsmacked." He flopped back in his chair, his arms dangling at his sides, while Joey wrapped himself tighter around his dad. "He probably wouldn't be able to say anything much, except wow.

"Wow.

"Wow.

"Wow!"

On the fourth and loudest "Wow!" Megan hurled herself at her uncle and pushed her face into his beard as dozens of mice emerged from their hiding place under the bookcase and the monitor showed the whole Mouse Council applauding.

"I'm so glad you're here, Uncle Fred," said Megan. "I'm so glad you know."

chapter thirty-two

There was one mouse who was bitterly disappointed.

He was the guy in charge of smelling salts. They'd rehearsed it a dozen times—how the uncle would learn the truth, and he would faint right there in his chair, and the mouse would run up his arm to dangle a little bag of smelling salts under his nose, and then the uncle would come around, and everything would be hunky-dory, and the mouse would be a hero.

Or maybe the other guy would faint—the thin one who was invited at the last minute. Of the two, the thinner one looked more promising because he did go a little pale, but then he recovered once that young male started hugging him. And as for the uncle, everything seemed hunky-dory without even a whiff of smelling salts.

First, both humans had a conversation with the Big Cheese, who joined them by webcam from Headquarters. Then they each had a quick chat with that talking mouse, and the uncle stroked the other three mice who'd arrived with him, greeting them like long-lost friends. Next, the full-grown humans listened while the two immature ones told them about mouse magic, and kindness, and trips to Silicon Valley, and accidental overhearings, and nice soft traps.

At the "nice soft trap" bit, both men roared with laughter, which meant that there was absolutely no chance either of them would faint, no chance a guy with smelling salts could ever be a hero.

He began to feel a bit more hopeful when the uncle started worrying about the threat that mice could pose to humans. "What if they turn out to be little cyber-terrorists?" he asked.

"Yeah, what if they want to crash all human computer systems?" asked the Jake guy. "And put an end to our civilization?"

Then the girl showed them the treaty—the one that all mice knew from the nation's Web site. And after that, the chance of anyone fainting dwindled to zero, because both men were smiling broadly now, each one hugging a kid.

• • • • • • • • • • • • • • • • •

For Megan and Joey it was of course a huge relief that both men seemed happy with the treaty—though Uncle Fred did have questions about the last part.

"I know why you put in that bit about mice helping to stop climate change," he said. "You really are your mother's daughter. But no way, kiddo. Maybe they could help us out with a little spying on bad guys who pollute rivers, stuff like that. But climate change? What, they're going to keep the Greenland ice cap from melting? Change ocean currents? Make Washington get its act together? That sounds impossible to me."

Far off in Silicon Valley, the word "impossible" exerted its usual magic. Megan could see on the monitor screen how the Big Cheese made himself as tall as possible as he said, "The word 'impossible' does not exist in the mouse vocabulary. Once you have helped us to acquire the necessary technology, our nation will be excellently equipped to slow up or even reverse climate change. Not by cooling down ice caps or moving ocean currents, of course, but by changing human beliefs, human attitudes, and human behavior, as you will now see."

• • • • • • • • • • • • • • • • •

Megan had seen a lot of mouse presentations, and the one about how mice would tackle climate change was much slicker than most, because (as Trey whispered to her) it had been put together by guys who hung out in the best advertising agencies.

First, three mice trotted forward with snappy salutes. One of them gave a quick signal, and the presentation began with a screen reading:

Operation Cool It
Saving the Planet
The Mouse Way

Next came a picture of mice surrounding a Thumbtop, with the words:

Think of the Mouse
As the computer chip of the animal kingdom
We are small, but we are very, very powerful
We can help humans save the planet
One opinion leader at a time
One politician at a time
One family at a time

In the scenes that followed, mice showed how they would educate people who didn't know the truth about climate change—and change the tune of those who knew the truth, but for various reasons pretended they didn't.

You saw a succession of cartoon characters depicting senators and lobbyists and oil company executives and scientists and union organizers and captains of industry and reporters and talk-show hosts and television executives and typical American families who wanted to save energy (and money) but didn't know how. And everywhere you saw mice. Mice with Thumbtops. Mice getting onto computers to correct the facts when opinion leaders or politicians got the research deliberately wrong. Mice spooking certain talk-show hosts until they promised to tell their audience the truth about the climate. Mice eavesdropping on important people, then printing up sticky notes to leave where those important people would find them—then, knowing they'd been overheard, these important people would start to tell the truth. And mice dropping hints for their host families on how to conserve.

Megan couldn't follow it all, but she saw that Uncle Fred and Jake were both grinning as if they thought the mice had it just right.

"You guys," said Uncle Fred. "I'm impressed. If you can get

to those politicians and business types . . ."

"Knock some sense into those screamers on the radio," added Jake. "And show ordinary people that it makes sense to conserve."

The Big Cheese had reappeared on the screen.

"Of course we can do all that," he said, "when we have the right technology. When we fulfill our dream of a computer in every mousehole."

"A lovely dream," said Uncle Fred. "*Dream* is the right word. Because there's no way it can happen, right, Jake?"

"No way," agreed Jake sadly.

"What do you mean?" asked Megan. She felt a huge lurch of disappointment, like a hit in the stomach. After all their work in luring Uncle Fred and Jake into this nice soft trap, were they going to escape? Had her team failed after all?

"Simple," said Uncle Fred. "It would cost millions to make all the Thumbtops you'd need, even if they were assembled in China or Malaysia or somewhere. And neither of us have that kind of . . . Hey, what's going on?"

He'd noticed some very strange behavior in the mice on both sides of the continent. In far-off Silicon Valley, the Big Cheese had started a pirouette, and the rest of the Mouse Council joined in. The mice in the New York office were all pirouetting and dancing and flicking their tails in a happy frenzy.

The Big Cheese stopped spinning to say something that Trey translated.

"For a moment there, Mr. Barnes, you had us scared," he explained. "But if it's only the *costs* that concern you gentlemen, then there is no problem, as you will now learn."

He faded away as one of the New York mice stepped forward and introduced himself as the Director of Manufacturing. He waved a paw at the computer to bring up a picture of something that looked like a regular factory. Except you didn't see workers on the assembly line. You saw plastic sandwich bags.

Jake leaned forward to peer at the screen as the camera zoomed in on a sandwich bag. Then he leaned back with a soft "EEEK" as the bag gave a wiggle and a mouse stuck out its head, waving a plastic-wrapped paw.

And Uncle Fred's beard moved sharply south.

"Neat, huh?" said the director, as Trey translated. "That's your labor force—mouse power! See? No mouse hair gets into the product. No dirt, no germs. Everything clean as a whistle. And you know the best part? Mice work for free!"

Another mouse took over—the Director of Production.

Without labor costs, he explained, the economics would work just fine. The Engineering Department had drawn up plans for machines that could assemble Thumbtops without requiring thumbs. Yes, you'd need some money up front to pay for the machinery, and pay for the Thumbtop parts, but mice happened to know that Uncle Fred had excellent credit. He could borrow the start-up funds he needed. And by selling the products of the mouse factory, he would make more than enough money to pay back the loan.

"Products?" asked Uncle Fred. "That's plural? Products?"

"Of course plural!" said the Big Cheese. "Why else would we have invited Mr. Jake to come here? According to our research, his solar blobs will become the cash cow. They will provide the funds to pay back the loan, with plenty of money left over."

"The cash WHAT?" asked Jake, laughing.

The Big Cheese carried on as if he hadn't been interrupted. "The blobs will be an excellent source of power for cell phones and music players. That's something humans will value—especially when the blobs look like this."

The computer screen filled with blobs shaped into belt buckles and buttons and frames for sunglasses and barrettes and jewelry and pins for sun hats.

"Whoa!" said Jake. "What makes you think my blobs can go into all those shapes?"

"Trust us," said the Big Cheese. "On my instructions, engineers at some of the finest universities are devising ways to form the blobs into any shape you choose."

"These engineers," said Jake. "Are they—how shall I put this—are they *mice*?"

The Big Cheese said something in MSL that Trey translated as, "Well, duh!"

"Mice," said Jake, as if repeating the word would help him take it in. "Wow."

"So *mice* will help us set up a factory where *mice* will make Thumbtops and *mice* will help Jake finish his research on blobs?" said Uncle Fred. "Make that a double wow."

They gazed at each other for a moment, wide-eyed. Jake ran his hand through his hair just the way Joey did sometimes when he was trying to make up his mind. Uncle Fred scratched his beard in the way that sometimes helped him think.

From the monitor came the dulcet tones of Sir Quentin.

"My master bids you to summarily embrace the commitment that will ineluctably, nay, inexorably materialize into a multispecies, multigenerational collaboration."

"In other words," said Trey, "do we have a deal?"

"What do you think, Fred?" asked Jake. "What have we got to lose?"

"Not a lot," said Uncle Fred. "What have we got to win?"

"For us?" asked Jake. "For the kids?"

"For the planet?" asked Uncle Fred.

They were both silent for a moment, as if waiting for the other to speak.

"I think they're nearly there," Megan whispered to Trey.

"Maybe this will push them over the edge," he said. He signaled to the Youth Chorus, which was waiting to one side. They swung into a song as Trey translated their signs:

All hail the world's most helpful guys,
Fred and Jake.
For mice like us it's no surprise,
Fred and Jake.
They'll put computers in our holes
So we can play our mousely roles
To help our planet meet its goals,
Fred and Jake.

Then, at the prompting of the chorus master, they all made the sign for "Deal?" (You hold out your right front paw while your tail makes the shape of a question mark.)

Uncle Fred got it, and laughed. "Deal, Jake?"

"Deal," said Jake, and reached out to tap the paws of the chorus mice.

chapter thirty-three

What a difference a day makes, thought Megan, on the way to the airport.

Yesterday, when they'd come back from Springle Street, she'd been happy for so many reasons. The trap had worked. Uncle Fred and Jake were now in charge. It looked as if the planet was really in luck, finally.

And everyone else was happy too, as they'd all gone out to eat at an Italian restaurant where the waiters thought it was neat to have a cage full of mice under the table, catching any spaghetti strands that swung their way. Then Jake had taken them to the ice rink at Rockefeller Center. Not that he skated himself. There was a lot that he and Uncle Fred still had to talk about; things like machine tools and blobs and business plans and rental property and markets and mice. And their talking had to be at the side of the rink rather than on skates because there was no way—make that no way in a hundred years—that they'd get Uncle Fred on ice.

So the men talked and watched, but mostly talked, while the kids rented skates, and Joey shot off at top speed, and Megan went more slowly, partly because she hadn't skated for a long time, and partly because it was hard to skate fast with a cage full of mice.

But now look what was happening!

They were in the taxi, back to the airport. Curly, Larry, and Julia were overjoyed to be going home to Cleveland with Uncle Fred, and were letting it all hang out. In fact, they were trying to prove that three mice can play Chase My Tail in a birdcage that's a bit small at the best of times.

And halfway to the airport, Joey gave a yip and looked as if he'd like to join in the game of Chase My Tail himself, because Jake had just said, laughing, "Okay, okay . . . I give in. You can come to Cleveland."

Abandoning Aunt Em? Abandoning Garfield Middle School? Abandoning Megan?

And Trey? He'd have to go to Cleveland too, of course. He had to help set up the mouse factory—Planet Mouse, they'd decided to call it—translating for all the high-powered guys who'd soon be arriving by Greyhound bus.

Even the Thumbtop would be staying in Cleveland so it

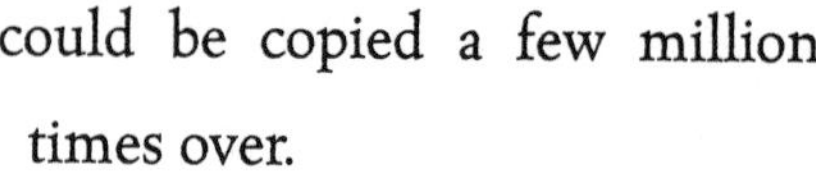

could be copied a few million times over.

Which left Megan flying back to Oregon very much alone.

At least Uncle Fred had made up for the Thumbtop-shaped hole in her life by buying her the sort of phone that can do e-mail. But it was still hard saying good-bye to everyone—especially Trey.

"I'll miss you, mousie," she said, cupping him in her hands so no one could see his lips move.

"I'll miss you too, human," he whispered. "But I'll e-mail every day. And it won't be for long. You'll come to Cleveland as soon as your mom gets back, right?"

Right, but how long would that be? The latest e-mail from her mom had said, "I love the outback! I feel I could live here forever!"

Thanks a lot, Mom, thought Megan, as she looked sadly down at the vast continent that would separate her from her friends.

Annie met Megan's plane and whisked her to the restaurant, where Aunt Em and her dad were waiting.

Everyone joined in the torrent of questions. Had she felt scared, with millions of people watching her on TV? How was New York? Did she get to skate? Were the chestnuts still roasting on Fifth Avenue? And Aunt Em wanted to know all about Jake's new job in Cleveland.

Megan did her best to answer. Wasn't too scary, being on TV. They did skate, and she smelled the chestnuts. And she told them about the new partnership between Jake and Uncle Fred in words they'd all agreed on. Jake had lost his Tick-Tock job, but he didn't mind a bit because now he could get back to his blobs. Through Uncle Fred, he'd found some guys who believed in the blobs, and who'd help him finish his research.

"Well, let's hope those investors are really serious," said Annie.

Megan thought about the Mouse Nation, and how serious mice can be, and as if Annie had intercepted the mouse thoughts, she shot to her feet.

"Your mice!" she said. "We forgot to pick them up at the airport!"

"It's okay," said Megan. "They went to Cleveland."

"Cleveland! Why would *they* go to Cleveland?" asked her dad.

"They wanted to," she said with a shrug, as if it were obvious—and the adults all laughed.

• • • • • • • • • • • • • • • • •

It wasn't too bad, being back in Oregon. For one thing, all the kids in her class were grinning at her when she came into Room 15—even Brandon.

And there was another flood of questions.

"How did you . . ."

"What did it feel like . . ."

"Was it you or Joey who . . ."

The questions were still coming when Miss Fitch arrived to quiet the flow, but not before Caitlin had whispered, "Seriously, it was so cool."

It wasn't so cool going home to a house with no mice. Megan found herself wandering from room to room feeling very much alone, because even though her mice hadn't taken up much space, the house felt far too empty without them, and far too quiet.

She jumped out of her skin when her new phone rang. It was Joey, who said, "Hi, I'm putting my phone on the floor for Trey."

"I have a gift for you," said Trey. It was great to hear his whiskery voice.

"A gift?"

"Look around your room," he said.

And then she saw it—the tip of a tail under the dresser. Trey had leaned on the Commander of the Greenfield Region to send a couple of volunteers from the clan at 249 Cherry Street to 253. When Megan kneeled down to peer under the dresser, two mouse faces peered back, two guys trembling with fright but holding their ground.

"Hi," she said in MSL.

"Hi," they replied with tentative waves of the front paw, then came out slowly so she could tickle them behind the ears, and feel much less lonely.

And Aunt Em helped with the lonely part.

Megan sometimes went to her house after school because they both missed Joey, and Megan liked hearing Aunt Em talk about him. Sometimes the big orange cat sat on Megan's lap and purred, and didn't seem to hold a grudge. Looking into its yellow eyes, Megan felt that maybe it remembered the night of the damp box and forgave her for it, and understood about the planet and the importance of mice.

And there were so many e-mails and phone calls from Uncle Fred and Joey and Trey that she almost felt she was *watching* the events in Cleveland. Watching as Uncle Fred and Jake rented a house with a huge garage that would be perfect for Planet Mouse. Watching as Joey set up mouse dorms for workers. Watching as boxes of machine parts were delivered, and as engineer mice arrived by Greyhound bus to help Uncle Fred and Jake set them up. And watching mice in sandwich bags learn how to assemble Thumbtops and work on solar blobs.

Megan usually had dinner at the restaurant. She had her own little table tucked away near the kitchen, where she could eat and do her homework, while Annie and her dad sat down to chat when they could spare the time. But sometimes Megan had dinner at Caitlin's house, because soon after she got back from New York, they started hanging out during recess, then at lunch, then after school, because they found they had a lot in common (and no one mentioned sticky notes that change in the night).

Caitlin wanted to be a scientist too, and Megan longed to tell her about the biggest scientific development of all time. Of course she couldn't say a word about that, but she could talk about climate change, which was something Caitlin's family took seriously. They listened, fascinated, when Megan told them about her mom's work in the outback with the hairy-nosed wombats.

One January night, Caitlin's dad Googled that part of Australia to see what it was like. And he said, "Uh-uh."

"What's the problem, Dad?" asked Caitlin.

"There's a huge dust storm," he said. "You've heard about the drought in part of Australia? Well, part of Australia is blowing away."

Megan checked her e-mail on her phone. No, nothing from her mom. Well, how could there be if she was buried under a huge pile of dust?

The next day, Megan was walking home from school when Annie drove up beside her and stopped with a squeal of brakes.

"I have a surprise for you," she said, leaning over to open the passenger door. "It's in your room."

When they got to the house, Megan ran up the stairs—then gave a little scream at what she saw. There was a body in her bed, all covered up except for the springy blond hair on the pillow.

"MOM!" she yelled. Then she realized that her mom must be in need of sleep and changed it to "Mom," more softly, but by then her mother was awake and sitting up, and holding out her arms.

"I wanted it to be a surprise," she said. "I guess it worked."

chapter thirty-four

What had Megan expected? That Annie and her mom would claw each other's eyes out? Not exactly—but here they were in the restaurant actually grinning at each other like old friends, with her dad in between, gloating as if he . . . well, sort of as if he were at a dog show with two prize poodles, one very beautiful and the other very smart.

Susie Miller explained why she'd come back weeks earlier than she'd expected. Her team had been driven out by the dust storm, which was one big symptom of the terrible drought in that part of Australia. She'd just about finished her research on the wombats, so she'd decided to head for home.

"I would have called," she said, "but there was a plane ready to go just as I landed in Sydney, and it was the middle of the night here. So I didn't call till I got to Los Angeles this morning—and Annie told me to come on up."

As they ate, Megan's mom marveled at the food, and wanted to try dishes from both sides of the menu—the Fresh and Local side and the Special Occasions side, where Megan's dad kept a small collection of items still in French.

"It was all Megan's idea, changing from Chez Red to Red Goes Green," said her dad. "She did the research. Our daughter is quite a kid."

"I know that," said her mom. "I'm so impressed. How on earth did you manage it, Megan?"

"Well, Joey helped," Megan mumbled, but she couldn't help going a bit red, and wished—oh, how she wished—that she could tell her mom the truth. But the treaty allowed for no exceptions, even for moms. Even for moms who were passionate about climate change.

Late that night, lying in a sleeping bag on the floor while her mom slept in the bed, Megan IM'd Trey.

"We're coming to Cleveland!" she wrote. "Please please please ask the Big Cheese if I can tell my mom. Humans HAVE to tell their moms."

"I'll try," he wrote. "But don't hold your breath."

. . . .

It was hard for Megan to say good-bye to Caitlin and Aunt Em and her dad and Annie and the mice under the dresser, but, as she told them all, she'd be back. And she found herself crossing the continent one more time. But this time at least there was a mom to lean against as she fell asleep, somewhere over Denver.

Uncle Fred was waiting at the Cleveland airport. As he drove them back to his house, they passed a huge billboard, and he slowed down so they could admire it.

It was a picture of Trey—you could tell because there was a tiny piece missing from one ear. He was standing next to a Thumbtop to show how small it was, and below his picture were the words:

Coming Soon:

The Thumbtop

Made in Cleveland by Mice

Which was true, of course, though nobody believed it. Megan's mom didn't believe it for a minute, but she laughed, delighted that her little brother had finally launched a real business.

"But you're not going to get rich selling those, are you?" she asked. "Aren't they simply too small?"

"I don't expect to sell many," said Uncle Fred. "Just a few, sort of as a gimmick. Our real business is this. . . ."

He'd driven around a corner so that now they came face-to-face with another billboard showing Trey, except this time he was surrounded by solar blobs that had been molded into useful shapes—shapes like belt buckles and buttons and barrettes and jewelry and pins for hats and frames for eyeglasses, all connected to a cell phone. Oh, and in the corner of the poster was a blob that was disguised as a pebble. It probably wouldn't sell too well to humans but could be very useful if you were running a tiny computer under a house, and could thread a cord through some gap in the wall to suck power from a secret stone.

The words on the poster read:

Get Ready For . . .

The Blob

Made in Cleveland by Mice

"We thought of showing a picture of a cow," said Uncle Fred. "Because that's what these blobs are—the cash cow that will keep our business going. Oh, and they'll help save the planet, by charging cell phones and things."

Susie Miller marveled that her brother had not only turned

into a businessman while she was away, but that he was actually now interested in doing something about the planet.

When they reached Uncle Fred's house, Jake was standing at the range, putting the finishing touches on dinner. Joey was doing homework at the table, with a mouse looking on—a mouse with a bit missing from one ear. As Megan came in, Joey leaped to his feet and handed her the mouse.

"EEEK!" said Megan's mom, as her daughter pressed Trey to her cheek and whispered, "I missed you, mousie!" while at the same time she reached her hand into the old birdcage to stroke the three other mice, who were pretending to be pets.

Jake wiped his hands on his apron and came over to shake Susie's hand. "You'll get used to the mice around here," he said. "They're our business partners."

And of course Megan and Joey shot him warning looks, and of course Megan's mom didn't believe a word, and laughed.

She did ask where the Thumbtops and the blobs were being manufactured, but she seemed satisfied when Uncle Fred waved toward the west, which happened to be the right direction for Planet Mouse, as well as for China. The one time she came to the headquarters of Planet Mouse to collect Megan, all she saw was the office, with its computers and filing cabinets. Way more businesslike than she'd expected from Uncle Fred. What she didn't see was the factory in the garage, where mice in their sandwich bags labored night and day to churn out Thumbtops for the Mouse Nation, and the blobs that would pay for them.

Megan longed more than ever to tell her mom the truth, but still the Big Cheese refused to give his permission. And Megan begged Trey to find out why.

"Strange are the ways of the mouse," said Trey. "But here's a hint: your mom believes in telling the truth, right?"

Megan thought about that one. Yes, that was one of the things her mom prided herself on. Calling spades spades.

"So you see the problem," said Trey.

"But for something as important as this, I'm sure she could, well, lie a bit!"

"For something as important as this," said Trey, "the Big Cheese is going to take his time."

The day came when the first Thumbtops and the first blobs made their way into human stores, and Uncle Fred and Jake and Joey and Megan and her mom celebrated at a launching party, where reporters marveled at the cuteness of the Thumbtop, marveled at the versatility of the blobs.

Which was great. But the real celebration happened the next day, over at Planet Mouse.

Megan and Trey watched safely from the back of the office (and the Mouse Council watched safely from the other side of the continent) while Uncle Fred wrestled with the cork from a bottle of expensive champagne, which he could afford for the first time in his life. Finally the cork came out with a loud bang, showering fizz over Joey and Jake and the old birdcage, which was close by.

"Let me propose a toast," said Uncle Fred, pouring glasses of champagne for himself and Jake while Megan opened a bottle of fizzy apple juice for herself and Joey. "To Thumbtops and blobs and Planet Earth!"

On the webcam, they could see that all the members of the Mouse Council had a tiny piece of toast, which they raised in their paws for a ceremonial nibble as the humans in Cleveland raised their glasses. Megan dipped a finger into her fizzy apple juice for Trey, while Curly, Larry, and Julia licked drops of champagne from their wet coats.

Now the Big Cheese said something in MSL, and a mouse stepped forward to translate, starting with a familiar low bow.

"My master wishes to convey," said Sir Quentin, "his

consummate gratification in the bi-species enterprise in which we are now successfully engaged."

"He means like, thanks, dudes," Trey said cheerfully.

Sir Quentin continued: "He particularly wishes to convey the profound gratitude of our species to the young human without whom none of this would have come about, and he hereby proposes a heartfelt toast to Miss Megan."

"Well, it wasn't just me," said Megan, but went a bit red all the same.

"This is indeed," said the Big Cheese, "the dawn of a new era that will lead to the betterment of the very planet on which we stand, enabling it to survive, nay, reverse the looming dangers that face it."

If the cloud of warming gases that had engulfed the world did indeed begin to thin out after these events, it could be because American politicians and American opinion leaders changed their tune, and American families responded to the hints of their resident mice with a serious effort to save energy, and put less greenhouse gas into the atmosphere. And the rest of the world followed suit.

A few humans would know how it had all come about, as

would generations of mice, because the history of Operation Cool It became an essential part of the curriculum that all must study. Indeed, most clans had pictures of Megan in the secret places where they lived, and celebrated Megan Day with extra cheese on October 26th, which was the day she had visited Headquarters and signed the treaty.

But to the kids in her new class in Cleveland, Megan Miller was just a normal girl who knew a lot about computers, and the climate, and mice. She sometimes had trouble controlling her hair, but not enough for them to tease her; and people liked her, even though she puzzled them sometimes by smiling for reasons she wouldn't explain.